For DIANNE
with the very best wishes
for 2014

PROSE SERIES 88

Canada Council for the Arts   Conseil des Arts du Canada

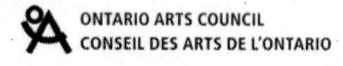

ONTARIO ARTS COUNCIL
CONSEIL DES ARTS DE L'ONTARIO

Guernica Editions Inc. acknowledges the support of
the Canada Council for the Arts and the Ontario Arts Council.
The Ontario Arts Council is an agency of the Government of Ontario.

MARINA SONKINA

LUCIA'S EYES

AND OTHER STORIES

GUERNICA

TORONTO·BUFFALO·LANCASTER (U.K.)

2011

Copyright © 2011, by Marina Sonkina and Guernica Editions Inc.
All rights reserved. The use of any part of this publication, reproduced, transmitted in any form or by any means, electronic, mechanical, photocopying, recording or otherwise stored in a retrieval system, without the prior consent of the publisher is an infringement of the copyright law.

Michael Mirolla, editor
Guernica Editions Inc.
P.O. Box 117, Station P, Toronto (ON), Canada M5S 2S6
2250 Military Road, Tonawanda, N.Y. 14150-6000 U.S.A.

Distributors:
University of Toronto Press Distribution,
5201 Dufferin Street, Toronto (ON), Canada M3H 5T8
Gazelle Book Services, White Cross Mills, High Town, Lancaster LA1 4XS U.K.

First edition.
Printed in Canada.

Legal Deposit – First Quarter
Library of Congress Catalog Card Number: 2011921283
Library and Archives Canada Cataloguing in Publication
Sonkina, Marina, 1952-
Lucia's eyes & other stories / Marina Sonkina.
(Prose series ; 88)
ISBN 978-1-55071-334-3
I. Title. II. Series: Prose series ; 88
PS8637.O537L83 2011   C813'.6   C2010-906772-X

CONTENTS

The Eyes of Santa Lucia 7
Runic Alphabet 49
Tractorina's Travels 73
Carmelita 129
Christmas Tango 191
Angels Ascending, Angels Descending 223

Notes 266

To the Memory of my Teacher Uri Lotman

THE EYES OF SANTA LUCIA

1

Not just once did Anton hear from the adults about an all-round orphan. And when they exhaled, *o-o-o-r-phan*, their stiff, fist-collected faces softened and went limp. So, Anton decided that to be a round orphan was good. No angles, no bumps. A circle.

While everybody else huddled in communal apartments, in the corners, or on narrow cots, a round orphan could fittingly live inside a circle.

It took Anton several weeks to perfect circles without a compass. To trace the line with an unfaltering hand was painstakingly difficult, given his circumstances. And when the cuckoo over a dresser called the hour, or neighbours behind the wall went on their screaming matches, Anton's fingers would lose the imagined trajectory, and he would have to begin all over again. But Anton was stubborn. He practiced on old blotting papers, on reverse sides of the drafts covered with his father's minute handwriting. And by spring, he was able to make – with one sweep – a perfect circle of any diameter, and then fit an all-round orphan inside it: two dots for the eyes, dash for the mouth.

Anton didn't have much use for bodies. They were a nuisance. So the sketch was no more than a head and a neck hinted at by two insignificant lines that led nowhere. Just like Anton's, the boy's head was shaven; the round orphan too must have had lice.

Anton hid the drawing under his pillow next to a piece of pink chalk that he had found on a pavement just barely freed from snow. Pink chalk was a rare find, a treasure.

While his father examined caterpillars, spiders, and grasshoppers through a magnifying glass, Anton was not allowed to ask any questions or show any signs of life. He was supposed to be asleep, period.

Eyes half closed, Anton watched the manoeuvres of troops. The night, conspiring with a corner street lamp, threw across the wall whole armies: lanced warriors dashed forward, then vanished under the baseboard, engulfed by shadows. And sometimes, if the streetcar passed, the dissipated warriors grew antlers and emerged from under the floor in the shape of a deer; another shift, and the deer would morph into a sharp-elbowed man leaning over the desk. Pointed head, chin and nose elongating monstrously.

The wire mesh of the bed squeaked as the boy crept deeper under the old, cotton-filled quilt to hide from the night reshaping his father into a monster who stretched across the wall. For sure it wasn't his real father. It couldn't be.

His true father is now sailing on the icebreaker *Lenin*. Or on the submarine *Nautilus* together with Captain Nemo. Or perusing the tropics on a ship with magnificent scarlet sails! Here he is! Standing on the Captain's bridge, he notices a typhoon ahead: he conquers that typhoon. He is young, courageous, tall, good-looking. Not sullen, old and bald, forever stooping over his typewriter, clearing his throat at monotonously predictable intervals. He is a Captain, not an entomologist and geneticist – the two words that make people's brows go up: "He is a who, you said?"

Anton imagined his Captain Father and himself catching a dangerous spy, then extinguishing the taiga fires. They see the Ussurian tiger trapped in flames: They save the tiger, making a way for him in the wall of fire. Next to his Captain Father, Anton is never short-winded; nothing compresses his breast, he can stand erect.

Now his father is bravely drifting on an ice floe towards the North Pole. He promised Comrade Stalin he'd be the first to reach the apex of the earth solo! But then spring comes, the ice is breaking off, bit by bit, like pieces of a watermelon, one tiny slice is left, his father balancing on one foot! He taps out a secret code on the radio that Anton had assembled for him under his bed, specially for this ice-floating adventure. In the whole world only two of them know the code. Anton should ask Comrade Stalin – Father taps – to send a plane out for his rescue. And now he, Anton, together with another pilot, is perusing the hostile deserts of the Arctic. After hours of desperate search they discover a tiny speck in the blinding white infinity... And then... no, not like that... Somebody else, not his father, is a minute helpless speck. His father is cut out for heroic deeds: He is the one rescuing that dot, the someone else who has risked his life on an ice floe. The two of them – he never leaves Anton behind – are flying the polar plane and Anton shouts: "I see him, I see him!"

"We're descending!" commands his father. "Anton, prepare the rope ladder! Throw the rope through the hatch!" But the rope is frozen stiff to the floor. Then Father orders: "You, Anton, fly the plane! I'll manage the ladder!" Anton is now alone at the controls. He pulls and pushes all kinds of levers, and the plane descends. Father hacks the ladder free with an axe and releases it. Anton knows he has to go in lower and lower circles till the man can catch the rope. Anton has never piloted the plane but he is his father's son. He can do anything! One circle, two, three, closer and closer to the treacherous slab of ice! How small it is and how lonely is the figure of the stranded man ... Finally! Together they pull him in. The man is frostbitten and can hardly talk, but the first words to crunch like broken ice from his mouth are: "Dear Comrades, Father and Son, I owe you my life."

"Don't mention it," replies the Father Captain. "We could do it again."

"Any time," adds the son, and they take a course right to Red Square... There Comrade Stalin is waiting on top of the Mausoleum, the red carpet is plush under their feet. Leaflets, flowers, mountains of flowers, a wind orchestra, jubilant smiles...

Anton knows that someday he will run away to meet up with his authentic father. One thing is preventing him right now: an awkward but deep sense of connection with the grotesque shadow that is leaning over the table.

He was first aware of it while examining through a lens sharp-kneed grasshoppers, triangular-armed spiders, dragon flies with whispering-glass wings, caterpillars with ugly protrusions, twenty-legged centipedes. Unlike his father, he detests bugs. He is sure that because his fraudulent father was constantly dawdling over these knobby creatures, he, Anton, ended up with a hump on his back. The hump, though not that big, grows to one side: It gives him a grotesque look in any clothing he wears. Anton has adjusted to his deformity, though breathing is never easy. The hump compresses his lungs and he can't run like other kids; when he tries, he is just a laughing stock.

Anton can only lie on one side, but the good thing is that it is the side from which he can see his mother. Mother died long ago and now lives in a small wooden frame on a chest of drawers. When Auntie Luba had moved into their flat and father removed the portrait, Mother died again. But somehow Anton knew that Mother would come back and didn't worry for her, not as much as he worried for his Captain Father.

It was Father who needed to be taken constant care of, for whom new adventures had to be invented daily.

2

Auntie Luba arrived with a nest on her head. It was made up of transparent braids that reminded Anton of a particularly wonderful batch of *challah* he once saw in a bread store. What a huge line gathered for this *challah* on that day! The legless beggars, plenty of them after the war, got together for a fun ride near the bread store – back and forth, back and forth – on their low, make-shift platforms with ball-bearings for wheels. But when the rumor of *challah* came, they went crazy from the smell of the freshly-baked bread and rode right into the crowd! But vertical people formed an impenetrable wall, and the roller-boarding cripples didn't get a crumb! Auntie Luba, on the other hand, had a whole loaf of it on her head!

Auntie Luba produced all kinds of sounds when she moved, and it took a while for Anton to figure out how she did it. A starched blouse with a ruff said "tracsk-tracsk" when she raised her arms. Her black skirt stridulated as she mounted herself onto a chair, and her high heels were strict and stern like a pointer at school. Every time Anton heard their tap-tap-tap, he'd pull his head into his shoulders.

When Auntie Luba moved in with them, father put a screen in front of the boy's bed, and Anton couldn't watch the great battles on the wall any more. He listened in to the rustles and whispers of the night. Aunt Luba giggled as if somebody was tickling her. But who would make their way to their home at night to tickle Auntie Luba? That Anton could never figure out.

Every morning, Aunt Luba made Anton do *hygienic exercises*. She flapped her arms in front of him like signal flags while he had to squat from twenty to thirty times. "Up, down! Up, down!" she ordered. "You want to remain a hunchback forever? Then keep your back straight!" What was amazing was that in the morning she had no nest on her head, but a short sparse growth instead, of an indefinable colour. But the white blouse with a ruff and black skirt stayed.

After *hygienic exercises*, Anton wasn't allowed to have breakfast yet. First, he had to clean up the mess under his bed. His hump prevented him from crawling beneath the hanging metal-net belly, so Aunt Luba gave him a broom on a long handle and watched, arms to her hips, him poking with that broom here and there fishing out his meagre treasures: a slingshot, an old cartridge case, some charcoal for drawing, a pen-knife and pieces of bark he needed to carve things, and all sorts of springs and rusted parts to assemble the radio one day. These he imperceptibly drove away with the broom to the very corner and Aunt Luba didn't notice. "A real garbage pile, this place is, no air to breathe," she sniffed.

Aunt Luba lived with them for about three weeks, but Anton knew from their first meal together that she would soon be gone. He knew that and, for the time, followed her orders.

On the first day of Aunt Luba's arrival, Anton entered the room when the table was already set. He'd never seen white napkins with red cockerels before: "A present from

Auntie Luba." He stopped short, afraid to look up at their new guest.

"Is he always late for dinner, your son?"

The Insect Father withdrew his head into his shoulders, exactly the way Anton did, but said nothing. "Come over, sit down," Auntie Luba said, patting her hand on the seat next to her. Anton hesitated. Instead of climbing into the chair, he first dragged it away from her and tried to straddle it, all the while facing their guest to hide his deformity.

Aunt Luba squinted her eyes, examining the boy.

Then she put her knife and her fork down.

"Oh, that's what it is... kyphosis!"

The Insect Father looked away, then drew Anton to his side. And by the way he did it, hand dallying on his left shoulder, Anton knew Aunt Luba was a goner.

Intuiting the day of her disappearance, Anton returned his mother to her old place. And by the time Auntie departed, and the screen was removed, Mother was back home.

***

Anton didn't like to go outside much. But the Insect Father insisted: Fresh air was essential for the development of a healthy mind and body.

Boys from the courtyard teased Anton: "Give us a humpity-bumpity ride, eh? What's in your hump, camel?"

When he approached them, they didn't beat him but simply gave him a chase and shooed him away like a cat. Hobbling off, he groped for air – a fish out of water – so funny to watch.

Anton would find refuge in the shoe-maker's workshop. His huge arms covered with a thicket of curly hair, his black beard concealing half of his chest, Leo the Kike looked like the pirate Barmaley from the famous children's story. He always wore an old mariner's shirt, smeared with blacking, so you couldn't tell anymore the black stripes from the white ones. Topping this off was a greasy leather apron with two enormous pockets. Leo the Kike mangled all thirty-three letters of Russian alphabet, as they say.

"So, Antosha! Are they mishtrating you again?"

"Nah, they are just teasing…"

"Boorhish people. Bachbarians. Teach their childhren bad zings…"

Leo the Kike extracted a chocolate nugget from his pocket: "The Bear of the North." The outer wrapper showed a bear climbing a diagonally fallen log up to the azure sky.

"Have a bite!" urged the shoemaker.

But Anton carefully unwrapped the treat, examining first the outer layer, then the shiny foil and finally, the transparent waxy coating. Having made sure that everything was in place, he wrapped it all back and hid the Bear in his pocket.

"Saving it for your Dad, eh?"

"Aha…," said Anton, climbing onto a high stool next to the polish caldron, his usual post. He peeked over the pot-edge to better see the bubbles gurgling in the black slop.

Leo the Kike placed on a boot-tree a wreck of a shoe and the magic began. With one precise movement he freed the shoe out of its old shell, a worn-out sole that had given away its last breath to the toils of the roads. Now the shoe looked like a pallid skeleton: too naked, too fragile to come into contact with even a road paved with feathers.

Anton liked the astringent smell of turpentine. He liked the way Leo the Kike turned the shoe this way and that, then put it away for a moment. On the shelf he kept different pieces of leather. He took one piece, cut out a new sole, attached it with the small shiny tacks fanning out of his mouth, then cut off overlaps with a knife and adroitly rounded all the edges with a special tool. Anton watched a leather ribbon coiling down to the floor in a neat stack. Leo the Kike dipped a flat stick into the bubbling cauldron – the moment Anton held his breath for – and traced the join between the sole and upper with a shiny border. Now the shoe was ready for new adventures, its second life.

Anton climbed down from the stool to collect the leather snake and all the rubber shavings left on the floor from other jobs.

"Father promised to buy me a talking parrot," he said, dawdling a little, shifting his weight from one leg to the other. It was a lie, but he wanted to thank Leo the Kike for his gifts. And the only way of doing it, in his mind, was to tell him something extraordinary.

Anton's cheeks flushed. After all, it wasn't a total lie: He'd simply blended two fathers together. Couldn't his Captain Father one day bring the parrot from some tropical country? And couldn't his Insect Father, who knew so much about every creature, teach that parrot to talk?

"I must go now," declared Anton. "So much business to do!"

"You'll have to show me your parrot one day," Leo the Kike said, laughing. "When you get some free time, busy man."

"I will," promised the boy.

Indeed he was in a rush. He had to peel potatoes before father came from work, to mend his father's socks and do his own homework. But first he had to get over to Uncle Tolya, all the way across the yard, before Uncle Tolya closed his *edemption* shack for the day.

To avoid the gang of boys flicking pen knives against the wall, he took a longer route past the back side of the grocery store. But he found the path blocked by a refrigerator truck. The man in a padded jacket was heaving frozen cow carcasses out of the vehicle, dragging them by a rope over the ground to the zinc chute, then barreling them into the opening. "Thump, thump, thump." Anton counted each hulk thudding onto the still-frozen ground. Crash! Bang! At the other end of the chute, underground workers shouted and swore. Anton peeped inside the truck filled with carcasses. By the time they unloaded, Uncle Tolya would have already closed.

Anton bent over to measure the distance from the ground to the truck's underbelly, then dipped below. Crawling clumsily, he reached the front wheels; waited till the man with carcasses turned away, then dived out at the other end.

3

Inside a long shack, Uncle Tolya was sitting on a wooden crate puffing on his cigarette. Black inside and out, as if built from planks pulled out of fire, the shack didn't have one single window. It smelled of fungus and mildew. Emaciated mice darted about, paying no attention to an obscure bulb clinging to its twisted cord. The sign outside once read "Empties Redemption Centre." The letter "R" had disappeared and until the previous year Anton still had thought *edemption* was some kind of transparent, invisible rat poison that people were bringing to Uncle Tolya in different-size bottles. Uncle Tolya was picky: Some poison suited him, and some he rejected. But he must have tried *edemption* on his shack's little inhabitants: They looked so thin, and altogether unhealthy. That's what Anton thought before he even went to school. But now, a first grader, he was big and knew better: *Edemption* simply meant empty bottles.

Uncle Tolya was wearing a grey overall with black oversleeves. There was something ratty in him, some kinship with the rotting wood, with the decay of the underworld.

Uncle Tolya flicked the cigarette butt onto the dirt floor, then poked his head out a hole in the side wall to serve his waiting customers: grey and black coats, mostly women and children in oversized garb, and a couple of men in urgent need of cash for the "morning after." On the

– 18 –

ground, a little to one side, a glassy snail of string bags bulging with *edemptions*.

"What are you shoving these into my muzzle for?" Uncle Tolya shouted to an old woman in a grey woolen head scarf. "Sour-cream jars I'm not taking on Tuesdays! How many times do I have to repeat?" But she held her ground, as if frozen, with a jar in each mittened hand extended out to him.

"Two hours in line, please have mercy…"

"Fuck your mother – Don't you understand plain Russian, old hag? Next!" barked Uncle Tolya.

Anton sighed in disbelief: such an old *babushka*, really ancient, still had a mother, while he had none.

With unexpected agility, the "hag" bent to one side over her sacks, extracting new bottles.

"How about some beer empties?…Will you take those? Left from my son…"

Uncle Tolya shot a stern glance at the bags.

"Who is going to wash the labels off? Me? You know the rules: Get them off, then come back."

"But you'd be closed by then, I stood for two hours already…"

"What about milk bottles? You take them?" A young woman with a baby in her arms was elbowing her way forward to take the "hag's" spot.

"Depends what kind," snapped Uncle Tolya without looking at the young mother. "One litre – maybe; others NO." Taking advantage of the woman's hesitation, a hunk of a man struggled forward.

"Don't jump the queue here, shameless scum!" women in the crowd chorused.

"No queue for vodka bottles, comrade citizens!" snarled the man.

"Who said so? Since when? And you woman, yes, you! – with a baby – standing here, counting crows in the sky! Letting crooks in!"

The crowd started a commotion, closing ranks in an attempt to squeeze the offender and that gawk of a girl with a baby out.

Anton felt sorry for these two women. He didn't like Uncle Tolya at all. He'd gladly avoid this place, never show up here. But the *edemption* shack was the only place he hoped to get what he was looking for: bottle shards. Not the ordinary green pieces of glass strewing the dirt floor inside, but the rare, smoky-blue ones, from foreign bottles.

He had already put by several valuable things for Lusya: a pink chalk to draw the hopscotch; the leather garland for her necklace; and the "Bear of the North." She could eat the chocolate and use the wraps for her *secretik*.

What he needed was a suitable piece of glass to cover the *secretik*. A lot depended on his find. A beautiful glass could turn the *secretik* into magic; an ordinary one would make it look like any other girl's.

While Uncle Tolya was fighting the *edemption* people, Anton examined the shack's floor more carefully: cigarette buds, broken glass – nothing special. It was getting late; his father would soon come back from work. The boy picked up a green splinter – just in case – and hobbled out.

Convulsively, Anton gulped in the prickly, crisp air of early spring, partaking of the great work of earth unfolding in front of his eyes. He felt the snowdrift's secret sorrow: how it couldn't help itself anymore, the loosening of its shape and dignity, first imperceptibly, then into open nakedness. The treachery of melting had begun underneath, in the snow's deep bowels, where it first touched the earth; then the yielding sprawled through the snowdrift's spine and blackened it with soot, remorse and desperation. The snow cried and bemoaned its fate, its memories of lost power, its grip on the earth. And now sobbing, it was retreating into nothingness, pulling its arms away like white flames. Anton bent down: On the strip of dirt freed from the shackles of winter there wallowed a magnificent shard of red glass. It wasn't just red, it was ruby-red, with dark-green veins pulsating inside. Sealed in its depth was the flame of its foreign blood: the bliss of the hot beaches under never setting sun, the ecstasy of the festive, care-free existence nobody in the observable world could fathom. Anton's dexterous fingers grabbed the ruby. He would examine it later; now he had to clear out of here, before somebody snatched the treasure away from him.

4

It had been almost five months since he had fallen in love with Lusya. Five months of fear that she would get weary of him. He camouflaged that fear and his thirst for her presence by rapid talk, and little gifts he spent most of his time looking for. Lusya must be finished with her homework by now and would soon go out. He ran to Lusya's house. Socks and potatoes would have to wait.

At the portal leading to her unit of flats he stopped. He never shouted like other kids, hands cupped to their mouths – "Lusya, when are you coming out?" – till Lusya's mother showed up on the balcony and broadcast in broken Russian, her unbent arms on the railings: "Please stop to shout! Lusya, he is busy now. He make the homework."

No, he, Anton, always waited.

Lusya's real name was Lucia. Only six months old, she had arrived, together with three thousand "civil war children," from Spain. Her parents were real Spaniards and they never learned to speak Russian properly. Lusya, on the other hand, was only a little bit Spanish, not much really, because she spoke exactly like Anton. Yet everything about her was extraordinary. She was always dressed festively, not like other girls. Her ironed skirt had many neat folds, and her little lacquered belts looked so tender on her waist. She smelled sweetly: as did a cinnamon bun that Anton had seen once but never tried. A deep cleft in her chin he found irresistible.

Boys teased Lusya in a dirty way. "Lussy, Lussy, show me your pussy." But Lusya passed by as a queen, without as much as twitching her shoulder.

Yes, she was very proud, in a quiet way. She smiled shyly, into her palm. And when she adjusted a polka-dot satin ribbon in her hair, she kept her emerald-green eyes cast down. Shadows from her eyelashes covering half of her face mesmerized Anton. They flew to him in his dreams. The polka-dot ribbon and the matching socks showing from the lacquered shoes collected Anton's shimmering happiness like a prism. Lusya never teased him, and if there was nobody else around to play with, she agreed to play with Anton.

He was sitting now on a bench next to her entryway, waiting patiently. From time to time he checked the treasure hidden in his pocket, its delightful smoothness. Spring bloomed, dripping icicles sang their arias. Neither his deformity, nor the encroaching evening with his Insect Father bothered the boy right now.

The air thickened in the premonition of almost intolerable happiness. Anton's heart pushed against the bars of its cage. Lusya stood in the entrance doorway. She stiffened, evaluating the situation.

"Lusya," Anton whispered rising from the bench. "Will you play with me a little?"

The girl, a year older and almost a head taller, looked dreamingly over his head. "All right..." She paused. "Did you bring me the boat?"

Now her eyes were pouring steady calm light over him. Anton's feet wobbled; words rough and dry like last year's leaves stuck in his throat: "It isn't ready yet. Tomorrow, for sure."

"You promise?"

"Yes, you'll see!"

At the end of March, when the snow firmly packed by months of blizzard finally yielded to the sun and gushed down the pavements in torrents of water, the kids came out to launch their boats. They slapped them together out of litter released by the melting snow: wood chips, fragments of plywood, even newspaper scraps.

But Lusya had to have a real boat: carved out of wood, with masts and sails and all the rigging and a crew to boot. Anton began to work on her boat before the snow fell. He had been collecting bottle cork from Uncle Tolya and rubber cuttings from Leo the Kike through the whole winter. It was the sailors he got stuck on: He made two of them, then ran out of Plasticine.

"Do you mind if I make sailors out of acorns?"

"Acorns? Won't it look funny?" Lusya said chuckling.

Anton quickly calculated: He had already removed all the saddles and the spurs from the Plasticine cavalry he had built two months before. Of course, he could pinch off riders' legs too – after all, these were cavalry men, not foot soldiers – but legs are thin. Wouldn't be enough for a whole crew of sailors. Besides, the cavalry was sitting right on his father's desk on a piece of plywood. Father would notice and ask questions.

"I don't have any Plasticine left," Anton finally confessed.

Lusya cocked her head to the side, smiling enticingly.

"I got a whole new box for a birthday present. Can give you any colour you want…"

From constant use, his own Plasticine was crumpled and crimpled into balls of indiscernible colour: something brownish, with impregnations of green and dirt-yellow. He imagined untouched sticks, with even, machine-made grooves, each piece nestled into a separate cardboard compartment according to its shade, like a rainbow, from light green to intense purple to tender pink. He sensed the marvelous, industrial smell of this rainbow and ardently wanted to become its owner.

"Look what I've got for you..." He reached for the ruby, but his hand hesitated, then pulled out the candy. He wanted the ruby to be a splash of surprise; he'd give it to her last, and see how her face bloomed.

Lusya unwrapped the "Bear of the North," then sent the candy into her mouth as she surveyed Anton dreamingly with her languid eyes, the bow of her lips moving rhythmically. A starched white handkerchief appeared from the pocket of her blue coat: She gently blotted her mouth.

"It's not because of the Plasticine, please don't think anything..." The very idea she might suspect the candy was a payment for her generosity was unbearable.

"Of course not," said Lusya chewing calmly.

Anton scratched his head under the cap; when he was nervous the stubble made him itchy.

"Thank you," said Lusya. "You're a kind boy."

Nobody ever talked in such a manner in the radius of his acquaintance. "He is a good boy; she is a good girl." That's how her parents must carry on at home, Anton thought, his afternoon quietly lighting up. In the meantime, Lusya was examining the wrapper against the sun:

"That's the best. Even Tankya doesn't have wrappers like that. Come, I'll show you something."

Shuffling rather than skipping along the way Lusya

did, Anton followed her to the courtyard fountain, dumb since birth. Along the outside of its round cement wall that had never known a touch of water, the girls had dug small depressions in the earth. The bottom of each hollow was laid with foil. Shiny trinkets were placed on top: candy wraps, shards of glass, pieces of coloured ribbon. A piece of plain glass covered the cache. A layer of soil made the *secretik* invisible.

Late autumn was the best time for *secretiky*. Fallen leaves camouflaged the spot; then snow fell and in spring you removed the layer of earth and dug till you hit the glass, a window revealing the treasure, forgotten over the long winter. If somebody else found your cache, fights would erupt, in spite of the rules that you'd have to relinquish all your rights.

"You hid it here? Anyone can find it," Anton said, bending over, next to Lusya.

"I'm not that silly! This one is fake! The real one is over there!" Lusya waved her hand away from the fountain, as she continued to dig. Under the ordinary green bottle glass showing finally beneath the layers of last year's litter was nothing but dirt. The real *secretik* was half a meter away from the fake one. And it was splendid: golden and silver candy wraps, white pigeon feathers and coloured glass beads forming a star.

"You're the only one who's seen it," whispered Lusya putting her arm around Anton's neck and pulling him closer. Her eyelashes almost touched his cheek: "Give your Honest Pioneer Word that you won't tell anybody."

"My Honest Pioneer Word."

Lusya let him go.

"Where is the glass you promised?"

Anton dipped into his pocket, feeling for the ruby.

"Lucia, come home!" shouted her mother from the balcony. "The teacher for piano is arrived!"

"*Estoy viniendo!*" Lusya called to her mother. Then she turned to Anton: "I have to go now!"

"Will you come out later?" he shouted after her.

"Don't know! Perhaps!"

With a light shrug of her shoulders she flitted out of his world, immediately turning his treasure into a useless trinket.

Anton's day died in his hands. Nothing was left of it, except the persistent croaking of the crows in the tops of the naked trees.

He rolled his shoulders restlessly, sniveling, then slowly walked towards his home.

5

The first thing Anton needed to do was darn his father's socks. Otherwise, what would Father wear to work? The boy had learned the skill while watching old ladies on the bench. One of them gave him a cracked wooden darning mushroom she no longer needed. Not for nothing did Anton have long, pale, adroit fingers that he could almost braid together. Anton could sew and mend all kinds of clothing, his father being hopeless when it came to any housework. Anton would peel a potato in two seconds. As for school homework, there was this "Perhaps" from Lusya, hanging on one silvery thread... and his father never checked on homework anyway. One way or another, he had a bushel of things to do while Lusya was running her gentle fingers over the keyboard.

Anton had once visited her flat and now could see clearly the dining room, the brightly glazed vase on a table, and Lusya's straight back at the piano, in something airily, delightfully pink...

Her parents never allowed her to invite anybody from the "street." The fact that Lusya once had broken this rule was Anton's greatest reward for his awful humiliation a month before.

On that day Anton had gone out into the courtyard to confront a frightening scene: Lusya was sitting right on the dirty pavement, smearing tears over her cheeks, her hair dishevelled, the ribbon and the coat lying in the dirt, the laced hem of her dress torn, one foot bare. Girls were volleying her shoe to each other, laughing and grimacing; then, bored with it, bean-pole Tankya scooped up some snow with that shoe and poked it under Lusya's nose: "Go ahead, eat it." That was a signal for the bashing to begin. The girls crushed Lusya under and took turns kicking her. Lusya made no attempt to defend herself.

The sun grew black in Anton's eyes. Without giving it any further thought, he attacked Tankya, the beanpole, twisting his tenacious fingers into her hair. She jumped away, screaming. Then he tried to peel the other girls off Lusya, working his elbows like hatchets. "Look, he just went off his rocker! The slime-ball!" screamed Tankya. But Anton thrashed left and right. He was alone against a whole swarm of girls, each of them taller and older than he. They crushed him under and sucked him in. They mauled him and lashed him over the face with slimy, rotting flowers out of the garbage. Then they pushed him inside the iron garbage container, the size of a giant's coffin, threw a dead cat on top of him, and slammed the iron lid.

Anton shouted, beat against the lid to no avail. Much later, Leo the Kike, who went to throw away his cuttings, pulled Anton out. The boy was barely alive.

After this mishap, Lucia bestowed a great honour on the boy: for the first and only time she invited him to her place. Anton took off his shoes and gingerly stepped on the mirror of the parquet in the living room. The sweet smell – the same smell he sensed around his idol – enveloped him. The grand piano watched him in dark silence as he tip-toed after Lusya to her room. Two ornate black-lace fans on a carved table bowed their heads, catching the light breeze that moved the curtains.

"Here. We're going to make theatre," announced Lusya, closing the door behind them. "Do you want to be my page? And I'll be your Princess." And without awaiting his response: "Let's begin then!"

Out of the lacquered drawer came a Spanish Grandee in a soft hat of black velvet with a red feather, black cloak, a toy sword dangling at his side. Anton was dazzled.

"And who is this?" asked Anton holding his breath when the Princess pulled the second puppet out of the same drawer.

"This is Matador," she said. "It belonged to my grandmother. That's what we got out of Spain, these two. Touch it, gently."

"What does Matador do?" Anton asked, stroking the golden brocade, the silk embroidered jacket, the coloured waistband of the puppet.

"He fights a bull. Like this, I'll show you."

Lusya spoke rapidly in Spanish, manipulating the Matador and the Grandee. Both of them attacked the cat, Marcela, who served as a bull.

Finally, Marcela emitted a heart-breaking "mew" and escaped under the bed.

"Enough," Lusya declared. "My mother doesn't allow me to handle the puppets for too long. They are too old for that. Marcela, you were a good bull. Come out, I'll give you some milk."

She looked at Anton meaningfully.

"Well, my page. We're now going to do something else. Ready?"

She climbed up on a chair and fetched down from a high shelf a folio with gold-embossed covers. Barely able to hold it for the weight, she nestled on a sofa next to Anton.

Interspersed with rice paper were pictures by old masters. Lusya traced with her finger, reading the names of artists in unfamiliar script: El Greco, Goya, Surbaran. Anton could already easily read in Russian, but that his Princess could make sense out of these strange letters so effortlessly! A bird of Paradise flitting from one exotic flower to the next!

They were sitting close to each other, Lusya leafing through pages, making sure the rice paper didn't crease. Suddenly he stopped her leafing hand, stunned by the strangeness of a portrait they came to. A young woman in a bright dress — half of her face sharply lit, half still consumed by darkness — stood tall, gazing impartially at the spectator. Her dark hair was decorated with a wreath of roses. In her left hand she was holding something long and sharp, like an unusually long branch, or a feather, the likes of which Anton had never seen. But it was the object in her other hand that startled him. On a platter floated two liquid, transparent eyes. Alive, they were staring at Anton.

"What is it?" Anton whispered.

"This is Santa Lucia, the martyr. I was named after her."

"Why is she carrying... these... on a tray?"

"They tore her eyes out because she was a Christian. But she didn't die. She grew another pair of eyes, instead."

"For real?" Anton rubbed his own eyes as if to make sure they were all right. "You mean, she could see with them? With the ones in her face and on the tray?"

"Yes, but the eyes on the platter are magic. They see things hidden. For example, if you lose something, you ask Santa Lucia's eyes and they'll tell you where it is hiding.

Or if you're lost in the woods, the eyes can show you the path."

"How do you know?"

"Everybody knows that!"

"May I copy them?" asked Anton timidly.

"I can't loan you the book; my mother won't allow it."

"You have water colours?"

Lusya hesitated, looking over Anton's head at the closed door. "My parents are soon coming back. There is no time."

"I'll be fast, you'll see."

She thought for a moment, then returned with a glass of water and an unopened box of paints. Anton dipped a brush into water, then scooped some dark brown pigment, then green and brown again. Several strokes, and there appeared a platter resembling the one in the painting. He kept painting, forgetting to breathe normally, a bizarre whistle coming out of his chest with each exhalation, his lower lip now sticking out, a thin thread of saliva beginning its journey towards his chest. And finally, there appeared a pair of bulging eyes floating on the platter.

"I didn't know you could paint so well…" Lusya patted him on his nape, looking at the picture from some distance and moving away so that his saliva didn't accidentally touch her.

"You made them not frightening at all," she said. "*Son blandos*. Tender and a little sad." She examined Anton's production more closely. "But Santa Lucia's eyes are brown, not green."

Anton looked at her gravely.

"They are magic eyes. And green. Like yours."

"You like my eyes?" asked Lusya, opening them even wider. "Here is a hanky. Wipe your chin off."

Then she covered Santa Lucia with rice paper, closed the book and put it away on the shelf.

※ ※ ※

Since that day, Anton had always carried the Magic Eyes in his pocket. But during the night they had to hide behind his bed, slipped into the space beneath a loose flap of wallpaper. When he stumbled onto the red ruby glass, he knew right away who helped him to find it, directing his steps.

6

Lusya didn't come out to play for the next two days. When Anton finally saw her, she looked so forlorn that his heart grew heavy with pity.

"I'm having my wart burnt... my mother is taking me to the doctor's," she murmured, looking down at the tips of her shoes, her skipping rope hanging listlessly in her hand.

"Just don't go," Anton blurted out, himself suddenly overcome with a pang of pain.

"How can I?"

"Why do they have to burn it? See what I've got?" He collected his hand into a fist. On the right knuckle sat a small rough mound. "I played with the frogs last summer, and that's what happened. But I'll never have mine burnt." Anton was embarrassed by his own words. How could he compare himself to his Princess? She was perfect. No wart could make him uglier than he already was.

"With my birthmark, nobody would want to marry me, that's what my mother said."

"I... I will!"

Lusya laughed. Anton cast his eyes down.

"Is it big, your wart?"

Lusya rolled down the white round collar of her dress: A brown spot covered with black hairs sprawled down towards her chest.

"Mine is not from frogs. I was born like that..."

Anton was baffled. In his mind, he was the only one to have any deformities, by virtue of his indefinable but certain affinity with dead insects. But Lusya, his enchantress, the Light of his Life, couldn't possibly have anything like what he had just seen.

"You know what they'll do? They'll fasten me to the table and then burn me with a red-hot iron. *Zh, zh, zh,* like that…" She cocked her head to one side to see the effect. Anton shuddered. Burn her with a red-hot iron? That was insufferable. No, he couldn't allow that to happen. He had to prevent it, to undertake something urgently.

"Let's run away, then!" he whispered looking to the sides.

"Run away to where?" she scoffed, flicking the tip of her tongue around her lips.

"To my father. He is the Captain on a big ship. He is in charge of everybody. He'll give an order and they'll sail to Spain, to your relatives…"

"All my relatives were finished. Done with, in the war," said Lusya matter-of-factly, raising her head. Anton followed her gaze: The pigeons had taken off from the dovecote on the roof, and were now circling in the sky. "You have no Captain Father. You're just making things up. Your father studies insects. You told me so yourself."

"This is my father for here. But I have another father over there. Honestly!"

Lusya chuckled.

"You're silly! There can be no such thing as two fathers. Understand? I know that for certain."

"But what about Kolya?" retorted Anton. "He had a brother in Kiev. He himself told me. And this brother has another mother. So Kolya has two mothers, right? I have no mother, but maybe I have two fathers instead, see?"

"Yes, I see. That you're still a little boy," Lusya said. She sighed and thought of something. "All right! If you have another father, how do we get to him? Where is his ship? Tell me, just tell me!"

Anton hesitated for a second.

"First we take a train. We ask the Auntie conductress to take us to the boats. We get off at the seashore, and there everybody will know my father's ship."

Lusya unfolded her rope and began to skip.

"Su-ppose, su-ppose – there is a ship some-somewhere. We still need an exact address, silly!"

"There is no address on the water... addresses are on land."

By now she was skipping away, and he was losing her.

"Lusya, wait, wait! We don't need to go to the ship, we can hide at Burnt Man Barren. They won't find us there, I promise!"

Burnt Man Barren was a scary place: muggings, assaults, rapes, even murders. Children believed that, before the war, a man was tied to a tree and burned on it alive. They said you could still see his silhouette on a scorched trunk. Burnt Man Barren was adjacent to the railway track, separated from it by two fences. The endless freight trains swished by at full speed, and nobody ever saw one stopping. It took your breath away when you counted the cars – on a bet – ten, twenty, thirty, and soon Anton would run out of breath and lose the count, shivering in the brutal blasts and swirls of wind that could knock him over and suck him under the wheels any moment.

7

The day he finally managed to talk Lusya into going to Burnt Man Barren they climbed, as he usually did, over the first fence only to realize they were trapped. The hole in the second, much higher fence, standing a metre or so from the first one, was now hammered tight with planks. Anton scratched his head trying to figure what to do.

"Let's turn back," Lusya declared.

"Wait, I know another path, through Motovka Depot!"

"But it's going to get late! I'm not allowed to come home after dark."

"There'll be another break in the fence. It can't be too far... you'll see! Let's go. Please."

Lusya stepped away and looked hard at Anton. "Why have you dragged me here anyway? Why? I don't want to count your trains!"

"I thought if they force you to have this thing burnt... if we needed to hide someday... we could come here, but if you really don't want to..."

Lusya sniffed. She was a big girl, after all; he, but a little hunchback. She made a step forward with proud, regal reluctance.

Squeezed by jagged, sooty walls on both sides, they now continued to walk carefully, avoiding the snowy slush mixed up with human and dog excrement. As if locked in a prison cell with the ceiling taken off, the only thing they could see was the fading eggshell of the sky. But Anton didn't mind. He loved enclosed spaces, preferred them to open, unprotected vistas. And now he felt strange exaltation being so close to her, watching her making these tentative, cautious steps in the sludge. Anton's senses were sharp: He could see and smell and hear better than other people. He noticed the transparency of the huge pale disk hanging over his head – no more than a sketch of a moon in the dark blueness of the sky. And beneath was snow mixed with dirt and her small footprints filling with water the moment she lifted her foot.

Minutes later, the moon had already come fully into its body, all luminescence. It transformed everything around – darkening and expanding the walls on both sides, snatching the half-belt on the back of Lusya's coat and sculpting it into a furry living thing. Anton was happy: He wanted nothing else from life, nothing but this moment, a Page following his Princess into eternity.

And then the glad monotony of the inner wall suddenly faltered: Here it was, the other break Anton had hoped for. He looked up the wall. The hole was way above his head.

"I know what to do… You climb on my shoulders, and I'll hold you tight. See that plank up there? You grab it and then jump down on the other side and wait for me."

Lusya glanced at Anton, her eyes frosted.

"And you? How will you get over?"

"Don't you worry I can climb better than a monkey. Come, Lusya, come!"

And he stretched his arms towards the girl.

Lusya stepped back.

"No," she whispered. "No…"

What he read in her eyes was not just fear, but disgust

with him, disgust with the very idea that she would have to touch and even rely on somebody so pathetically deformed yet wanting to play the role of a strong and healthy, grown-up man.

"No," she repeated. "Never."

"As you wish," said Anton feeling a dry lump in his throat.

And again they walked, locked between the two walls, Anton gasping, struggling for air and lagging behind so that she couldn't hear that forced, pathetic sound his lungs were making. But then the fence abruptly came to an end, and they found themselves at large again. Warehouses, sheds, piles of lumber, heaps of coal. In the dark the railway tracks glittered.

The high beams of an oncoming train blinded them: a freight. And then something extraordinary happened: They heard the screeching of its brakes, hissing of the locomotive, and the train shuddered to a stop. The children waited in total silence, their eyes wide open. Anton had never before seen a train stopping here. What they thought was a cattle car turned out to have barred windows. Behind them were faces. Emaciated, spectral, they were staring into the darkness, while the children were staring at them. Into this suspense a folded piece of paper flew through the bars; then another one. White doves were alighting at their feet, some falling between the wheels. And immediately, without warning, dogs appeared out of nowhere, their ferocious barking shattering the silence. Taut leashes, the guards straining on them, searchlights dissecting the sky. Then the train hiccupped, as if choking, the wheels moved, and a minute later, the vision was gone.

All that was left were the tracks glittering in the dark, the blinking eye of a semaphore down the line, and pieces of paper scattered white on the ground. Anton picked one up.

"Leave it! Don't touch!" shouted Lusya. In the light of the moon her face was deadly pale. But Anton had already stuffed the paper into his pocket, as he did almost anything his sharp eyes noticed, just in case.

She stood there dumbfounded and then a terrible scream split the air. Anton never imagined anything like that could come from anybody's throat.

He slouched against her, covering her with his arms: "Don't, please Lusya! It's over! These were bad people, in the train. But we're safe. Nobody saw us, I swear!"

"How can I go home now? What will I say? If my parents find out they'll lock me up! They'll…"

"Nobody will know… Tell them you played at my place."

"I will never, never lie to my mother! It's all your fault! Your country is terrible! My mother hates it! Why do we have to stay here? The war is over, I want to go back home to Barcelona!" The words spattered out of her, more and more coloured with an exotic foreign flavour.

"You will go home one day, I promise! My Honest Pioneer Word."

He pulled a tattered rag out of his pocket and held it out to her. As he watched her wiping away tears with her own handkerchief, he didn't dare to touch her anymore.

✿ ✿ ✿

That night Anton couldn't fall asleep. As soon as he closed his eyes, the searchlights were disembowelling the black sky, German Shepherds tore off their leashes, and Lusya screamed at the top of her lungs. He remembered he still hadn't given her the ruby and thought he should find a way of doing it; this and the boat. Spring was coming; the girls would be opening their *sekretiky* soon, and launching their boats. Even if she never forgave him for the disgrace he had brought upon her, even if neither the ruby nor the boat could mend the harm he had inflicted, she still had to have the best. He'd make sure she lacked nothing; she could depend on him no matter what. The thought comforted him and he was finally able to fall asleep. In his dream, the ruby caught fire, burned through his pocket, the flames reaching higher and higher to his heart. He was trying to grab the ruby, scorching his fingers, throwing it to Lusya. Soldiers with dogs came to extinguish the flame.

Their appearance woke Anton up: The soldiers proved to be real. They were searching the flat, looking for something. Father's books and papers were scattered on the floor, and a huge Brazilian butterfly, the pride of his father's collection, lay smitten out of her glass case, tipped over onto one wing like a crashed airplane. The ceiling light illuminated sharply the dishevelled figure of his father. With no colour in his face, he was barefoot, in underpants. He tried and couldn't get his leg into his trousers.

"It's nothing, nothing Antosha. Keep your spirits up. T'-w-will all end well." These were the last words his father said as he kept fumbling and failing to insert the buttons of his fly into the holes. Then one stranger took away his father's typewriter; the other picked up all his insects; and the third one took Father himself.

All of the next day Anton stayed at home listening for sounds from the staircase: quick tramping, then silence, a thump and silence again. He boiled himself a potato and ate some bread, then crouched in the corner. The sound of his own breath, short whistling exhalations escaping from his breast, now scared him. Night fell. Shadows thickened, intensifying his fears: He expected *those men* to come back any minute. But more than anything, he worried about his Insect Father. Where did *they* take him? He was a helpless man, unable to as much as darn his own socks; without Anton he would perish, that much was clear. Under the dishevelled desk something was glistering in the dark. Anton crawled across the room afraid to make any noise. His father's microscope lay on its side amidst shards of glass. He tried to unscrew the lid, and his whole body throbbed with soundless sobs. Daddy, my daddy, my kind good daddy! He managed to dismantle other parts and stuff them in his pants pocket. When he found his daddy, they'd reassemble it together and put it back on the desk, so that everything would be as it had always been: the light of the lamp snapping his daddy's bent back out of darkness; the projection of his head on a wall, stretching upwards or shrinking, or moving sideways at the eerie will of the streetcar headlights.

Anton tried to comfort himself by thinking of his other, heroic father, but nothing came of it. The Captain proved to be no more than a shadow, easily yielding to the quiver of his daddy's hands, lips unable to form a word. It was up to the son to find the father then; to return him to the life they had had before.

Anton waited till the timid spring dawn diluted the sky into liquid grey, then he soundlessly opened the door, looked around and tiptoed down the stairs.

It was early. The yard was still empty. Leo the Kike and Uncle Tolya were closed. Anton climbed inside the dead fountain and squatted, protected by its round cement wall. Chilled to the bone, he hugged himself with his long arms and stiffened, half-dozing yet alert. When neighbours began to emerge from their houses, Anton scrambled up to his feet and, half-crouching, went to the vaulted gate separating their building from the street. That would be the best place to encounter people, to inquire about Father.

Anton loathed these gates. He could smell the stench at a distance: At night drunkards relieved themselves under the protection of the thick arches, swaying like ghosts back and forth against the wall. By morning, yellowish stalagmites grew on every vertical surface, and you had to jump over streams of frozen urine to make it into the street.

Anton waited. Finally he saw the first familiar face. It was a neighbour and he eagerly hobbled forward. But the young man hurried away. Could he fail to recognize Anton? A woman approached the archway. She glanced at the boy, but when he intercepted her gaze, she too turned away. He was used to it. People often were embarrassed at the sight of his infirmity. Yet, though he didn't know what it was, he sensed there was something different here.

Without strategizing any longer, he let his legs carry him wherever they wished, and they brought him to his usual outpost, on the bench near Lusya's portal. Sooner or later, she'd show up, on her way to school. He waited. Then the air swelled and pushed into his chest with a familiar hot wave. Lusya, his enchantress, was standing on the porch. Red beret, red mittens to match, dark blue coat. In the dismal light of early morning, her face was pallid, her eyes looking vacantly at the world around her.

His tender joy; the anchor of his life; the sweet breath of his bitter days: What happened to you at home? Did they find out? But he couldn't tell by the look of her.

And then Lusya saw him. Her face changed into one expression of concentrated pain.

"What are you doing here? Go, go away! My mother is coming!"

"I wanted to tell you, I'm sorry about yesterday, and also, my father... they took my father away..."

"I can't play with you anymore... Go, Antosha, go..."

"But why?"

"My mother said you dragged me to the Barren because your father is an enemy of people and he ordered you to kill me!" Lusya quickly turned around, her voice now a whisper.

"You believe that I...?"

But at that moment her mother appeared on the porch.

The woman flicked a startled glance at Anton, jabbered something in abrupt Spanish and pulled Lusya away.

Anton stood motionless, but then he struggled after them, flushed from the strain of trying to walk straighter than he possibly could. He had to rectify the injustice, to kill the lie.

"Come, Lucia, come. We're getting late." That was said in Russian for Anton's ears.

Lusya responded to her mother in Spanish, then freed her hand from her mother's and stopped for a second, cocking her head.

"Lusya, it is not true, about my father, Honest Pioneer Word!"

She continued to look at the boy with a shy, vague smile.

"Where is the piece of glass you promised? And the boat?"

"The boat I'll finish tomorrow. And the glass is here..."

Anton fumbled in his pants pocket: In one there were pieces of microscope; in the other nothing but a hole. His heart dropped. He was done for! What a fool he was for letting that hole in his pocket grow till it engulfed everything precious he had, ruining him, destroying his life! He swallowed.

"I... I... must have left it at home."

"Aaa... As you wish then!" Her face took on a dull, indifferent expression.

"I'll bring it to you... tomorrow... And my father... he is not an enemy of the people, please do not believe that." His lips trembled, forming almost no sound.

But Lusya had already turned around, catching up with her mother.

Anton froze, nailed to the ground, then waved.

She didn't turn back.

He wandered aimlessly around the courtyard. He had lost the ruby out of his own negligence. And his father... he hadn't looked after him well enough. That's why it had happened... many a time he was ready to exchange him

– 45 –

for a more adventurous and glamorous one, so they came and took the meek one away. Clearly, it was all his fault.

Heavy adult despair descended onto the boy. He was doomed: Nobody and nothing could help him now. He looked at the sky; it was all aflame, the greyness melted away, replaced by blissful azure. Bright morning light turned tiny icicles adorning each tree branch, each cornice, into translucent, scintillating jewels.

And suddenly he remembered. The eyes of Santa Lucia! They alone could save his father! People are useless, but the Magic Eyes had found him the ruby glass once; they'd help him again, they'd find his father! That's what he'll have to ask for first. Magic Eyes! I'll look after you! I'll fold you ever so carefully, I won't stain you, tell me where they took my father!

Anton turned around and ran awkwardly, sagging to one side, towards home. He mumbled on the way something that came to his mind, a prayer, a supplication. He believed he had to ask the Eyes really, really well, ask, in a verse, with all the power of his heart, for the miracle to happen.

> *Magic eyes of Saint Lucia,*
> *Show me paths, far and near;*
> *In the sky, or on the plain,*
> *Put me on my father's trail.*

The door of the apartment was wide open; two men were dragging his father's desk to the staircase landing. He stole past them to the place where his mother had lived before. But her photo was gone, together with the chest of drawers, her home.

Then he knew it was now his turn. His bed stood alone, exposed. He dashed to it and plunged underneath. There, in the little cache formed by the covering unstuck from the wall at the baseboard, he saw the edge of the paper with the Eyes of Santa Lucia, still intact. But in the urgency of his desperation, forgetting his hump, he had got stuck under the bed and lay flat on his belly unable to reach the Eyes.

"So that's where we're hiding, young fellow!" said the man who looked exactly like one of the guards in Anton's dream. "Comrade Petrov, can you lift the other end of the bed? There is this dwarf hunchback here. Stand up. Stand up straight! What's in your pockets? Get this shit out! If you try to run away, I'll shoot."

※ ※ ※

First time in his life Anton was setting out on a real orphan voyage. He was going to an orphan house, to this perfect circle where – he knew with all his vast, eight-year-long experience, with all his crooked, hunched spine – there would be no *secretiky*; no "Bear of the North"; no boat with rigging made out of cork and leather shavings; no father; no mother; no Lusya; no Leo the Kike; no Uncle Tolya, the master and lord of mice and empty *edemptions*.

They were taking him into a new home, a circle he had so many times tried and finally succeeded in drawing without any compass.

He fumbled in his pocket. There, instead of Santa Lucia's eyes, was an unfamiliar piece of paper. Under the light flickering into the Black Maria at intersections Anton managed to make out uneven scribbles:

> *My Beloved Olechka! Please do not send me parcels any more. I won't need anything here. Take care of our boys. If you meet a good man who can help you raise them, do marry him. I will love you into eternity and will forever remember how...*

The truck suddenly lurched up to the curb, causing the paper to slip out of Anton's hands. As he bent down to pick it up, someone nudged him out of the Black Maria and onto the street.

He never did manage to learn what was it that the letter writer forever remembered.

RUNIC ALPHABET

To R.L.

1

In the plant nursery, Witoslaw handed the money over to the girl behind the cash. Five minutes before, he hadn't known he would be buying a tree.

The tree had a name attached to it on a white band clinging to its slender trunk. The Latin version he skipped, but the English he read with curiosity: "Japanese Snowbell." So far, the name meant little to him, except that the tree, like himself, was a foreigner, an exile in a new land.

In spite of its vulnerable look, it was already twice as tall as he. The most remarkable things about it were the clusters of delicate white flowers that studded the branches from bottom to top. Permeated by the sun, the petals both retained and exuded light. If pure joy, yearning for some tangible form, could materialize out of thin air and move into the matter, it would choose this tree.

Though the tree was right in front of him, he couldn't quite convince himself that it wouldn't disappear – much like the face of an exquisite woman glimpsed by chance behind the window of a passing train. He had read somewhere that the Japanese have a special word (which he couldn't recall) for this fleeting, yet perfect love: when your fate presents itself in front of you in a flash, only to be dragged away along the tracks in smooth, hardly perceptible lurches, while you're still standing on the platform, spellbound, already fully aware that you will be yearning for this face for the rest of your life.

Witoslaw approached the tree and brought his squinting eyes close to its modest bell-shaped flowers, the way Ariadna would have done. The petals gave off a delicate, tender fragrance. The aura of happiness and quiet exaltation enveloped him, as it always did in the presence of beauty.

Like beauty itself, the tree was mysterious: It stood there, silent, motionless, amidst varied but insignificant plants in plastic throw-away pots. It could not complain about the uncertainty of its future. All it did was fill his chest with accelerating and expanding palpitations. The more he looked at it, the more the world around him seemed to be changing, coming into sharp focus as if viewed through special lenses that eliminated the fussiness of its outlines. Every speck of reality found its way directly into his mind, unfragmented, unbroken.

In that state, scraps of conversation, people, street signs, a ribbed metal bottle cap on the pavement would stop drifting past and fall effortlessly in their places forming a pattern whose meaning would sooner or later be miraculously revealed to him.

Witoslaw knew that such states of sharpened consciousness were rare, and he yearned for them. Yet, out of superstition, he hesitated to call these moments "inspiration," fearing to destroy that elusive butterfly by pinning it to the dull regularity of classification. But without that butterfly, his paintings would be nothing more than the sparkless renditions of a well-trained professional.

The artist touched the leaves of his tree: They were a miniature version of lilac. At the end of the sloping line, nature suddenly diverted from its rather overused oval, and took a smooth, but firm dip inward, then picked up on the forward thrust in order to finish the drawing with the light stroke of its pointed brush. A weak gust of wind sent a shiver through the branches: The leaves fluttered, infinitely responsive to air's every whim. The flowers on each branch looked like tiny parachutes ready to lift the whole tree up into the sky.

※ ※ ※

Back home he stood the tree in the middle of the lawn, in front of his house. Mentally, he drew a straight line from the tree trunk to the window of his studio. One day he would paint it. Ariadna would have loved him to paint it like that, in full bloom.

He tried to balance the tree and was surprised at how heavily it weighed on his arm. His purchase came with a bundle of native soil now tightly swaddled in burlap and criss-crossed with ropes. This dry, stuck-together soil – a sealed depository of vital juices, familiar bacteria and ferments – was the only thing connecting the tree with its past life. Like an anchor thrown overboard into alien waters, not reaching the bottom yet, it was now suspended in mid-fall.

The tag still attached to its trunk affirmed that the tree's life had been put on hold: a rough draft, an unanswered request for a place under the sun in this land of tough, red-necked, muscular cedars, firs and cypresses that shamelessly expanded upwards and downwards, grabbing the air, the earth, and the light, scattering their seeds ferociously.

A gust of wind entangled itself in the tree's branches and it fell. Helpless, with half its flowers pinned under, it lay on its side, like a slain angel with wings crushed. Witoslaw rushed to its rescue. What he had to do was to restore its vertical line. Everything seemed to depend on that. Vertical meant life. Horizontal meant defeat, death, and decay. Even brought back to its normal position, the tree somehow looked helpless. Not an angel anymore, but a homeless orphan changing orphanages, always in transit with meagre belongings packed away in a grey sack huddled at its feet. Perhaps, it's the tag, thought Witoslaw, pulling a worn clasp knife from his pocket to remove the white band with its hardly-visible letters. Then he started digging.

"See, I found a home for you," he said. "Just be patient. Soon I'll bury you, then you can start living for real…" He paused: "Isn't that strange? When they bury me, I'll be dust. But you'll grow roots, and then, perhaps, I'll grow roots too and won't look for another place." Witoslaw was making a pact with a tree: He promised it a home. It would be their new home, for both of them. "But you will have to take to this soil, to accept it. You agree?"

The tree stood there silent, the wind gently picking at its branches.

2

The nursery's instructions were to dig a hole five times larger in diameter than the bundle of earth that the tree carried. This was a new, progressive method, they said, allowing the roots to spread horizontally with greater ease. The work seemed overwhelming. He would have to remove the sod, then replace it, after he finished the job. It would take a good portion of his morning, and the day would be lost for painting, the light he needed gone.

He looked at the spade he'd bought at a garage sale: The edge was dull. Making a deep enough hole would take ages, but he didn't have a file at hand. All he wanted was to get on with the job and finish it as soon as possible. Never having planted a tree before, he didn't feel confident. After all, this tree was a whim; he had no intention of becoming a gardener. He was simply struck by its fragile beauty and desired momentarily to possess it, a foolish bargain. He knew that the only way to possess something was to paint it.

Witoslaw was told in the nursery that the flowering lasted only three weeks. Somehow, in his mind, he stretched this number to an infinity, to a never-ending feast arranged for the pleasure of his eyes alone. He tried to cheer himself up. With the Japanese Snowbell right in front of the studio window, he would finally track down that ideal line permeating every form in the world, the line that so often eluded him.

And if the tree were to lose its flowers after he painted it, so be it. By the time that happened, the memory of that short-lived splendour would stay with him forever. He would learn to think fondly of the tree's subsequent plainness while waiting for the next spring.

He started to remove the sod. The ground beneath the black topsoil was a yellowish mixture of sand and rocks.

Soon the hole looked deep enough to completely cover the bundle of earth the tree had come with. But the labour of the five-times diameter remained. Witoslaw groaned and pressed on with his dull spade. When he finally stopped digging, he slumped onto the edge with his feet in the hole. It did look like a grave, maybe for a huge spilled dinosaur egg. After a while he emptied the sack of planting soil that he'd brought for good measure into the centre of his excavation, where the yolk would go, and mixed it well with sand. Then, firmly holding the tree down, he unfastened the ropes, removed the burlap and started filling the hole with earth.

At length, he stepped back: The vertical thrust was exact.

3

During the next week the tree shed all its flowers. At first, this looked like an innocent, if somewhat sly, game. As if the beauty wanted to reach beyond its prescribed borders. As if it didn't matter where perfection manifested itself: on the branches or on the earth. The fragrant snowflakes generously sprinkled the circle of black soil around the roots; the soil inside the circle looked like a minimalist painting.

On the fourth day, however, decay touched the flowers: They imploded and collapsed. A brownish mess cushioned the base of the tree. Black birds came to pick for worms in the exposed earth.

Every time Witoslaw had to pass by the tree, he averted his eyes. He felt that he had betrayed it. He had promised it a home but instead was killing it. Or perhaps it was the tree that had betrayed him by surrendering to decay.

Only in the evening, when the ultramarine shadows diluted the outline of the trunk and the branches, did thoughts of the Japanese Snowbell ebb away. But at night, melancholy would take hold of the artist. He imagined the choked cry of the roots searching blindly in the earth. What exactly the roots were looking for at night – water, a particular combination of minerals that give them life – he didn't know. Those voiceless cries, suppressed by the weight of the soil, tormented him no less.

On one such night, after staring into the eyes of insomnia for several hours, Witoslaw decided to get out of bed. He couldn't find his bath-robe but didn't want to wake up his latest mistress by looking for it in the dark. He walked over to his studio, naked, shivering from the night breeze. Boxes still unpacked after the move into this house cast diffused rectangular shadows on the floor. His unfinished canvasses were stacked facing the wall. I might as well empty some boxes, he thought, giving up any hope of sleep. In the dark, the coarse sound of the tape torn off the cardboard was brutal, like sudden pain.

His eyelids were heavy with fatigue, yet he didn't turn on the light, relying instead on one street lamp for a complete redecoration of his studio. The fugitive light from outside the window turned the newspapers scattered on the floor into feeble beacons that guided his eyes through the labyrinths of frames, boxes, canvasses, and the white papier-mâché cubes and spheres that he used for his still lifes. The chairs were grotesque monsters wrestling with each other in the centre of the room, some mounted on the backs of others, their legs up. His Japanese Snowbell had also changed. Its trunk laid a dark shadow across the window pane.

Without looking, Witoslaw submerged his hands into the first box that came his way. Albums, mixed up with old postcards and books and more albums – he had to find homes for all these vagabonds forced under the same roof by moving. Right now, in the stillness of the night, the task seemed enormous, beyond his reservoirs of energy.

He fumbled through papers, ready to give up, when at the very bottom of the box his fingers stumbled onto something cold and metallic. He jerked his hand away as if he had grabbed an electric wire, but one second was enough to shake the remnants of night-stupor from him. He recognized an ornate handle on the lid of a small chest.

Inside it were Ariadna's letters. There were also tapes with recordings of her voice, a black and white photograph of her face, a slim volume of Italian poetry she had given him, and some other trinkets that would mean nothing to the outside world, had the world by some fluke suddenly brought them into broad daylight. He shuddered at the thought of their imagined exposure, though he knew perfectly well that the world didn't care.

He had packed these possessions according to a hierarchy known only to his heart. Ariadna's photograph, his most cherished treasure, was at the bottom, safely tucked under the velvet lining of the chest: The photo had to be separate from the letters and tapes piled up on top of it.

When packing it, he tried not to leave any spaces unfilled (he always pretended to himself that his box was more crammed full than it really was) and inserted in each corner small rolls of sketches that he had made of Ariadna on their last day together. On top he put numerous drawings that he later made of her from memory.

There were moments when his life, he thought, was still an open book for Ariadna. She continued to read it with rapture in her death the way she had always read it when she was alive. Somehow, even after almost twenty years, she kept the protective wings of her soul over him. There were moments when he didn't doubt it. Then there were darker days of insipid conviction that she had abandoned him forever. On such days it seemed to Witoslaw that she knew nothing of a long and convoluted chain of events whose meaning so often eluded him too. Yet he wanted to hope, against all odds, that what was hidden from him would somehow become transparent to her on the account of her unusual, if precarious, status: being dead for the world, yet alive for him. He even believed that her knowledge, miraculously intimated to him, would somehow ultimately save him...

It cannot be that she doesn't know how I, after the news of her death, have also succumbed to stupor. But I, being the only guardian of all our moments together (58 hours, 42 minutes, I once counted), the only keeper of the quiet radiance of her face, the only one who knows how all of her – the gentle slope of her shoulders and the mole under her chin – assumed this melancholic quality, when she was leaning over the book – I, being the only witness, couldn't afford dying together with her, and had to drag along my guts and my heart that never stopped sobbing for her, never stopped sobbing.

4

Sitting on the floor, with the box weighing coldly in his listless arms, he tried to regain his breath, watching his everyday life closing over his head. It was always the same, every time he touched what was left of her: a quick spasm in his throat, then obscurity, darkness, objects around him losing all their meaning and purpose, their contours becoming more impenetrable, more enigmatic than usual. One might look at a vase, or a wall and ask: "What is it?" or "Why is it here?" and find not a hint of an answer in one's own memory.

He felt like a buffoon from a fairy-tale of his childhood who had accidentally crossed some forbidden line and was now being punished with impending death. And while he lay there prostrated, awaiting the worst, some fairy turned up with a bucket of magic "death" water and sprinkled him from head to toe – to let him die fully and irrevocably. But once he was filled to the brim with his own death, the fairy would empty a handy bucket of "life" water on his body and he would jump to his feet, feeling fresh springy life in every muscle.

"Death" water first, then "life," then – the resurrection. Only many years later, when all that was left of her were his memories and these faded letters now obscurely glimmering in the dark, did he understand the meaning of this strange baptism.

There were no witnesses to his transformation except the tree behind the dark window pane and its shadow on the floor. At night the tree continued to shed its flowers, caught up like himself between death and life.

No, Ariadna knew nothing about this tree, as for so many years now, she had known nothing about his life. She knew nothing about his wanderings, his doubts, his spasms of wintry immobility when he couldn't so much as keep a brush in his hand, overwhelmed by a sudden fear. So many things had happened without her. The map of the world had been refashioned; old walls had been destroyed, new ones erected; he had given up the brilliant colours he was famous for as a young man, in favour of a translucent milky, silvery palette. He had now moved to another city, another continent, and had a new lover, the "newest" one.

5

Immediately after her death, he had felt a desperate urge to contact her husband, and ask him for one exceptionally generous gesture: Could he not perhaps give him something that was left of her? It didn't matter what: her childhood photographs, or even that dark blue dress she was wearing the last time he saw her. He couldn't have thrown it away, that would be unthinkable. I will not abuse your hospitality; I'll just pick up whatever you can give – and disappear.

With time the hand of insanity loosened its grip, and Witoslaw found himself standing alone on the crust of the earth observing clouds and kingdoms passing by, while she was hidden inside, deep in the black soil.

Now she descends into the earth, now she is on a level with telephone cables, electrical wires, dead water pipes and pure water pipes, now she descends to deeper places, deeper than deep, there lies the reason for all this flowing, now she is in the layers of stone and ground water, there lie the motives of war and the movers of history and the future destinies of nations and people.

The lines came to him from somewhere but he couldn't remember who it was...

Silently Ariadna and Witoslaw were whirling round and round, each in their dwelling on the same earth. The tectonic plates were shifting, rubbing at each other's shoulders, pushing out hot lava and pumice, and they were far apart. But sometimes – today was such an occasion – they would meet in the darkness of the night, inside an ornate chest sitting now on his lap.

The desire to look at her face overpowered him. The photo was his last resort, kept for the emergency cases: days of despair when his brush would fail him, or when he was packing his suitcase up before visiting his daughter in yet another city.

Usually, Witoslaw was unwilling to superimpose the anguish of his own life over the pure line of her forehead which, for so many years now, was unfailingly leaning towards his soul. As if he was afraid that the photograph's powers would diminish, from too frequent a contact with this world. But today was a different day. His tree was shedding flowers – it was dying. He was trespassing the promise he gave it, and he needed Ariadna's help.

Contemplation of her face always filled him with great tenderness; it melted all the harshness this world imparted onto him. He was ready to forgive himself for aging so rapidly, for producing such mediocre art, for continuing to live after she was dead. Her eyes, quiet and grey, with a distinct darker rim around the pupil, dispensed mercy that fortified him and brought him back to the mysterious source of his life where everything became possible, fully transparent and pliable.

He didn't need any props to remember how her dark chestnut hair fell in a straight cascade over one cheek – as if some invisible breeze was still stroking her face – leaving the other one exposed to the very temple, and further down to the lobe of her ear. The smallness and vulnerability of that ear never failed to move him. Somehow he imagined that her gentleness started there – inside that little shell – and then spread over her face, her hands, her arms, her whole body, spilling over into the world. Every time he looked at her face the world became inhabitable again.

He found it handy to keep a little dictaphone inside the chest. He pressed a button without turning on the light, and her warm low voice stepped into the room in the middle of a phrase: He must have forgotten to rewind the tape the last time he listened to it: "It is night here. I'm almost asleep, but in your city it must be morning already, and you're wide awake... How strange time is..."

He was both elated and becalmed by the rich modulations of her voice. It was uncanny; she was long dead, yet so close, so alive, hiding somewhere in the mechanics of the talking box. She had a strange manner of gliding off the vowels at the end of words, as if she was tired, or simply knew the excessive effort was unnecessary when talking to him, as if both of them could do without words. Often she would read him poetry, most of it by heart:

> *Look how lightly the dragonflies*
> *Carry a rainbow on their wings.*

She would pause trying to remember the next line:

> *Without dropping it into the pond*
> *Full of water lilies.*

Witoslaw loved those moments of hesitation. They gave him a more direct access to the life of her soul than words themselves. When she read from the book, he would hear the rustle of pages under her fingers as she whispered:

"No, that's not it, and this is not that," trying to find something she imagined he would like. The illusion of seeing her eyes moving along the page made him suffer again.

There was silence on the tape, interrupted only by her breath. But it was an illusion: There was nobody in this room but him, naked in the middle of the night, clad only in his aging, greyish flesh. He shivered.

On one occasion she must have forgotten to turn off the tape-recorder at the end of a poem and he heard the rough sound of the chair being pushed back, then some muted clattering, and then water running, pots clanging. She must have started cooking, unaware of her uninvited visitor, forever listening to her, frozen in the corner of her invisible kitchen. What meal was she preparing in that moment, now twenty years ago? Who would have gathered around her table? These acoustic fossils, these leftovers of her life accidentally immortalized by a primitive machine, became a no-man's land that he greedily appropriated while she herself was gone, leaving him with the sounds of bygone pots and pans.

"I want to spend every waking moment with you," he once said to her on the phone. "Describe to me things you see right now. The street you're walking on, trees, people."

Ten days later, on another tape, she took him for a walk.

"See that trolley with horses? It's a hot day here, the end of the holidays, lots of tourists, gaudy crowds, twin girls with balloons just passing by... One has the red one, and the other – yellow."

Her voice was fading, gradually taken over by the noise of passing cars, the remote jingle of a bell from the trolley with horses. Soon it re-emerged:

"See an old lady dressed in frills. She is pushing a supermarket cart with two ducks, also in frilled caps, and aprons, and pink ribbons. I often see her in this park... I think she is a fortune teller. I should ask her next time to tell me what will happen to us... I cannot breathe without you much longer, I can't... "

Her voice was now threadbare; she couldn't talk for a while. But he continued to walk by her side, through this silence. He didn't want her to cry: Her tears would have torn his heart. She must have read his mind and forced her tears back.

"Now we are coming closer to where I live," she said in a lifeless voice.

"Do you see those tall trees? Right there! Two monkey puzzles, H-m-m... I always thought them ugly... Let me move into the shade here, away from the crowds. That's better, now I can talk to you. Can your hear me, my love?"

Her voice came back to life again: "Oh, look at these red-breasted robins! They flit from bush to bush, peck at some berries... what do you call this bush? Sycamore?"

Again there was a pause, and he could hear cars passing by, children shouting, and some far-away whistle. "Now lift your head. See this clown high up in the sky? He has a hat with a pompon, one pant leg is striped, and then below, I think, are his feet in huge white shoes. Oh, look, the right shoe is melting away... Now the leg is disappearing... Do you see it? I wonder what you are looking at in this moment in your snowy city. I'm looking at the clouds but I can turn around and I see you, standing behind my shoulder."

6

Witoslaw stopped the tape-recorder. In the silence of the night, he heard the uneven beats of his heart. He knew that in a moment the clown would turn into a monster with fuzzy sleeves dispensing torrents of rain. And she would be running away from the rain, and he next to her, forever bound to the sound of her breath and water pouring down her face, her chest, her hair; and she would forever be looking for a shelter for both of them in that park with the monkey puzzle trees, as she was turning left or right, towards a big cedar. He would have no say in her itinerary, trying to keep up with her again and again for the last twenty years along the imagined route preserved by this tape. All he could do was follow her, breath to breath, shoulder to shoulder, getting soaked in a rain that hadn't ceased for twenty years. He couldn't stop the rain, no more than he could stop her from dying.

If he could, he would have sheltered her, saved her, found the way for them to be together while she was still alive. Fate plucked two of them out of a million, put invisible tags around their wrists so that they could stand out in the crowd and be seen anywhere they went. Then the same fate smuggled them from each other to different continents, jailed then into small impenetrable cells, chaining her to her husband, him to his then wife.

In their naiveté or arrogance, they tried to cheat their destiny. They kept plotting and scheming, picking cities on the map in which to meet, however fleetingly. But the chosen dates collided with unforeseen obstacles in their other lives; weeks collided with weeks, months, then exploded, and died. Hotels and pensions they planned on staying in, dodged them leaving nothing but the echo of their names.

Then, in desperation, as their last resort, they found this little machine. It could swallow thousands of miles without blinking, simulate reality and raise the temperature of their longing for each other tenfold. Finally they realized the only place they could stage their lofty, tender and forlorn trysts was in the metal intestines of a plastic box.

Witoslaw listened to her voice, and peace came to his soul, grief melted into joy and he didn't know the difference between the two anymore – where grief ended and joy began. Nor did it matter.

The morning came and pain didn't exist, nor death, nor remorse, nor self-pity. What did it: her voice talking to him again? Her face? All he knew he was free: sore in his heart, tired, but free.

7

On the floor he noticed two dry ginkgo leaves, pale in the uncertainty of a bleak morning. They must have fallen out of her letter while he was scrounging for her photograph.

When the day came for Witoslaw and Ariadna to part, she had gone to the park near the station from which his train had just pulled out. There she sank under a tree, as she wrote later in her letter, into a state of oblivion. When, finally, she came to her senses, she found herself sprawled on a bright carpet of small, unusually shaped yellow leaves. These were two-lobed, simple triangles with the sides only slightly curving away from the straight line. There was something rudimentary, even primordial about their shape. Held by a stem upside down, they could pass for an Indian tepee, she wrote him. But if you flipped them back, they turned into the tiny fan of a fairy. Or perhaps, it was a shard of some Runic alphabet, just one surviving vowel, a muttered litany of never-ending a-a-a-a.

These were ginkgo leaves, a "blueprint, a rehearsal of God's future craftsmanship" as she put it. Another name for it was *Ginkgo Biloba*, or Maiden Hair. "If you bring the leaf, this little fairy's fan, against the light, instead of the usual net of convoluted green veins running in all directions, you will see a membrane as smooth and polished as the perfectly combed hair of a young woman." Maiden Hair had survived dinosaurs and the Ice Age, remaining unchanged for 260 million years. But then the Creator, as if embarrassed by his first crude attempts, must have perfected his skills and come up with more refined and intricate patterns: oak leaves, maple leaves, tulip tree leaves. Japanese Snowbell... God then swept the original prototype under the carpet of the remote provinces in Southern China where, millions of years later, the Buddhist monks found it. They believed in the sacred powers of ginkgo: It could cure a melancholic heart and return a lost love...

Witoslaw carefully put the fragile leaves back into the envelope.

He didn't notice how the room started to come to its senses in the grey milk of dawn. As in a developing negative, objects appeared one by one, first in an outline, then in flesh: canvasses, wrestling chairs, a chest turned inside out, the letters, the tapes, the tape-recorder, the rolls of drawings scattered around him.

Soon not a trace of night was left. The day was standing there erect and plain-faced, all up for grabs, as crude as the deeds it would be filled with. Unlike the night, which belonged to him, the day was everybody's flea market.

He looked out onto the street. Separated from him only by a windowpane, his Japanese Snowbell was like an unfinished painting in the morning mist.

He suddenly understood what he was looking at. The tree was Ariadna herself, that part of her that had never died, but continued to live all these years without revealing itself. In that tree, in the ephemeral beauty of its bloom, she had finally found the home that for so many years eluded her.

Her previous attempts to find form for herself had all

failed – he was witness to that. One late afternoon he saw a familiar silhouette crossing a bridge; the same dark brown hair flying in the wind, the same small stride. It took him running half-way across the bridge to catch her up, but then he saw Ariadna's awkward scheming: The woman was old, with a heavy jaw and muddy eyes.

His beloved hadn't turned into a tree the way nymphs in sun-drenched ancient groves had: shrieks and heavy panting, eyes coming out of their orbits and near surrender to the lustful arms of gods at the end of a messy chase. No, she had prepared him for her metamorphosis long ago. Having sent him two leaves, now dry, a message written in a lost script, she entered the tree calmly as familiar essence enters familiar essence, blood enters blood, water enters water, beauty enters beauty.

He could see her now beyond the window, separated from him and his easel only by the sheet of glass. She was standing there waiting. Once again she had moored to his heart, uncertain of herself, with a bundle of earth as her only possession.

He couldn't betray her a second time, by letting her die again. This time she would live ... Promise me you will live. Promise me this time, for I won't, I can't survive your death all over again.

Later in the day, he returned to the nursery. He recognized the girl who had sold him the tree.

"My tree is dying," he said. "I bought it from you three weeks ago."

"What tree was that?"

"Japanese Snowbell. Do you remember I bought it?"

"No, not really. We have lots of customers."

"I must have a receipt somewhere."

"Is it really that bad?"

"By the look of it. It's dropping all its flowers."

"It may be in shock. But if it dies, you have a warranty for a year. You can bring it back and be reimbursed."

"I don't want to bring it back. I want it to live."

"Try to water it well. It needs good drainage. Wait till next year and see what happens."

Back home, Witoslaw poured some water into the dark circle around the tree. In its thirst the earth greedily sucked up two buckets. It gave him pleasure to imagine roots absorbing water through hundreds of capillaries and then redirecting it to the trunk, and from the trunk to each branch, and from each branch to leaves and flowers. He gently rubbed a leaf between his index and big finger, checking it for resilience. It was flaccid. Was it so tender because of its nature, or was it slowly and imperceptibly succumbing to death? It was hard to say. "Of course you're in shock. When you accept a new soul into you, you're always in shock. New soul going into new soil. Drink, we'll somehow manage together. You have your own home now, not just a tape-recorder inside a box or memories inside my heart for I too will go one day… Drink. You are free now. We are both free. Like in that poem you read to me once, remember?"

She is free. Free from the body.
And free from the soul and from the blood that is the soul,
Free from wishes and sudden fear
And from fear for me, free from honour and from shame
Free from hope and from despair and from fire and from water,
Free from the colour of her eyes and from the colour of her hair,
Free from the furniture and free from knife, spoon fork,
Free from round seals

*And from square seals
Free from photos and free from clips,
She is free.*

The dying cinders of sunset were pouring over the top of the Japanese Snowbell. High above his head, clouds with a crimson lining were blowing soundlessly their high-order sails, drifting away into some unknown land. He turned around and saw Ariadna standing behind his shoulder.

Another flower, a perfectly chiselled tiny bell, detached itself from her branch and parachuted pensively to his feet. It was crimson in the rays of the setting sun.

TRACTORINA'S TRAVELS

1

Tractorina Ivanovna read in the newspaper that in five billion years the sun will turn into some kind of a White Giant or Red Dwarf, scorching and engulfing the earth in the process. They'd write anything these days. But suppose it's true? Then, what's our Government thinking? We've sacrificed our lives for the bright future of our children and all of a sudden – phew! No more. Shouldn't it be the Party's number one concern to preserve our achievements for generations to come? But these days there is no Party and nobody cares. With *Perestroika*, people lost their moral compass. Look what's going on! Three pages covered with murders, robberies, rapes. A mother drowned her two babies in the tub. What kind of a mother is that?

Tractorina Ivanovna put down two bags of groceries on the sidewalk, then straightened up and tried to catch some air. Lately, it would take her several feverish gasps, cut in half by the painful stab in her side, before she could muddle through the ordinary business of breathing. Humped over, she helplessly waited for the mysterious obstruction in her chest to melt away. Her back and knees were hurting: What do you expect at seventy-three, *babushka*, the doctor had said. I don't sell spare parts here. Go get an elastic bandage and wrap it around your calves to support your varicose veins. Better still, stay home.

But stay home she couldn't. Her son Sasha was finally coming to visit. After ten years of absence, that is. A stepson, in fact, but her only child nonetheless. True, he was coming for a very brief stay, because the young people are very busy these days. We weren't like that at all, but what can you do? Even a two-day visit demands extensive food hunting. You have to do things properly, to give them a good welcome. If it were not for the elevator, stuck between the third and the fourth floor for a month now, she wouldn't complain. But dragging groceries to the sixth floor puts a lot of pressure on your veins. In the old days, they'd have fixed the elevator in two weeks, but now a month had passed and still nobody showed up.

Tractorina Ivanovna walked over to the bench at her apartment entrance to rest before the ascent. Fat Nina from the fifth floor and Larissa from the seventh moved to the edge of the bench to make room for her.

Nina's husband had died of a heart attack two months ago, but Nina hadn't lost a pound. Some people are like that: Nothing can get to them.

"What did you get over there, eh?" asked Nina bending down, her flesh rolling over her spread thighs.

"Potatoes and bread, nothing special," replied Tractorina Ivanovna reservedly.

"Those I can see. And what's over there?" Nina pointed to Tractorina Ivanovna's other canvas bag.

"A bottle of sunflower oil." Tractorina Ivanovna imperceptibly covered a bag of buckwheat with the edge of the canvas.

"They 'pushed' oranges this morning at the Serpuchov intersection," said Nina. "I told my granddaughter: 'Run!

Leave everything and run.' But she shilly-shallied around till it was too late, the blockhead!"

Tractorina Ivanovna wiped dewdrops of sweat off her forehead. Oranges! What good are they when it comes to feeding the family? Something much better had fallen into her lap today, and all things considered, the day turned out well, her sore legs and minor injuries notwithstanding. True, her luck declined in the afternoon, but it's the first hour, between eight and nine a.m., when the stores have just opened, that counts – the hour when the saleswomen's fierce resistance to customers' demands is still muffled by an early morning chill as sleepy fingers reluctantly tie up the straps of their stained aprons around vast waists. "We've just opened, no fire to extinguish here, step back, or you won't get a thing from me!" It is this hour that makes or breaks the day. After ten, the sun shines over the earth in vain, wasting its benevolence on empty counters with blood-smeared trays, grey blobs of fat here, a bone there, and flies, God knows why they woke up so early in the season, fat green-bellied parasites, already at work.

Still you can't quit; the distribution of food is as mysterious as God's ways, and while a cold-headed and shrewd strategist will most likely win, you can't be too arrogant about your wits either, for arrogance has never put dinner on anybody's table. The best hunter doesn't plan. The best hunter leaves a fat chunk of randomness to fate, demonstrating a not-by-bread-alone fortitude both at the end of an aborted line and in front of the closed-for-inventory sign popping up in the least expected places. In other words, the ultimate winner is the one who measures success not by one day, or week, or even a month, but by the ability to hold up after years of roaming through the empty counters. The quieter you ride, the further you go, as the saying goes.

This morning, around eight-thirty, as Tractorina Ivanovna was lining up for salted herring at Miasnitskaya grocery, they suddenly "pushed" buckwheat in the Bread Department, an arm's length from her line. Tractorina Ivanovna, alert in spite of her aching joints and varicose veins, in one awkward leap thrust her body to the counter across, outwitting everybody except one rangy youngster. The victory of an astute mind over ailing flesh, of the intuition of a seasoned chess player over the novice's rigid calculations, the victory that guaranteed her a kilo of buckwheat – a one-person ration – all she needed for Sasha's arrival. Of course, she had to give up her herring line, but try to shoot two birds and you'll miss both. Tractorina's heart was beating with cautious joy as she watched the cloud of dust rising over the light-brown flow of buckwheat that poured from the metal scoop into the canvas sack she had fashioned out of her old apron specially for buckwheat hunting.

"If you're trying to short-change me, young lady, you won't succeed!" threw Tractorina Ivanovna to a fifty-something saleswoman, pointing to the needle that was vacillating around the 700-gram mark – well below a kilo.

"Put on your glasses, *babushka*, then go shopping," barked the woman, quickly removing the sack from the scale.

"Don't hold up the line, move on!"

"No shame left in people, no respect for old age… What will become of you when you get older?" muttered Tractorina Ivanovna more for the sake of formality than out of true anger, for the buckwheat was good, very good indeed – clean, with not much husk.

She'd pick out all the black grains in no time; then cook it, half water, on a slow fire, and then wrap the hot pot in three layers of old newspapers and snug it between two pillows overnight, to keep it warm for Sasha's arrival. One night's worth of sleep without a pillow is no hardship: as long as the buckwheat *kasha* is fluffy, the way Sasha has always loved it.

Though the salted herring problem had remained unresolved – and you can't drink vodka without herring or some other *zakuska*, Tractorina Ivanovna had to move on to the next item on her list, namely, borscht. She ran out of fingers on her right hand – cabbage, beets, parsley, potatoes, tomatoes; then switched to the left – carrots, peppers, sour cream, dill. Where to get even half of these?

Tractorina Ivanovna crossed the street and stumbled into a line so dense that from the tail end of it you couldn't see what the head was getting. She quickly took stock of the situation, avoiding direct questions which, as any experienced hunter knows, can invite bad luck. People may mislead you hoping to gain your portion in case you quit. So have patience. Wait and see what happens. And Tractorina Ivanovna waited. Who knows, it could have been cabbage, carrots or lemons, even bananas. Bananas is climbing up a dream ladder too high, but tea with lemon would be nice. Deep down, in the guts of the snake, she discerned the underground tremors of agitation. They were about to erupt. When the head of the snake line had secreted two dark figures, each with a double necklace of toilet paper rolls around their necks, Tractorina Ivanovna's mind went into high gear. After all, it wasn't carrots or anything she could use for borscht. It was toilet paper, a luxury item that had vanished decades ago from Moscow bathrooms, replaced by a solitary nail piercing neatly cut newspaper squares. What would Sasha's wife from Siberia think about this? Tractorina Ivanovna sighed and remained in the line that was folding around itself in three dark loops; an hour and a half of waiting, in Tractorina's rough estimate. Hunting for the missing borscht ingredients with rolls of toilet paper around the neck? Impossible. The goldfish had to be let go. Besides, too much greed never brought anybody luck, the lesson Tractorina had learned almost forty years before.

She never forgot that long gone December night, when she was determined to get a new pair of shoes – a Bulgarian import! – for Sasha. She stood for ten hours in front of the store that had closed for the night. People wrote their numbers on their palms. Hers was 26th. The last woman in the line was 120th. When her feet went numb with cold, she'd hide in the nearby apartment building entrance and then come out again. But after seven a.m. she had to keep her post at the closed door, and that's when the snow began to fall, in heavy dense waves. By the time she stepped into the store, everyone looked like white ghosts twice their natural size. When she finally laid her hands on dark blue leather, her fingers couldn't feel anything but cold. Nevertheless, she danced back home brimming with joy: Her endurance had paid off and next spring her dear Sashenka would wear shoes to school, not felt boots with galoshes.

She leaned over Sasha's bed and listened to his breath. There was no school on Saturday, but she woke him up anyway, whispering her usual pet words to soften his landing from the world of dreams to the floor of reality. She sat him up and, supporting his wobbly back, collected his sleepy foot in her still cold palm and tried to push his toes into the crunching leather. Sasha whimpered with pain: The shoe was too small. She kept kneading his foot this way and that as if it were a piece of wet clay that could shrink from her efforts. Then she gave out a wild scream and ran out of the flat. Never again, not even at the funeral of her husband, did she cry more bitterly. Ever since that night, the cruelty of fate had acquired a sinister bluish gleam and a smell of new leather.

Now standing in the toilet paper line, Tractorina Ivanovna made an attempt to shake the painful memory off. She got on tiptoe, counted the heads in front of her, told the lady behind she was going to come back and quietly left the line.

It was with the sour cream and sausages that Tractorina Ivanovna goofed. She still didn't understand how it all happened. She had already spent more than an hour in a Milk and Sour Cream line, when some kind of a spring inside the crowd popped, the invisible hand shuffled the cards, and chaos descended on them all: the yearning, the thirsting, the forsaken. And like a cork out of a bottle, Tractorina Ivanovna was shot to a no-man's-land, in no proximity to food. She lost her balance as the centrifugal forces pushed her to the ground. Crawling between boots and galoshes in the slush of melting snow, she groped for her wallet and keys smitten out of her bag. Sudden pain pierced her hand. Shards of broken glass had slashed her finger: That was her jar for sour cream hunting. As she was licking her finger – thank God, nothing serious – somebody kicked her in the ribs, but she struggled back up to her feet and was suddenly rewarded for her perseverance. God did not forsake her, but gave her crumbs from his table, namely, a spot in a suddenly formed sausage line. Sausages for Sasha! The core of the meal that could replace herring, even borscht!

"Disperse, babushkas, don't obstruct the path! No delivery today." A voice that could only belong to a man in charge overpowered the buzz of the crowd.

"Stop bullying us! What have you done to the sausages? We saw them with our own eyes!" People pressed forward, but the man in the white overalls held his ground: "In your dreams you saw them! Clear out of here, folks!"

"What do you expect from these swindlers? They'll begrudge snow in winter to their own mothers!"

It was at this moment that Tractorina Ivanovna fled. Her feet, not her mind, knew that her luck for today had been used up and that the best thing, in fact, the only thing to do, was to run.

Resting on the bench from the morning calamity and nursing her cut finger, Tractorina Ivanovna was glad sausages had proved to be a mirage. The truth is she had only ten roubles left till her next pension, and she needed to take Nastya to the circus, and the family on a city tour. But how far can you stretch ten roubles?

Yet happiness doesn't reside in sausages: We didn't have banquets before the war, and we can live without grease now, as her departed mother used to say. The main thing is that Sashenka is coming.

From the letter received from Sasha, two weeks before, Tractorina Ivanovna found out that her boy had been living in Norilsk, the city of permafrost, far beyond the

Arctic Circle. He moved around from one job to the next, changing addresses. The reason he had been out of touch for so long, he wrote. Tractorina Ivanovna's heart went into palpitations when she learnt that her little boy was now married and had a seven-year-old daughter, Nastya, a first-grader! Sasha further wrote that he had cobbled together quite a bit of money at a smelting plant where he had been paid triple for health hazards, and now they were going to buy a little house in sunny Sochi in the Caucasus, right on the Black Sea. Would Tractorina like to come with them? Sochi is not like Norilsk: no snow there at all! No matter where you look, you see palm trees. Lemons and oranges hang right off the trees. Pick as much as you want.

The time has arrived for Tractorina Ivanovna to have some sunshine in her life after all the hardships she had endured. They will keep a small goat in their back yard; fresh milk every morning, fun for the little girl to play with a goat too. Wife Zina will find a job at a local sanatorium for military men as an orderly and that would give Mother (he called her Mother again, just like in his childhood, that was nice) free meals and an access to the facilities; bask on a chaise longue on the beach the whole day. Or, if she wanted to, she could help Nastya with her school work, though Nastya is a straight-A student, and they never had any problem with the girl. And by the way, she is dying to finally meet her granny.

Tractorina Ivanovna read this letter bit by bit, gasping for air at each paragraph: She felt how the frozen bleakness of Sasha's long silence yielded to exuberant joy that expanded in her chest, then shot high into the azure in a cluster of multicoloured balloons. And Tractorina

Ivanovna's heart, attached to those balloons, floated free in the air. But then something happened. As her eyes moved down the page, balloons collapsed and popped one by one: Sasha was advising his stepmother to sell her apartment before moving to the South. To sell the apartment in the *House of Labourers*? Except for evacuation during the war and her brief stay in Siberia, Tractorina Ivanovna had never left the apartment.

The *House of Labourers*, a cross between a fortress and a prison, was part of a two-wing complex built for the exemplary workers of the subway construction, one of the most celebrated of Stalin's industrial projects of the '30s. As a child, Tractorina nicknamed the building *Grey Waffle* because of the grooved concrete finish of its gloomy façade. The other building, adjacent to it, the *House of Specialists*, was meant for managers supervising the workers. From the exterior, the *House of Specialists* looked no different than the *House of Labourers*, except for the yellowish, less sombre hue of its walls. But inside the *Yellow Waffle* (as Tractorina still called it) the apartments were twice the size of the *Grey Waffle*. Even so, with a separate kitchen and a bathroom, *The House of Labourers* was luxury at the time when most Muscovites dwelt in communal bathless apartments with one kitchen shared by ten families. But Tractorina came from a family of "hereditary labourers". It was her father who gave her the name she'd get into trouble with all her life. In the '20s, nothing was more glorious than the Soviet tractor, the "iron stallion" that had replaced the horse of Tsarist times. The beacon of the industrial revolution, the symbol of the first Five-Year-Plan that had walked in front of the girl all her life.

Tractorina's father, however, made himself a celebrity

not on the horizonless fields of Our Great Motherland, but inside her dark, plentiful womb. In the '30s, during the celebrated construction of the first, best and fastest subway in the world, he had manually drilled the first tunnel between the two stations, exceeding drilling norms by 100 times, the newspapers wrote. Even though his star inexplicably faded after the war, as he was stripped of all his honours together with the free food parcels from a special distribution depot for the privileged, the Government, in its kindness, didn't take the *Grey Waffle* away from his family. How was it possible now to sell her flat in that *Waffle*, a flat that belonged to the past as much as to the present?

Very simple, explained Sasha, as if reading his step-mother's mind at a distance of thousands of miles. The Government, always trying to make people's lives easier, had decided to give the apartments to its long-time tenants for free. As an owner, you have the right to sell your property to anybody you want. The market price of the apartment would be no less than fifteen American grand. Fifteen thousand American dollars? Tractorina Ivanovna shivered. Her hands had never held more than five hundred roubles, in small bills.

You don't need to worry about anything, Sasha wrote. He already had a buyer in mind, a trustworthy fellow, a chief engineer from his plant. If Mother agreed (Tractorina Ivanovna was pleased he called her Mother), Sasha would come at the beginning of April with his family and do all the paperwork for her: She would only have to sign. Needless to say the money was all hers, unless she wanted to contribute some towards their new house in Sochi. On a strictly voluntary basis, of course.

Sasha's letter brought Tractorina Ivanovna's life to a troubled stand-still. During the day she dreamt about the long strolls into the sunset, hand-in-hand with her little granddaughter. Trees and bushes always in bloom, palm trees rustling their gentle greetings to the newcomers from the North. But in her sleepless nights, palms and orange bushes collapsed like back-stage props and the necessity of selling her home gripped her restless head with its stone hand. The source of her anguish wasn't the money – she would give all the money to Sasha without a second thought – but rather *propiska*, the stamp in her passport allowing her to live in Moscow. *Without a stamp you're a worm; with a stamp, a human being,* as the popular saying went. She would lose her *propiska* on the day she sold her apartment. And not only that. She would have to say good-bye to the dear old objects that had shared the journey of her life but could not be moved to another city. Give up her Singer sewing machine? Or her tea mushroom, a spongy jelly-fish creature, floating in a three-litre glass jar filled with used-up tea brew and excreting carbonated sour liquid she drank every morning before breakfast to soothe her heartburn? Then there was her mother's carved wooden chest, with an old rag doll buried under the heap of moth-balled winter clothing. Two days before her death, the mother took the doll to her bed and caressed it, and sang it all the lullabies of Tractorina's childhood. That's how Tractorina Ivanovna knew her mother was going to die. All the women in their family – Tractorina's grandmother and her two aunts – played with dolls before their deaths, taking them for their children. But the doll belonged to the chest, and, in Tractorina's mind, couldn't be transported separately.

Tractorina Ivanovna's injured finger was now throbbing with pain. She brought it closer to her face: It was badly swollen. Rather than dallying here on the bench, she should hurry back home and apply the verified domestic treatment, a sappy aloe leaf sliced in half, whose bitter juice would immediately stop the infection. Tractorina's thoughts, distracted for a moment, ran over the familiar circle. Her aloe plant, what to do with it? Just like the Singer, or the chest with her mother's doll, you couldn't take it with you on a train. Tractorina Ivanovna sighed. It was time to get going.

"Look at her, this one-legged cripple!" Larissa sitting next to fat Nina pointed to a toddler pushing a pram with a baby. Tractorina lifted her head. Behind the boy his young mother hobbled along on crutches.

"No leg, but she pops babies all right. Her hubby's running around her like a chicken without a head! Why is that, can anybody explain it to me?" Larissa spread her arms in a gesture of total puzzlement.

"One leg missing, so what?" said fat Nina. "The rest of her must be in good repair."

"How come she's got such a cute hubby? Look at her; moustached like a man, this Armenian!"

"They say her leg was cut off by a streetcar. She was eleven or ten then."

"You mean he married a cripple? Couldn't find anybody better?"

"Knocked her up twice, plus he does all the chores: shopping, cleaning, even cooking! Either she has bewitched him or he is a total fool."

"How do you know he cooks? Did he invite you over?" snapped fat Nina.

Tractorina Ivanovna scooped up her bags and got up from the bench.

What a vicious tongue this Larissa had! No wonder she had never been married and now envies this Armenian. But who is to blame? You have to do everything in the right time. She, Tractorina, had lucked out. She had married twice, first time to a violent alcoholic, Sasha's father, but the second time, to the light-hearted, honey-voiced Pavlusha, a man of easy laughter, the soul of any party. None other than God must have put Pavlusha in her path thirty years ago, in spite of the fact that God, this opium for the populace, didn't exist – as Tractorina had known firmly since her cradle. But how else to explain the convergence of bizarre circumstances that brought them together at the Vagankov Cemetery, the place most inappropriate for that purpose? Tractorina was burying her first husband, the alcoholic, who had burnt himself to death together with three of his buddies. Only a week before they had gone on a "Raise the Virgin Lands" campaign to Kazakhstan and got so drunk one night that they forgot to turn off the primus burner under a kettle. Four charred remains came back to Moscow in aluminium caskets and were buried side by side. Tractorina noticed Pavel at the furthest grave: He was the first to throw frozen clumps of earth on the coffin of his remote relative, one of the four.

In the long nights after the funeral, Tractorina cried for her dead, good-for-nothing husband. She imagined his disfigured corpse, all alone under the crust of hard earth, and felt sorry for the wasted powers of this wild man. He could bend coins with his fingers, or, in a moment of rage, snuff her out with a slap of that very hand. Now all his mad energy and jeering and heckle were nothing but dust.

After the funeral, Tractorina and Sasha returned to their *Grey Waffle*. And it came to be that Sasha had nobody in the world except his stepmother, and Tractorina had nobody in the world except Sasha.

Yet Tractorina held her ground when Pavel came to visit her with a bottle of champagne and paper flowers that secreted blue dye into the milk container Tractorina used for a vase. She didn't say much and avoided looking at the visitor, combing her fingers through Sasha's flaxen hair while the boy was examining the stranger with frightened, round eyes. But Pavel was good to Sasha: In one deft movement, he flung him on his shoulders and raced through Tractorina's kitchen slithering funny glottal sounds with his throat. Then he gave Sasha a badge and a broken clock from a submarine. Sasha opened up the clock, saw all kinds of wheels and gears inside, and his love for his new father was sealed.

In the summer of 1958, Tractorina and Pavel got married and started their new happy life. Pavel pampered his wife. Once a year, on March 8th, he'd bring her fresh mimosa that Georgians sold on the Three Railway Stations square. Tractorina would bury her face in the fragrant fluffy balls and blush, her eyes filling with the humidity of gratitude. Pavel would laugh and flick her on the nose: "Ah, canary bird, look at your nose, all yellow!" Then he'd go and do dishes and wash the floor in the kitchen. It was Women's International Day, and on that day Tractorina was the queen and Pavel was her page.

When Pavel got tipsy, he'd never get into a rage. An uncertain apologetic smile would meander over his face, touching his lips, then moving to his eyes. His hand would reach for the guitar on the wall and he'd draw out in a deep baritone:

> *Telegram leaves are flying*
> *Darling, I'm far away.*
> *Look for me at the construction ground*
> *Darling, I'll think of you on the First of May.*
> *Today it's not the personal that counts,*
> *But only the quota of the day.*

Tractorina loved to watch Pavel's fingers thrumming the strings harder and harder, his voice growing richer and larger. He'd pace the length of the room, from window to wardrobe; then squat and make an abrupt gesture as if ready to pull a dagger out of his cloak; then laugh it off, turn around and switch to a conspirator's whisper:

> *My heart is fretful, all a-flutter,*
> *A bird hitting the bars.*
> *The cargo is being crated...*

Holding her breath, Tractorina would wait for her husband's voice to climb up again and then together they'd take a giddy ride down:

> *My address ain't a street, or a flat,*
> *But the whole of the USSR!*

As they tapped and clapped in sync to a vertigo rhythm, the boisterous train of their happiness rattled, squeaked and hissed, till it arrived at the next stop, a new toast proposed by Pavel: "For the Fulfillment and Over-Fulfillment of Our Five-Year Plan!" "For the Brave Geologists, Conquerors of Siberia!" countered Tractorina, clicking glasses and draining hers in one gulp. Then her spirit softened and expanded, till it covered her whole country with one protective veil. She saw the blue ribbons of rivers, and the darkness of woods, and the golden waves of wheat rolling over the vast flat expanses, and at the same time her body grew cozier and smaller, till it turned into a tiny lark fluttering and dissolving in Pavel's embrace.

2

Holding two bags of groceries in one hand, Tractorina Ivanovna tugged with the other at the heavy brass handle of the entrance door. But the door wouldn't budge. After more than half a century of living in the *Grey Waffle*, its features were as familiar to her as the features of her own face. Now, petrified by the very idea of saying good-bye to her home, she saw it again with a fresh eye, the way she must have seen it in her childhood.

The handle, shaped like a Corinthian column, had held an eight-year-old Tractorina in awe every time she approached it. She knew she didn't have the strength to pull it and, therefore, had to wait for neighbours or strangers to let her in. One winter day – all landscapes of her memory wore winter boots and coats – after waiting for a whole twenty minutes, Tractorina, unexpectedly for herself, stuck her tongue out and licked the heavy brass handle. Whether she did it to punish the stubborn door or simply out of boredom, she didn't know, but her tongue immediately adhered to the icy brass. At first she didn't feel any pain, but being chained to the handle with her own tongue was the utmost degree of humiliation. She wailed like a puppy, hopping from foot to foot. Finally, in one act of desperation, she pulled her tongue off and, screaming, shot up the stairs to her sixth floor. Sixty years later she still felt squeamish when she had to touch that handle, as if the tiny patch of her skin, invisible yet imperishable, was yet glued to it. Tractorina pulled at the handle with all her strength, and finally the door yielded. There was no light in the hallway. New bulbs were stolen the same day they were put in. But Tractorina Ivanovna knew every cranny of the *Grey Waffle* by heart and could find her way in complete darkness. Her nose told her that the regular crop of drunks had recently visited their usual hideout, between the radiator and the metal mesh of the elevator shaft. On cold winter nights, they'd "squeeze" a bottle for three and, drowsy with warmth, relieve themselves right on the chequered tiles of the floor. Would anybody dare to do such a thing inside the *Grey Waffle* in the old days? Disgusted, Tractorina turned her head to invisible rows of mailboxes on the opposite wall. Like all the other boxes, hers was scorched, with fragments of bubbled paint peeling off. A week ago, teenage hooligans had inserted burning rolls of paper through the round holes in the metal doors and burned the mail inside. Groping in the dark, Tractorina Ivanovna unlocked the door and pulled out what seemed to be a letter. She didn't know anybody who could have written her, except Sasha. But Sasha had already sent her a letter and was himself coming in less than a week. With an uneasy feeling, she hid the envelope in the pocket of her coat and began her ascent.

The first floor of the *Grey Waffle* had neither apartments, nor windows, and Tractorina Ivanovna moved cautiously in the dark listening to her laboured breath. But on the second floor, the light from a barred gap in the thick wall gave away the presence of people: Cigarette butts, candy wrappings, matches and empty cans littered the metal mesh that covered the dead space between the elevator shaft and the stairwell. Out of habit, Tractorina averted her eyes from the mesh where more than half a century ago a dead cat, lying on its side and exposing its dirty underbelly, had grinned at her with a terrible grin of death. After that, little Tractorina had avoided using the stairs. But a plate nailed on the wall near the elevator read: "Persons Weighing less than 40 kg are Prohibited from Using this Machine." No matter how hard she jumped inside the devilish box, she couldn't trick it into motion. The elevator deemed her too light for a solitary ride home.

Once again Tractorina had been forced to rely on the mercy of strangers.

On the third floor Tractorina Ivanovna stopped for a rest. "Lena Plus Volodya Equals Fuck" was written in chalk at the door of Apartment 9. Hooligans desecrating state property again. Where is the House Council looking?

You couldn't recognize *Grey Waffle* anymore: People from Tractorina's times were vanishing; there was some kind of scheming going on, swapping a big flat in the *Grey Waffle* for two smaller ones in remote areas, or vice versa, depending on the divorcing or marrying priorities of the growing population. The newcomers were accidental people from suburbia and the villages, the peasant stock outfoxing the Government, making their way to the capital by hook and by crook. These were people with no education and respect for their neighbours. They bred chickens on their balconies and cooked garlicky meals whose miasmas penetrated the heavy oak doors no longer able to contain smells or sounds the way they did in the thirties, when whole families disappeared, arrested overnight, and nobody heard anything about it in the morning.

Tractorina stared at the door of Apartment 9, cushioned by black imitation leather and fortified by bars, an unheard of novelty in the *Grey Waffle* where all doors always looked exactly the same: raised square panels, painted grey. When last summer, the Gusevs, a family of four, had moved out of Apartment 9, only one man moved in, replacing the whole family. Tractorina Ivanovna nicknamed him a "Minister," for he always wore a dark leather jacket and carried a black briefcase as he hurried to the black car waiting for him at the entrance with a chauffeur dozing at the wheel. Sometimes the chauffeur was seen in the yard playing dominos with the local guys, but he never spilled the beans as to who his boss was. It was clear, though, that the man with a briefcase was a big fish. Nina, who saw and knew everything, said that the chauffeur had never left the wheel even at night. Must be guarding the car from vandals, Tractorina Ivanovna thought, but fat Nina was sure the chauffeur guarded his boss, not the car. They all have personal guards these days, she said.

Already out of breath, Tractorina Ivanovna negotiated another flight of stairs and paused on the fourth floor. Had she wings, she'd have gladly skipped this one. She avoided looking at what was leaning against the drab beige wall next to Apartment 25: a coffin lid with a carved wreath on polished wood.

Not that Anna had been buried in an open coffin. As Anna lay next to her open grave, watching through her closed eyes the grey sponges of clouds, the snowflakes landed on her cheeks and forgot to melt, but Anna didn't mind. Affairs of men were strange, affairs of God still unknown, and so she waited. Somebody suggested that they should protect Anna from the elements and cover her with the yet un-nailed lid. That's when they noticed Anna's black shoes sticking out and realized the lid was shorter than the coffin.

Her nephews deliberated whether to carry her back home or bury her with feet uncovered, but then the cemetery worker spat on the ground, stamped his foot and, calling Anna's relatives non-humans, disappeared. He returned with a fitting lid, albeit not matching the coffin in colour. When Anna was finally buried, her two nephews took the shorter lid, of more expensive wood, back to her apartment and left it in the hallway, hoping to sell it one day. No shame left in young people, no conscience.

If Anna hadn't died from a blood contamination – the rumours were they had stopped sterilizing syringes in the hospitals, she and Tractorina would have celebrated the sixtieth anniversary of their friendship this year. Anna was wise; she knew how to listen. She would have told Tractorina whether to sell the flat or not. But now Anna was dead, and the old woman had nobody to turn to for advice and consolation.

3

It was easy to remember the exact day they met: July 17th, 1945. On that day, sixty thousand German prisoners marched through the streets of Moscow and Tractorina watched them as she sat perched on metal railings erected before the war for mass spectacles. Next to her a wisp of a girl dangled her feet, and God Almighty, did she ever reek of cats! Tractorina tried to jump off the rail, so bad was the smell, but the density of the crowd wouldn't let so much as an apple fall to the ground. Trapped, Tractorina wiggled, and began to count prisoners: There were twenty in each column. She counted the convoy on horseback and then the guards on foot. The prisoners in drab uniforms, with no insignia, were different from anybody else in the street. They carried nothing in their hands as if they were the only ones freed from all worldly obligations, and now unburdened, could go wherever they pleased. At the head of the column walked empty-handed generals: They looked straight ahead, their faces stiffened with pride and arrogance. From time to time, black crosses between the collars on their necks caught and refracted the sun.

The prisoners avoided any eye contact with people flanking the street. And they were watched in total silence. It was an ominous, stupefied and mournful silence: The enemy that had burned, killed and tortured was now defeated. And somehow, following the old tradition, the Russians felt sorry for the prisoners marching to their fate.

A woman threw a loaf of bread over the head of the convoy, then ducked into the crowd which stood there in silence, unwilling to humiliate the enemy by shouts of hatred and spite. The last column was followed by tanker trucks with hoses below their grills like an elephant's proboscis spewing water to wash down the pavement. They were carrying out Stalin's order to clean the Moscow streets of German filth.

On her way back home, Tractorina still felt the lingering trail of cat-stink. She turned around and saw the smelly girl following her. It turned out the girl had only recently moved to the *Grey Waffle*. Her name was Anna. She had flaming red hair, and nobody plays with redheads. Her eyes said how badly she wanted to befriend Tractorina. But Tractorina looked at the girl's arms covered with scratches up to the shoulders – and hurried back home. "Don't go away," said the redhead in the serious voice of an adult. "I'll show you something, if you promise not to tell anybody. What's you name?"

"Tractorina. If you call me a tractor, I'll kill you."

"I'll call you Vasilisa, Vaska, a cornflower in the field. Or do you want to be a daisy?"

Vaska was a boy's name but still not as vexing as Tractorina.

That evening, they both climbed to the attic of an abandoned shed, and there, half buried in the straw, were four kittens curling around a shaggy, bony cat. The kittens were still blind, so new they were from birth, and their mother, weakened by the toils of labour and war, had enough milk for only two of them. The other two, Anna said, would die of hunger. She turned away from her kittens, then suddenly stopped and flipped around, agile as a monkey. She thrust her hands deep into the straw and pulled out a German postcard with a dashing brunet gent hugging a smiling blonde: "Happy Birthday, my Sweetheart. Forever yours, Fritz."

It turned out Anna knew a bit of German, God knows where she had picked it up. But Tractorina/Vaska lashed out at her brainless friend: How dared she collect such muck? She nailed Anna's small body to the ground and kept punching at her till Anna screamed for mercy and tore up the postcard in front of her tormentor's eyes.

"Tractor! Bitchy MTS!" shouted Anna, shaking hay from her skirt.

Later that fall, an open truck overflowing with German caps, swastika armbands and other regalia, arrived in their yard. Anna's German again came handy as she explained to the prisoners that they had to burn all this trash in the boiler room of the *Grey Waffle* basement under the indifferent eyes of the guards. When kids heard Anna speak German, they were in awe. Nevertheless, they called her a German sell-out and slut. But when one young German prisoner winked at her and gave her a three-mark coin with the profile of Kaiser Wilhelm, the gangs from both the *Grey* and the *Yellow Waffle* herded around Anna like a pack of wolves. The trophy coins were highly prized for their special jiggling sound among boys who played *rass-hibalku* and *pristenok*. Later, Anna exchanged the coin for a trophy knife with several blades, the likes of which nobody in the *Grey Waffle* had ever seen. Then she swapped the knife for a trophy harmonica and the harmonica, in turn, for a porcelain ballerina in pretty golden slippers, which one girl bought from her for a loaf of bread. With every transaction Anna's popularity grew and soon kids from the yard were competing for her friendship. Tractorina, however, didn't hold many hopes for herself. She didn't expect Anna to forget the thrashing. But as it turned out, Anna kept no grudges. She invited Tractorina to her shed again. Now there were six new-born kittens instead of four. In the corner, sly, horsy Nurka was breast-feeding the seventh one. Nurka slept with every cripple that came back from the war and every year Nurka got pregnant, as if she had pledged to repopulate her devastated country single-bodily. But then, after fulfilling her duty, she'd escape the maternity ward and leave her babies behind. Twin boys she had sold to the gypsies, who poured into the streets of Moscow from The Komsomol Square, the square of the Three Railway Stations. Nurka believed in reincarnation: The kittens were her abandoned and sold babies. They alone could give relief to her bursting breasts. With Nurka's help, Anna had saved a whole litter of kittens from being drowned in a puddle or under the tap.

At the end of the war, both Tractorina and Anna went to study in a construction technological school; and Tractorina, the daughter of a highball worker, got a well-paid job as a welder, but Anna remained unemployed. It turned out she had been the daughter of an Enemy of the People since 1937. How she had managed to hide the fact all those years remained a mystery. How she and her aunt, Anna's sole guardian after the death of her parents, had landed in the *Grey Waffle* was a bigger mystery still. But it wouldn't have entered Tractorina's mind to ask those questions then. And now it was too late for her to withdraw her friendship. The trail from Tractorina's apartment on the sixth floor to Anna's on the fourth was so well-trodden that no weeds of discord could take root.

Nevertheless, for some time Tractorina was torn between two allegiances: one to her people, and the other to her friend. She had chosen Anna, but thought of this choice as a sign of weakness rather than courage. Secretly, she regretted it, and wanted to hide the slackening of her principles from both Anna and herself. As long as Stalin was alive, she looked over her shoulder when talking to Anna.

Yet men too sniffed Anna's orphanhood at a distance and didn't want to be contaminated by strands of loneliness oozing from her long red hair. On many occasions, Tractorina did her best to make up for her friend's isolation: Twice she had invited Anna to her weddings.

When, in the sixties, Pavel stole several wooden boards and was sentenced to five years of "chemistry," it was on Anna's flat bosom that Tractorina disbursed herself of tears and bewilderment: "How could he be stealing from the State?" cried Tractorina.

"C'mon!" Anna said in her raspy voice. "What difference did it make? The officials would've squandered the wood anyway. So he sold two boards for cheap, what crime is that? Why can't they sell lumber in the store, so that people don't steal, you tell me!"

She had been fearless, her dead friend, and could say what Tractorina knew, but would never admit even to herself: that there was no point in Pavel or other moonlighters ditching the leftover wood after they had finished building the barn for the collective farm Octabriskaya. Nor was there any point in returning the leftovers to the administration as the rules prescribed, for the lumber would be left to rot. What Pavel and his friends had done was the only sensible thing: They sold boards to collective farmers who needed lumber to mend their houses; with this money they bought vodka and hired plumbers, again a necessity. No plumber would touch a pipe without getting drunk first; and without plumbing the barn would be considered unfinished and no money would be paid to the moonlighters for their work. Tractorina knew all that. She also knew that Pavel could have been saved from "chemistry" with a bribe. The judge hinted he wouldn't be immune to it had a whole boxcar of lumber been stolen. But who would risk his career for two boards? The boards were removed from the peasants' houses and carried into court as evidence. Pavel was sentenced to five years of labour at a hazardous production plant near Norilsk. The term didn't include the time he had already spent in jail during the preliminary investigation.

"In five years, Sasha will be twelve," said Tractorina, holding her head with both hands.

"Eat, Vasilisa," said Anna, moving a bowl of fried potatoes toward her friend. Tractorina drank some tea but didn't touch the bowl. When they returned from Siberia, the boy could go back to his old school, grade six. In the meantime, she would weather it somehow. Good welders are in high demand everywhere.

Anna only shook her head: "If you leave, don't count on coming back. In five years' time your *propiska* would be shot. You might as well say goodbye to it now." That a wife should pick up a child and follow her man to Siberia was folly in Anna's view, not a noble sacrifice. If you're drowning, why drag the whole family with you?

But Tractorina looked at it differently. It was any wife's duty, she believed, to be with her husband through thick and thin. The more so in her case, for her Pavlusha was weak. Deep down, she knew he was made of soft stuff, fit for a plucky song about adventure, but not for the adventure itself, if you can call adventure the stink of fear. In fact, she was convinced that, without her, Pavlusha would perish in Siberia. And then there was another nagging under-thought she wouldn't dare to share with Anna: Unfair as Pavel's punishment seemed for his small misdemeanour, Pavel had put his hands on what belonged to all of society; therefore, he betrayed the people's trust, the trust our State is built on. She should have stopped her husband from committing the disgrace. The fact that she didn't know about it was but a lame excuse. Therefore, indirectly, she was guilty of stealing as well. Husband and wife are one and the same devil, as they say. Now together they had to rectify their guilt.

Anna stubbed her cigarette on a metal lid and immediately reached for a new one.

"You never know what fate will bare," she said. "Sometimes it's her face, sometimes it's her ass. I'll keep an eye on your apartment. Stay overnight sometimes, so people don't suspect anything. The first year we'll manage somehow." But Tractorina had no money for the future maintenance fees. "Don't worry about the money, Vaska," said Anna coughing. "We'll figure out something. Get settled first, find a job. And then we'll see." As if she had some plan for her, different from that of the Government.

At Sasha's school, Tractorina told the principal the family was moving to a new district and Sasha would attend a new school there. The principal swallowed it alright, and Tractorina quickly got the papers she needed. But at her plant, the truth was sniffed out, and Proshin, the Party Secretary, fried Tractorina for several hours before agreeing to let her go "on her own accord and will," as he made her write in her work records.

For her journey, Tractorina packed only two suitcases: a small one for herself and Sasha, and a bigger one for Pavel. New warm underwear, padded pants, five pairs of woollen socks, three new sweaters and mittens she knitted; also canned food and dried fish, things indispensable in a harsh climate.

They were going east, and Tractorina watched unending snowbanks running along both sides of the train. What lay outside was foreboding, but pure and eternal; what was inside the train – the stink of unwashed flesh, the heavy snoring of the bodies sprawled on the six shelves of a doorless compartment – was brutal but temporal, the ransom she had to pay for reuniting with her husband. And she was determined to pay that price and take in stride the drunken banter of her compartment's companions, the poisonous air, the urine sloshing on the toilet floor, as well as Sasha's whining: He needed to pee and couldn't outwait the lines at each end of the car.

A stocky sailor sitting across kept his sharp steady gaze on her. She avoided looking at him. Then she got up and tried to get her bag from under the shelf that served as a bed. The sailor got to his feet.

"I'll get it out for you," he said lifting the shelf. In the small space their bodies collided. Tractorina stepped back, repulsed by the smell from the sailor's mouth.

"I can manage it myself, thank you."

"I'll take it out, I said," repeated the sailor, putting his hand on her waist. "What's your name, sweetheart?"

"Never mind my name," said Tractorina.

"We're an angry girl, aren't we? Mistreating the glorious Soviet fleet, ah? Be careful, honey!"

At night, when the lights were out and the communal snoring found its common pitch, the sailor climbed into Tractorina's shelf, pressed his body against her back, and painfully squeezed her breasts. Tractorina bit her lips and swallowed her scream. Sasha nuzzled up closer to her, snivelling in his sleep.

4

After seven days of travelling, Tractorina finally knocked at the door of the barracks on the very edge of a tiny settlement 100 km away from Norilsk. Beyond the settlement was the taiga.

"I must've made a mistake…" Tractorina raised her eyes to a young woman who opened the door. "I'm looking for Pavel Nitkin."

"No mistake, this is the place," said the woman, squinting her green liquid eyes at Tractorina. They were steady and shameless like the eyes of some insect, or a lizard – two cylinders with no cracks to peep through into the soul of their owner. The woman turned around and went back into the hut, shutting tight the door behind her. Tractorina and Sasha remained on the porch. It was minus thirty outside and already quite dark, though the sun had done only half of its daily toil. They waited in silence watching whiffs of breath come out of their nostrils.

Finally, the door opened again and Pavel showed up. Tractorina was taken aback by the sight of her husband: His skin was a wrinkled burlap sack only half-filled with his body, so much weight had he lost in the three months she hadn't seen him. He was pale with irritation and indecisiveness.

"Ah, so you finally came, didn't you?" he said, challenging the obvious.

Sasha leaned forward ready to jump and hang on his stepfather's neck, but Pavel stepped back.

"Falling on my head like snow. Could've sent me a telegram, at least. "

"I sent you one," Tractorina heard the echo of her own voice. "I thought you'd meet us..."

"There was no fucking telegram." Pavel spat on the snow.

"Don't swear in front of our child, Pavlusha, please," Tractorina whispered. Her arms, stretched for an embrace, fell alongside her body. She'd never heard him swear before and was shaken by the unexpected change in his demeanour.

"I did send it, honestly. The telegraph people sometimes make mistakes too." She drew the boy closer to her body as if to shield herself and protect herself at the same time. "This woman, who opened the door... does she... does she work with you?" asked Tractorina as if she needed a positive answer, or still believed at that moment she did. Some part of her, the desperate and lonely and loving part, hoped that her husband would deny the truth throbbing in her whole body. Tractorina knew well women with such eyes: predators, sniffing out and hunting down men on the loose, men far away from home. Hyenas, gnawing at souls weary from the burden of their loneliness and guilt. Such women have small deft hands capable of cooking meals out of nothing; they darn the same pair of socks five times, till socks become new and solid like steel; they knit blankets out of one knotty thread they pull out of a shabby sweater and the thread never breaks and never ends. They caress their victims with weak cunning hands and poison the victim's quivering flesh with memories;

they seal their stolen love with treacherous whispers and vodka before and after meals.

This was the woman who had appeared in front of Tractorina on the porch.

And this was the woman who let her and the child in. The woman threw a worn-out striped mattress on the floor, a bed for her unexpected visitors. She hung an old sheet across the room to separate them from her and Pavel's perfidious nest. She put unpeeled potatoes, a loaf of bread and two onions on the table, folded her arms over her small breasts, and sat there watching them eat. Sasha attacked the food with the loutish vigour of a starving child, but Tractorina's mouth froze. She briefly glanced into the eyes of the woman who was feeding her son: There was no remorse or guilt or mercy in these eyes the colour of a frog overheated in the sun. Instead, there was the sheer insolence and jeering of a conqueror over its weaker victim.

Tractorina had always known what was right and what was wrong, but with this woman her knowledge somehow didn't count and for the first time Tractorina became afraid. And the moment she became afraid, everything invisible and unknown turned its claws against her. When she and Sasha had finally settled for the night on the thin mattress, the strange unfamiliar sounds of the barracks crept into her soul, and beyond the hut's woeful protective boundaries, she heard the crackling of trees stabbed in their chests by relentless frost. She thought about the secret life of the taiga and the brutal lives of the people populating this land, people respecting neither law nor order. She lay there probing the darkness with the dry searching eyes of insomnia, till in the small hours of dawn familiar low-pitched grunts and moans flooded her heart with helpless despair: These were her husband's love groans, now bestowed on another woman. Humiliation scorched Tractorina's guts, but in that terrible cauldron of pain and jealousy and degradation, her fears turned into ashes, and by morning she knew what she had to do.

She would go to the Party Committee at Pavel's mine and tell both the Party Secretary and the Chair of the Union how one ideologically corrupt element – and here Tractorina realized she didn't even know the woman's name – how this element, never mind the name, was ruining the Soviet family, undermining the directives of the Party that had proscribed Pavel Nitkin to correction through hard labour. Not only was the insect-eyed woman undermining the Party's plans, but the Party's ideology as well. Tractorina would write all this in a letter and ask the Party to take the appropriate measures. She'd also point out that her husband, Pavel Nitkin, had became so haggard and spent not because of his diligent work in the nickel mines, but because of the disgrace this woman was nightly imposing on him. Tractorina knows her husband well, she'd add. He is a people's person; he loves good song in good company, but the nonsense of the night, that dark, suffocating nonsense, was never much on his mind, not in the last two or three years, thank you very much.

For a moment she hesitated. Would it be appropriate to disclose such intimate details to the Party *troika*, positive as these details no doubt were? In the wee hours of morning, Tractorina felt it would be prudent to delete them from her would-be letter. But then Pavel woke up and stuck his wrinkled face from behind the sheet screen: "You've got bucks for the return ticket?"

"All the money went for your clothing and for the one way ticket," replied Tractorina and reinserted the last paragraph into her letter.

People plan and God laughs, as Tractorina's grandmother used to say. When Tractorina arrived with her letter at the administration building of the mine, all hell broke loose. There had been an accident at night – nobody could say what exactly had happened – but the political committee took off from their oak desks as locusts from the sprayed fields to supervise the rescuing of corpses from the grip of the earth's intestines. The whole mine has collapsed, some were saying.

Tractorina wandered aimlessly watching people with stretchers run by. In the chaos of it all, a stray dog dashed out of the blue and attacked her. Dogs here were as dangerous as men. Luckily, Tractorina's long coat and boots protected her... But that was the last straw, and next day, Tractorina sent a telegram to her friend Anna: "Help send money return ticket."

A month and a half passed before the money arrived. And then together with her now constantly coughing stepson, Tractorina retraced her steps through the snowy tundra and taiga, all the way back to Komsomol Square, the Square of Three Railway Stations, and to the *Grey Waffle*. She opened the door with her key and aired the apartment. Then she went to the bathroom and tore off the sky map that Pavel had pinned to the walls. Then she climbed the ladder and removed the rest of it off the ceiling. From the toilet seat, Pavel had contemplated for hours the immobile constellations over his head, dead butterflies caught in the web of blue meridians. In the evening Tractorina cooked some food for Sasha and went to bed. She slept fourteen hours straight. Two days later, Tractorina went down to the fourth floor to visit Anna.

"I'll pay you the money," she said. "Can you wait a couple of weeks?"

"The money you'll return in the Neverland, at our first meeting," said Anna. "Let's find you a job first."

✿ ✿ ✿

Anna was already there, in the Land of Peace, while Tractorina was still loitering here in the Valley of Tears. But, who knows, maybe the time of paying debts was at hand, and soon they would meet again, on Anna's territory, and then she would hear her secret tender name again, that had died together with Anna.

When was it when she returned from Siberia? In sixty-four or sixty-five? Tractorina couldn't remember exactly. By that time Anna had become a respected accountant at a railway repair yard and was able to put a word in for Tractorina to the chief manager. They didn't need welders, the manager said, but if your friend knows how to operate a crane, I will take her.

5

Tractorina was an expert welder. She loved the white-hot metal; she loved the acidy smell of ozone generated by the arc. But of cranes she knew nothing. She was also afraid of heights. The nape of her head touched her shoulders as she counted steps on the ladder attached to the base of the crane. That same ladder she would have to climb up every morning and then down at the end of the workday for the next twenty years till her retirement.

There were two things she never did get used to: peeing in the bucket and swearing. The bucket was positioned in the corner of the operator's cabin, behind a piece of plywood. She had to stop work when she needed to relieve herself, and that way everybody knew what she was up to. Men below cracked jokes, waiting for her to finish. As for swearing, she never took to it, though the men pretended they didn't understand her instructions shouted in ordinary language. People say that, during the war, soldiers couldn't carry out the orders of their officers unless the orders were obscenities. But thank God, we're not at war anymore. It's time to teach these men some decency through proper personal behaviour.

※ ※ ※

Slowly, Tractorina's life returned to its old groove, redeemed by the very job that had intimidated her at the beginning. Eight hours a day she hovered high up under the sky looking down at people and their machines. And people depended on the precision of her eye, on her clockwork movements. She mastered perfectly the art of lifting the wheels and axles, engines, fuel tanks, pumps and compressors, and transferring them to their next destination.

Nobody knew Tractorina's past, and she relapsed into her former state of widowhood by moving her wedding ring from the right hand to the left. And a widow is not a divorcee; she gets fewer catcalls and more respect. The childless Anna kept an eye on Sasha when Tractorina worked night shifts. The boy grew up a reserved and taciturn teenager. You didn't hear him much. He was somehow passive. In summer he watched fat greenish flies crawling over the blobs of sooty cotton in the spaces between the window panes, insulation left over from winter. Or he watched his stepmother bending over and scrubbing motley black and white crusts of pigeon excrement off the balcony cement. The yard was empty, most kids gone to the Pioneer camps. But Sasha refused to go and Tractorina didn't force him. He occupied himself by playing with compasses and submarine clocks – old presents from his vanished stepfather.

With time Tractorina's sullen resentment mellowed and retreated into such deep reaches of her being that an accidentally dropped word or the familiar tune of a ditty couldn't squeeze blood out of her heart anymore. She locked her wound in herself, and walked stern and erect: She was wronged, but she didn't wrong anybody and that was the source of her strength.

Yet when a new disaster struck she wasn't prepared, as if disaster were a loaf of bread distributed by the Soviet Government: Each individual acquires only one and no more. But unlike Soviet rationing, one person can get two or three or four misfortunes, of different tastes and flavours. Tractorina's was unexpected, as all disasters are, and like all disasters, it was totally unfair. At the beginning of September, the first days of school, Sasha vanished. He wasn't at home when she returned from her night shift and had been absent from school for two days already, it turned out.

After a month's search the militia found the boy thousands of miles away, in Norilsk, reunited with his former stepfather and his unwedded wife, the insect-eyed woman. How could it possibly have happened? In the drawer under the old compass and other metal junk, Tractorina found a note written in the familiar scribbles of the man who had betrayed and rejected Sasha on the frozen porch of his barrack almost a decade ago. Had they been keeping up the correspondence all these years? The letter described the undiscovered diamonds of Dudinka and the glory of a quick Siberian buck. Troubles stretch time to infinity, and when you wake up and hoist your sails in the morning, you don't believe you'll ever moor to the evening. But when you live with misfortune long enough, it begins to sate itself on the day, sucking all the juice out of minutes and hours like a spider out of its victim. And the day, now thin and transparent, flicks by, leaving no traces or memories on the one who lives it. The nights, on the contrary, stretch to forever, and your soul becomes a night soul, the soul of sorrows and secret tears.

Tractorina forgot to feed Sasha's goldfishes. Only when her index finger poked through a dull whitish film covering the bowl did she notice that the fishes were floating bottom up. Then she knew that Sasha was not coming back.

6

When Tractorina Ivanovna made it to the sixth floor, she didn't know what had exhausted her more: the weight of her groceries or the burden of her memories. She sat on a makeshift stool in the corner of the small hallway of her flat, too weak now to remove her coat or shoes. But she sensed the encroaching stab in her rib and stiffened, her face assuming a frozen expression of complete indifference as if it could cheat the pain and allow her to breathe. Then she remembered the unread letter in her pocket. The handwriting on the envelope was familiar. It was Sasha's. Tractorina Ivanovna emitted a small moaning sound: It turned out Sasha wouldn't be able to come to Moscow – the plant's monthly plan was unfulfilled and his boss was delaying his holiday. He was sending Oleg, his best buddy, instead. Oleg would help Tractorina with all the papers in connection with the apartment sale. He'd help her to pack, get her railway tickets and whatever else she might need. The page trembled in Tractorina's hand. The verdict was pronounced: She would have to sell her apartment and move. Old stubborn pride stirred in her. She hadn't made up her mind yet, but they had decided for her! She looked at the dates in the letter. Sasha's envoy was coming the following day.

✿ ✿ ✿

Tractorina expected her visitor to look presentable, something like the neighbour from the second floor: imposing, solid, leather-clad. And indeed the man who rang her door bell was wearing a leather jacket, but worn to the point you couldn't make out its colour anymore. Only the patches on the elbow stood out: dirty beige. The one thing her visitor had in common with the "Minister" was his massive briefcase, from which he extracted a pile of papers. But neither the briefcase nor the paper made him any more trustworthy in Tractorina's eyes. She perused her guest's puffed face, his unclean nails, and quickly decided she wasn't going to put out vodka bought for Sasha. The man paused and then took his own bottle out of his briefcase.

"This is called The Sixty-Ninth Parallel. Distilled out of reindeer antlers. Any glasses in this household, Tractvanna?" Oleg looked around. Reluctantly, Tractorina got up and took two simple glasses out of the sideboard.

"For the success of our enterprise!" The visitor filled two glasses to the brim and held them up. Tractorina Ivanovna disliked the way he scrambled together two parts of her name. It was disrespectful. She covered her glass with the palm of her hand.

"I don't drink these days, Oleg. Sorry, I don't happen to know your patronymic."

"Oleg Ivanovich. You're Tractorina Ivanovna, and I'm Oleg Ivanovich. Beautiful! See, we can be relatives! But call me simply Oleg. I'll tell you something, Tractvanna. In old times, when Russian boyars invited guests to their feast, they'd give them glasses of a cone shape, sharp like a knife at the end. You can't put it down till you drink it all up, like that" – Oleg emptied the glass into his throat – "and you're saying you don't drink. How come?"

"My stomach rebels," said Tractorina gravely. "And how do you stand them up when they are empty, these glasses?" she asked more out of politeness than curiosity.

"Upside down, like so. Do you have anything for *zakuska*, Tractvanna?" Oleg took stock of the table: boiled potatoes, bread, canned peas and sardines, a clove of garlic.

"Not fancy, not fancy at all… We in Norilsk get marinated mushrooms for *zakuska*, even tomatoes sometimes. You know our temperatures? Minus fifty easy. Any day. But nothing missing. You have to feed the working class. Looks like you're leading a hard life here, eh?"

"No complaints," said Tractorina dryly.

"Excuse me for a personal remark: Why don't you put some front teeth in your mouth? Must be hard for you to chew on food like that?"

"Where would I get the money, Oleg Ivanovich? The dentists are not for free anymore."

"Is that so? Rascals! They plunder pensioners, the thieves." Oleg waved his hand in the air and shook his head. It wasn't clear who the plunderers were: dentists, or the world at large.

"That is true," agreed Tractorina. "People have lost their principles. It's all greed."

"But you'll be good now, Tractvanna! We'll sell your apartment and you'll have a decent life."

"I'm not selling it,"

"Not selling it, eh? Decided not to go to the South with your family, then? That is a grave mistake, dear Tractvanna. But this is totally your decision. I am not to meddle in family affairs. I was just sent as an envoy, a helping hand. But if help is not needed, that's fine by me."

Oleg Ivanovich started to collect his papers. Tractorina watched him in silence.

"So what would be the message to Sasha from his mother?" There was obvious sorrow in Oleg's eyes. "If you've decided not to sell, I better go and catch today's train back to Norilsk. No point in hanging around here for another day."

"You came here just to organize my affairs on Sasha's request?"

"Of course on his, who else's? Exactly right, came here to help you, no other business." Oleg rose from the chair, but Tractorina stretched out her hand to stop him.

"Please understand me, Oleg Ivanovich. You're Sashenka's friend, so you're like a son to me... Tell me, why didn't Sasha come himself? It's hard for me to decide, all on my own..."

"May I smoke here?" asked Oleg, leaning over the back of the chair and straightening out his legs. She noticed that one sole of his shoe was coming off at the tip.

"Please," said Tractorina, while fearing the smoke would cause a fit of suffocation in her.

"So, you don't trust me... That's understandable," said Oleg, pulling at his cigarette. "But I feel I must be honest with you. No fooling around with people like you. I'll tell you why Sasha didn't come." Oleg leaned forward. "He didn't want to upset you, and said it was work. It was a surgery, Tractvanna, that's what it was. We were preparing for the worst, but thank God, the tumor was benign. He is recuperating now. The doctors said, move to the South as soon as possible. Norilsk is no good for your condition. Money can't buy health, right, Tractvanna?"

Tractorina's mouth involuntarily opened and she quickly covered it with her palm, pretending she was about to sneeze.

"Tumor," she murmured. "Sashenka has had a tumor… Where?"

"In the guts," said Oleg, waving rings of smoke away from Tractorina's face. "But they have removed it. You can live with shorter guts, not a big deal, you know."

"And when is Sashenka moving to Sochi?"

"As soon as he recovers."

"And he has already bought a house there, he says."

"Yes. One wing is all for you."

"Tumor in his guts…" repeated Tractorina Ivanovna.

"I told you it was benign," said Oleg twitching his nose and pouring himself another glass. He was visibly losing patience.

"Benign," murmured Tractorina. "Did you see it?"

Oleg stared at her.

"See what?"

"The house, did you see the house?"

"Ah, the house… Only in the photos. Brand new, with a fountain in front. My advice to you: Move as soon as possible. Don't hold them up. Zina, his wife, is looking forward to your help. A sick husband, a young child and now a new house. She needs another pair of hands."

Tractorina squeezed her palm. Her arthritic fingers cracked.

"What do I have to do?"

"Nothing. We have already found a buyer. You just sign." Oleg pulled the stack of paper out of his briefcase again and handed Tractorina a pen.

7

In the next two weeks the wheel of Tractorina's destiny steered into Oleg's confident and knowledgeable hands. And they worked magic: They packed two small suitcases for the road, put aside what was to be sent by freight, and got rid of the rest. Still Tractorina worried: How would she carry 15,000 American dollars received from the sale all the way to Sochi? People on trains are not to be trusted these days. Oleg laughed these fears off: "I bet you'd sew the money into your underwear. Don't do that, Tractvanna. Those times are long gone. We'll put the money into the bank. Have you heard about the power of attorney? The next time I'm in Moscow, I'll transfer the money to Sochi."

With relief and gratitude, Tractorina Ivanovna signed another paper he handed her. "What would I be doing without you, Oleg? I owe you so much..."

"You owe me nothing," Oleg said, laughing. "Take 300 roubles for the road, maybe you'll want to have dinner in the dining car."

"Me, in a dining car?" Tractorina flushed like a little girl.

"Well, take at least 200." Oleg peeled some bills off the wad he kept in his breast pocket. "Don't worry, this is part of your apartment sale." As a former employee of the railroad repair plant, Tractorina Ivanovna was entitled to a free ticket in a worker's sleeping car once a year. She didn't want a ticket for the luxury class, but Oleg insisted.

"See, life changes for the better. There can be singing in the streets here as well," he said.

※ ※ ※

Already on the platform, Tractorina remembered that she hadn't asked for Sasha's new address. Oleg put his suitcase down and quickly scribbled something on a scrap of paper. "I'm giving it to you just in case. But you won't need this. Stay on the platform and wait for Sasha, understand?"

"Yes, I understand, I won't go anywhere." Tractorina choked on her words as she and Oleg rushed along the dusty flank of the Moscow–Sochi train. She couldn't check her excitement: "What do you think? Will he come himself to meet me or with his whole family?"

"They'll all come. How else do you meet the mother you haven't seen for years?"

Finally they stopped in front of her car. Oleg helped her to climb up the steps, waved good-bye, and Tractorina went along the corridor to her compartment. For a second she stood frozen between the two halves of the sliding door: The whiteness of the sheets, straightened out as if with a ruler, bedazzled her. Light creamy curtains fell in airy folds over the window. Hooks with hangers for clothing attached to the wall over each cot; small net shelves folded neatly against the surface of the walls; shiny rails held impeccably white towels. But her old instincts went to work without any participation of her will: Before the horde stormed her Fairyland, she must secure a small slice of it for herself, right there, in the corner, under the ephemeral bliss of the silky curtains. She pulled out of a separate bag a piece of soap, a hairbrush, slippers, and a housecoat, all she needed for a two-day journey. Smoothly, the platform began to crawl backwards, withdrawing further and further, till it finally opened to space and the gleaming rails forking in all directions, the furthest reaches of them crammed with freight cars. Dry-eyed, Tractorina watched the drab warehouses, hangars covered with graffiti, rickety fences, abandoned sheds and dumps the train tried yet couldn't outrun for a long while. Finally, the motley of tracks merged into two straight beams, as if somebody had cleared their throat and pulled out of many discordant notes one unifying melody. And this melody ran past thick deciduous woods surrounding Moscow; past *dacha* places with cartoon-flat crowds of cottagers stiffened on the platform, the white blots of their faces smeared out by the train's movement. Occasionally, the melody would pluck out a bouquet of gladioli in a woman's arms, the modest boon delivered by her *dacha's* plots and now carried to the city; or a scarf on a woman's head morphed itself into a billowed sail yearning for the train.

※ ※ ※

After three hours of travelling, Tractorina realized she was still alone in her compartment: The new passengers wouldn't board till next morning when the train reached Orel, the first big city on its route. Tractorina looked around. For the first time in her life, the clean starched world was all hers. Finally relaxed, she checked the money hidden under her woollen stocking and held in place by an elastic band. The band cut into her thigh, and she moved it down, fearful for her veins. When she heard a knock at the door, she quickly adjusted the skirt. The conductor brought in a tray of steaming, tea-filled glasses in ornate silver-plate holders; they jingled, responsive to each movement of the springs. Tractorina reached into her pocket for change. "I'll collect later," said the conductor, placing one glass and two packages of cube sugar in front of Tractorina, and disappearing behind the smoothly gliding door.

Sipping her tea, Tractorina looked out the window. The skies were slowly paling. The trees and shrubs were losing the firmness of their form, stepping back into the shadows of the night. Tractorina changed into her housecoat. Trying not to disturb the starched perfection of her bedding, she lifted the upper sheet and slid her body in. These were not the familiar threadbare mouldy sheets thrust at you in any normal sleeping car in the whole vast country, sheets you had to dry out with the warmth of your body before falling asleep. These caressed and cradled you with the promise of bliss.

Whether from the sheer sensation of cleanliness and comfort, or the rhythmic clatter of the wheels, Tractorina soon dozed off. And in her sleep, her fears began to dissolve. A premonition of something warm, tender and utterly beautiful enveloped her; and then tears formed in the corner of her eyes and slowly rolled over her wrinkled cheeks.

The train jerked and shuddered as if choking on a fish bone, and Tractorina woke up. She sat in her bed not knowing where she was. Then she remembered, and began to cry in earnest, unable to control her tears. She cried for the happiness she was being carried to, the happiness that was befalling her so late in life as to be almost useless; and she cried for her long-lost youth; for her legs that had grown swollen in thousand-hour-long lines; and for her lonely body that had been craving a man's caresses all these empty years, till it had finally become old and twisted with arthritis. She cried for dead Anna who had been buried in a mismatching coffin; and for Andrey who had burnt himself to death at the age of thirty so many years ago; she cried for Pavel who had betrayed her so easily and so cruelly; she cried for Sasha who had chosen the betrayer over her, but then came back, a prodigal son, now dangerously ill.

The train gave off a high-pitched, mournful whistle, as if it too was grieving or atoning for something, and Tractorina Ivanovna continued to cry. Perhaps it wasn't herself she pitied after all, but her people. She saw what was going on after Perestroika – the country was but a wounded beast in its last throes of agony – and she was losing faith in the Party that had allowed it. For her there was no worse misfortune than the loss of faith. You can survive wars and poverty. You can live on almost no food. But you can't live without faith. When Tractorina's father was reduced to a simple clerk in the Transportation Ministry, Tractorina never doubted it was a human mistake, not the collapse of the Soviet Principle. People's envy and greed had let her father down, marring and undermining the State in the process. She had then a sudden insight into the nature of governing: The State was powerful, yet at times vulnerable as a child. And as a child, she thought, it needs our collective protection. We are all responsible for its well-being. Our acts of kindness are not a matter of personal choice, then, but a civil duty. In

Tractorina's logic, Sasha and Oleg's concern for her weren't just a private matter. In a small way, they were restoring an ailing organism – the system and the Party – to its former glory.

Tractorina didn't notice how the train had slowed down and stopped at a way-station. Fitful diagonal light from the lamp-stands snatched out of the darkness a platform with a file of women in motley aprons and sleeve-protectors, bending over buckets filled with local produce. The train would stay here only for five minutes, the loudspeakers announced, and the pale sleepy northerners, who woke up in the middle of the night for their first taste of Southern abundance, had to make haste with their transactions: Rose-cheeked peaches, sour cherries, fragrant apples, watermelons and cucumbers could be had for next to nothing. Tractorina Ivanovna quickly got out of bed and dressed. Then, sideways, sparing her aching knees, she stepped down onto the platform. The air was unusually warm. For a moment she hesitated which vendor to choose, then saw a little girl, not more than nine, with an iron butterfly on a wooden stick. The toy was methodically opening and closing its brightly coloured wings as the girl rolled the stick forth and back in front of her.

"Only two roubles." The girl looked at Tractorina Ivanovna with expectation.

"Where did you get that from?" Tractorina Ivanovna smiled. She hadn't seen toys like this since her childhood.

"My brother makes them and I sell…"

"Is that your mother?" Tractorina Ivanovna pointed to a large woman standing next to a little girl.

"No, my mom lives with another man, and I live with my brother. Will you buy it for a rouble-fifty?" said the girl.

Tractorina took out three roubles. "Keep the rest. I have a little granddaughter, Nastya. I'll tell her it's a present from you."

The girl quickly counted the cash: "Would you like some cherries, then?" With skilful movements, she rolled a newspaper into a cone and filled it with a scoop of cherries.

The train hiccupped in preparation for the journey. Tractorina Ivanovna grabbed her butterfly and her cherries, patted the girl on the head, and hurried to her car.

The morning light unveiled neat white stucco cottages. Sunflowers hung their naïve faces over whitewashed fences. Cows in the meadows looked sturdier and healthier than in the North. Tractorina lowered her window and inhaled the bitter smell of sage. The train was now running through the Ukrainian steppes.

Lit by the bright morning sun, the world suddenly righted itself. She was agitated. It was a world full of new hopes and promises: Soon she'd come face to face with the Black Sea and the mythical palm trees and tropical flowers and fruit. And yet all this Southern luxury was nothing but a backdrop, the elaborate frame through which her reunited family looked at her smiling. She would recognize them all at first glance: even the granddaughter and daughter-in-law she had never seen.

Tractorina Ivanovna fretted impatiently. Two hours before the final destination she had collected all her belongings, straightened out her beddings, and sat on a bench straight as a rod, waiting. Finally, with the help of a conductor, she descended the steep staircase a final time, a suitcase in one hand, the butterfly on a stick and the bag with cherries in the other.

On the platform she paused, panting with excitement: Overnight she had moved from a black-and-white film of darkly clad Muscovites into the colour film of bright cottons and satins of the South. Welcomers mixed with the ones who had just arrived; hands exchanged flowers; arms opened; mouths kissed. She stood there waiting. Only in her childhood had she known a similar thrill of anticipation, sitting atop her father's shoulders, as he marched at a stately pace towards Red Square in the front line of the May Day celebration. She waved her paper flowers and her tiny red flag with Stalin's portrait under the hammer and sickle toward something mysterious, yet magnificent, lying ahead. The anxious beats of her heart resonated in her whole body. Now again, as so many years before, she was at the threshold of a new mysterious world.

Listening to the anxious beats in her chest, Tractorina Ivanovna tried to spot a familiar face in the crowd. But the Brownian movement gradually subsided, leaving around her a space that seemed deserted. Finally, there were only two people left on the platform, a young woman with a little girl. "Must be them!" Tractorina Ivanovna dashed forward but then her heart sank. Where is Sasha? Can he be that ill? The little girl's eyes were pinned to the butterfly, and as her mother tried to pull her away, the girl twisted her body, a string puppet, walking backwards. "Why are they leaving? No, that's not them..."

When the woman with the girl reached the end of the platform, the girl's head still turned backwards, Tractorina's legs felt cotton-wool weak. She stood there unable to move. The platform was now empty.

A porter stooped over Tractorina and offered help with her luggage. "No, no, I'm all right. My family is going to show up any minute now..." said Tractorina and let the porter pass. But then she remembered something and called after him. "Maybe you can help me though... Is Karl Marx Street far from here?" Tractorina handed the man the piece of paper with Oleg's scribbles. The porter turned the paper this way and that. "Are you sure, *babushka?* We have Lenin's street, Engels' street, Marshal Budenny's street, but what you need we don't have. Somebody got it all mixed up."

"That can't be. The address is correct. If you don't know streets in your own city, you shouldn't be in this job in the first place, young man!" Indignantly, Tractorina Ivanovna turned away.

There was no point in standing there alone anymore, and Tractorina Ivanovna walked over to the bench in the shadow of the railway station. She put her butterfly on the ground and moved her luggage close to her feet. Then inhaled the unfamiliar salty freshness. Must be the sea. How lovely. The air was balmy to the touch: rich and redolent with a hint of decay. Tractorina Ivanovna unbuttoned her woollen sweater, wiped the sweat off her forehead, and checked the cherries: The newspaper was all soaked with red sap. They better come before the cherries get all soggy. And they will. She simply had to be patient. She had waited ten years for her son's return. She will wait again. Ten minutes, half an hour, two hours. He'll appear from over there, the side of the invisible sea.

The direction she, for some reason, was afraid to look.

CARMELITA

1

I came here two years ago, shortly after my father's death. More than any time before, I felt then at loose ends in spite of the large inheritance I had so suddenly come into. Turning into a rich man in the blink of an eye may present certain difficulties for someone who has been a "dishevelled loser" all his life, as my father habitually called me from the age of five, referring, no doubt, both to my frazzled hair, not a strand of which I possess now, and my inability to put to any good use the strange talents that I somehow managed to tease out of my indifferent and negligent fate. I think it was this little bouquet of quirks lurking in the fissures of my brain and disguising themselves as the early signs of *wunderkinderism* that prevented me later in life from mastering any worthwhile profession. The ability to multiply five-digit numbers in my head is one example of my arcane and totally futile gifts. It used to be a sure bait for the girls I fancied, if only for a few dashing moments of initial acquaintance, when – pencil in hand – they'd quickly sketch a neat scaffold on a scrap of paper, verify the results and then turn their sharp-chinned, sun-lit faces towards me in complete disbelief. "I can also do roots. Give me any number." Puzzled, they'd walk around me, a curiosity under a museum glass, pause for a moment and then flit off like sated birds from a feeder to join their rope-skipping flock in the schoolyard.

My other gift was a photographic memory, keeping intact page after page of books I had read twenty years earlier. As a teenager I stammered, but my most ingenious classmates laid siege to this predicament, teasing the string of battle dates and names of the generals out of me at the exams they forced me to write for them. For a while, my lopsided usefulness did keep at bay their desire to punch me the moment my round form got into their field of vision.

※ ※ ※

It was only by fluke that at the age of thirty I finally stumbled on something that could bring me a semblance of an income: It turned out I could make up elaborate stories and fables at the drop of a hat. (At one point I secretly fancied myself a writer, even a poet, though I couldn't show a single written page for my whimsy.) But people in the street didn't care about my misapprehensions when I'd appear on a busy corner, cap for coins on the sidewalk, and, strumming three strings on a banjo, follow the meandering paths of my imagination. "One word, ladies and gentlemen, give me one word," I called out. It was all I needed to start spreading the magic carpet of my fantasies under the busy and indifferent feet of the city. I preferred concrete words over abstract ones, and women over men, for women were a much more generous and empathetic audience for a lost soul like me. I liked women's bodies, and the way they moved; I liked their twitter, their quick shift of subjects, their wide-eyed compassion towards the hurting ones, and the girlish playfulness that illuminated with sudden innocence even the oldest and the most lived-in faces of their tribe.

Unfortunately, women didn't pay me back in the same coin. Was it my natural shyness or my appearance that deterred them? Yes, I am a short and rather heavy-built man with bulging eyes positioned wide apart on a head too massive for my smallish body. In spite of that, women always told me I had some charm, if only because they sensed I was ready to serve them. And – oh, my pathetic self-pity! – how many men with far less pleasing exteriors had I watched becoming happy husbands and fathers! I, on the other hand, was destined to live and die alone.

It was this final realization that elevated my fears of death to a degree of paranoia. I've heard that people who haven't used up the full measure of their lives have a hard time dying. Remorse must make the physical pain of passing into the Neverland unbearable. That's when it dawned upon me that I, for one, hadn't even started living, for I couldn't, in full honesty, count as life the tediousness and the boredom of days that had filled up 60 years of my existence. In a nutshell, I suddenly became afraid of the pain of dying. There must be some way out of this fear, I said to myself during the sleepless nights I was by now quite accustomed to. And I began to hope, in a very childish manner, that the love of one woman, never experienced by me yet, could deliver me from the fears of the final passing... Oh, the dreams of an old decrepit man! Get back to reality, my father had been hammering into my head all his life, and then, finally, his call reached my ears in the form of a huge inheritance that I reluctantly, against all my instincts, had to deal with.

This shift in my life was as unexpected as it was immediate: Suddenly, a man in whose existence nobody had shown the slightest interest became the longed-for target of an invisible, smiling, finger-crooking crowd. I began to receive invitations for dinners, gala concerts and charity events. (I had never owned a suit, nor a tie, so I had to get both to show up at the functions organized by my father's retinue.) The phone barking at me out of the corner of my half-empty apartment became my worst enemy. Needless to say, I would never think of getting a cell. The sight of sealed envelopes oppressed me. Like Satie, the composer, I stopped opening my mail. (Another of my photographic memory remembrances.)

It was at that point that I decided to drop everything, and guided by mere chance rather than choice, came to Zipolite, a small Mexican village tucked away on the Pacific Coast. I was looking for some meaningful way of getting rid of my money, if that oxymoron makes any sense. Well, it did then to me: An orphanage, a hospital for sick children, or a school for the handicapped lurked in my imagination as a summary rescuing plan of sorts.

Zipolite consisted of only one street lined with dilapidated bungalows and stalls roofed with palm leaves where Indians from the hills laid out their trinkets. This humble, yet nonchalant life strangely suited my mood. As the daytime heat receded, the local beauties came strolling along the main drag mixing with stray dogs and barefoot toddlers. A fat American with a shiny skull, owner of two local hotels, watched the crowd out of his hammock on the balcony of his *El Paraiso*. At night, in the back yards, villagers burned their *basura*. Plastic bags, containers and leftovers morphed into black pillars of stench that crawled over the beach, reaching further and further out into the ocean. Old tires provided an atavistic entertainment for the local youth who burned them every night in bonfires dotting the beach line. Till dawn, the air was unbreathable, and I was coughing away through the nights, struggling with insomnia. Days were no better: Sinking into a sweaty drowsiness, I was asking myself why on earth I had come to this forsaken village.

One late afternoon, unusual noises outside jerked me out of my slumber. I went downstairs, past the hammocks bulging with sun-tanning vacationers, past the vendors, to the ocean front. Part of the beach was sealed off with a red ribbon the agitated crowd was pushing impatiently against. I couldn't understand what excited these people. My eyes could see nothing but the expanse of the ocean beyond that ribbon. A man in a white shirt shouted in Spanish into a loudspeaker. Everybody in the crowd was holding something in their outstretched hands, I noticed. I came closer.

And then I saw her. She was on her haunches, on the other side of the ribbon separating the crowd from the smooth hard sand of the surf. While the agitated forward-pressing mass was facing the empty ocean, she alone was facing the crowd. There was movement all around her. She alone was still, except for her hair – a magnificent jet-black waterfall cascading all the way down to her thighs. With a strong thrust of breeze, her hair suddenly transformed itself into a wild bird, took off from her shoulders, spread its wings, soared, and then landed again on her back. For the first time then I saw her face. It revealed an austere and proud beauty: The chiselled cheekbones, the perfect arch of her eyebrows, the aquiline nose gave her both an air of arrogance and a fragile aloofness. There was grace in her stillness, but also loneliness.

The daughter of an ancient Indian priest must have looked like that, I thought. But there must be mixed blood, the blood of Spaniards, Moors and Jews running in the veins of her ancestors as well. She was young, not more than thirty.

Unaware of being watched, the girl herself was watching the crowd through a camera she had improvised out of her index finger and a thumb.

"*Buenas tardes*," I said, squatting inadvertently inside her fingers-framed world. She scrutinized me silently through her camera. I smiled and mimicked her gesture with my fingers. She put her hand down. "I don't really speak Spanish. *Buenas tardes* and *adiós* are about the only words I know. Do you speak English, by any chance?"

"I certainly do, but you're in my way," she answered with a splendid confidence and got up to her feet. As she was rising, I noticed a small diamond pendulum nestling between her half-bare breasts. On fire from the setting sun, it caught my eye with sharp multicoloured sparks. Her wrap-around skirt tightly hugged her narrow hips, concealing her legs but leaving her flat belly exposed.

With her elongated El Greco limbs and neck she stood considerably taller than me.

"You speak with a British accent. Where did you learn your English?"

She brushed her long hair aside and paused, examining me.

"Studied at the London Institute of Art for five years," she said finally.

"You're an artist then?"

She kept looking at me without saying a word.

I realized it was the expression of her strangely still, almond-shaped eyes that more than anything else gave her that air of aloofness. She looked at me through a thicket of dark lashes without squinting. If the ocean was capable of gazing at humans from its mysterious depths, it would be gazing out of these eyes. What softened the air of severity about her, though, was her skin and her mouth: The skin had an olive tinge, magically warm in the setting sun. Her mouth was moving, as if she was savouring the sight not with her eyes but with her sensual, bow-like lips.

Nodding to the crowd, I asked my new acquaintance what was going on. "They are releasing baby turtles into the ocean. They do it every year, at the sunset."

"Where do they get so many?"

"Hatch them in the village," she said indifferently.

"La causa noble de la liberación de las tortugas permite a los miembros orgullosos de la comunidad..." barked a megaphone.

"What is he saying?"

"The noble cause of liberating the turtles will allow all the members of the community... I didn't get it... to proudly go to hell, I suppose."

For the first time I heard her laugh.

"First visit to Mexico?" she asked then.

"It is."

"Mexicans are like children. They like entertainment and will pay to be told how great they are. Out of two hundred turtles one may survive."

"Do you know why they release these creatures at sunset?" I asked.

"No clue, nor do I care."

"Yet, you, too, came to watch the event."

"I came to watch people... I don't care much about turtles."

"You must be a photographer then, though I never saw anybody taking pictures with such a camera ," I said smiling. But she didn't take me up on it.

"I'm not a photographer," she said seriously. "I'm a painter."

"Well, isn't it close?"

"Opposite mediums."

She was abrupt and I didn't know how to keep up the conversation.

As soon as the sun sank into the ocean, the man in the white shirt cut the ribbon and people rushed towards the water, their tiny charges in their palms. They placed the baby turtles on the wet sand bared by a receding wave. The turtles froze stiff, shocked by their first contact with the elements. Finally, a wave washed some of them off into the ocean, but others, still paralyzed, had to be carried into the water. My eyes followed their first helpless movements: It seemed inconceivable that these tiny clots of life would survive their first night in the cold abyss.

The girl turned around and started walking away along the water's edge. The incoming wave licked the hem of her dress and she raised her skirt over her knees. Her legs were perfectly shaped. I found myself following her.

"By the way, my name is Joseph Parson. I'm from Canada. And you are?" I caught up with her and tried to keep one step ahead, not wanting to lose the advantage.

"Carmela." She dropped the word without turning her head.

"That's a lovely name..."

"Nothing special, thousands of girls in this country are called Carmela."

"Maybe. But the owner of the name is very special: a very attractive and intelligent woman."

I knew how awkward my compliments sounded and got embarrassed, becoming aware of my unprepossessing appearance, of my uncovered bald pate. I touched my chin: A three-day stubble only increased my shyness.

Carmela stopped walking and looked straight into my face: "So you like me, eh?" she said, smiling.

I felt relieved. The ice between us was broken.

"Would you care to have a drink somewhere along the beach?"

"Sure," she said, as if expecting to be invited.

It was getting dark quickly and the stars were already out. I looked up, but couldn't recognize the familiar constellations: They seemed to be at the wrong angle. The moon, like an overturned beetle, was lying belly up. The tables of a restaurant-bar were placed near the water, their feet sinking in the sand. We took the one nearest to the tideline.

A dark-skinned, Indian-looking waiter brought the menu, placed some glasses, and stabilized the shaky table. Then he put his arm around Carmela and kissed her on each cheek the way Mexicans greet each other. I opened the menu, counting on Carmela's help.

"Oh, Carmelita, sweetheart! Where have you been? We were looking for you everywhere!" The call came from a table next to ours. Three or four men sitting there seemed to be quite loaded. One of them made an attempt, with some theatrical flourish, to move from his table to ours, but couldn't disengage his dangling Frankenstein frame from the chair which was sinking deeper into the sand the more he struggled. His two pals were egging him on.

"C'mon, one more time, just lift your ass!"

"Stay put, Bob, don't you dare move!" shouted Carmela in English, waving a "no" to the man. She turned to the waiter: "Francisco. Go, talk to him."

"*De acuerdo*," said Francisco, parting his gelled hair with a quick movement of both hands.

I turned to Carmela. "Everybody seems to know you here."

"Sure. I come here every summer. See the white house on the bluff? That's my studio."

Carmela pointed towards the ocean, across the bay, but I couldn't see anything in the darkness.

"By the way, these three are also from Canada. They sleep by day, crawl out of their burrows at night and get drunk like pigs."

"How do you know them?"

"The tall one, Bob, was my model."

"He looks like a complete waste," I said. "Is he always loaded like that?"

"I don't really care. He is a picturesque type, that's all I want. Look at his head, his wide, heavy jaw. Look how his face narrows towards his forehead, a rare bone arrangement. He told me he is a *mestizo*, half Indian, half Norwegian."

"We call them Métis. First Nations people mixed with Whites."

"That's like our descendants of Spanish and Indians then. He is fighting for the rights of his people, he said, and he is obsessed with diamonds. He even gave me one." She touched the pendulum on her neck.

"That's a generous gift!" I said, grinning.

"He got his portrait in exchange, didn't he? He had nothing to pay with and I'm expensive."

"Where is he from, you said?" I was a little baffled by all this.

"Somewhere from the North, some kind of a knife..." Carmela shook her hand in the air.

"Yellowknife," I said. "It's true, they did find lots of diamonds there recently. The Métis consider the land theirs and want some share in it together with the Dené Indians. There's a dispute, you see. But the Dené don't recognize the Métis. They are not 'Indian' enough for them, and for the Whites, they are not really Whites. The Métis are falling into the crack between, neither here, nor there."

"A hard place to be!" said Carmela looking at the candle on the table whose reflected light danced in her squinting eyes. I couldn't get rid of the feeling that her remark was aimed at me rather than the fat Métis at the next table. But then I felt so unsure of myself in the presence of this woman.

I tried to explain something about Canadian policy towards the First Nations.

"What's the First Nations, anyway? Funny name."

I started to explain. A stray dog came up and rubbed against Carmela's chair, then looked at her with pleading eyes. The scruffy creature had separated from the pack and was hunting for the leftovers at the beach joints on its own. Carmela made an abrupt movement to scare the dog off, got up and started to readjust her chair. I could see she was quickly losing interest in my rhetoric.

"So you're a painter," I said, trying to change the subject. "That's interesting. I know there is a rich art tradition in Mexico. What style do you work in?" Carmela gave me a quick contemptuous look. "I'm sorry, I know little about painting. I mean, is it abstractionism or surrealism, or perhaps…" Embarrassingly, I was running out of words for styles and she certainly wasn't helping me.

"I paint lungs and vaginas," Carmela said calmly.

"I beg your pardon?"

"Not human lungs, though. The vaginas are human all right, but the lungs are from sheep. I take sheep lungs, I dry them out. You know what they look like when dry?" She was now truly animated. "Like small white balloons, sausage-shaped. And then I attach them to the painted surfaces. I have one piece in the Museum of Contemporary Art in Mexico City. You've been there? Perhaps you noticed the painted blue sky with clouds over the entrance arch. They look like painted clouds, but in fact, it's sheep lungs."

I didn't know exactly how to react, so I nodded and smiled, just in case.

The waiter brought the *sangría* I had ordered for Carmela. He'd obviously heard our conversation.

"She is famous, sir! Everybody knows her here and even in Mexico City," he said in his heavily accented English.

"Oh, shut up Paco!" Carmela snapped.

"*Poco tímida, poco dispuesta.* It is true, what I said. You go to a big museum, she is there, like Rivera." Francisco patted Carmela on the shoulder.

"Hey, chum!" shouted Bob, the Métis, across the table. "Get your hands off her! Better bring us another beer!"

Then he made yet another attempt to disengage himself from the chair.

Carmela said something to the waiter in Spanish, and he went over to the table where Bob sat with his half-drunk pals.

"If you wish to see my work, you can come to my studio," said Carmela softly.

Alone in my hotel room, I couldn't stop thinking about her: the way she tossed her hair, the way her long slim arms danced as she talked. She had this habit of turning her head away in the middle of the conversation as if gazing at something only she could see. But her eyes remained strangely still, both searching for something, yet indifferent to what they found. Her eyes watched you, but kept what they observed hidden.

2

Carmela's cottage was perched on top of the bluff overlooking the ocean, and I had to climb up the winding stairs, cut in the solid rock, to reach abundant bougainvillea camouflaging the entrance to her studio. The door was ajar when I stepped into an unusual space of movable canvas partitions, positioned at different angles to each other. Between them the fresh breeze from the ocean wandered freely. The partitions looked like sails and were perfect for exhibiting art. One wall of the studio was all glass and through it, down below, I could see waves beating against the rocks, and above them, the horizon. I felt I was drifting through shimmering azure that was both the ocean and the sky.

At first, I didn't recognize Carmela: Her hair was tired up in a bun at the back, exposing her long neck. But her dry, businesslike manner contrasted with her attire. When she stood against the light, her diaphanous Turkish *chalivari* exposed her legs to the thighs.

"Have a look at my work," she said, pointing to some elaborate frames leaning against the wall. "This was commissioned by the Museum of Modern Art in Mexico City. I need to make three more pieces."

I looked for paintings inside the frames, but found none. Instead, there were fabrics of different textures and colours, mostly in red hues: from scarlet velvet to pink silk. The material was collected in folds to form in the centre of each frame an ovoid shape. The sign read: *Retratos de familia.*

"Do you like it?"

I removed my sunglasses in order to see better, but they slipped out of my fingers. As I bent down to pick them up, blood rushed to my head and I had to sit on my haunches for a minute waiting for the fiery circles behind my eyelids to stop their clockwork prance. Carmela silently watched me.

"Oh, yes, they are quite unusual," I said finally getting up and catching my breath.

"Do you like them, though? Well, you don't have to. Come, what do you think of those?" She moved over to three identical objects perched on high stools. They looked like leather purses with metal buckles. "Just look inside them."

I opened one purse and instinctively shut it back. Abashed, I was staring inside female genitalia meticulously reproduced in pink leather.

"I came up with this idea and somehow it caught on. I have a rich client who wants ten of those. I can't fathom what for."

I imagined this woman spending her days readjusting the wrinkles, adding a little bit here, taking away there… I was instantly embarrassed by this thought and looked sideways. My glance fell on small statuettes on a low shelf in the corner.

One of them was a Mexican God with the face of a jaguar and an elaborate hairdress. Painted blood was dripping from both sides of his mouth. The other figure was a sitting man: one part of him flesh, the other, skeleton.

"These are replicas," explained Carmela. "The originals are in the Anthropological Museum in Mexico City."

"I hadn't realized before I went to that museum," I said, "to what degree the whole culture was based on premeditated slaughter. When I first saw all this art collected in one place, I was truly repulsed."

"Magnificent artisans, though," said Carmela, turning the skeleton-man in her hands. "Yes, it is morbid, I agree. But life is morbid – it contains death. They didn't deny the reality, that's all. Aren't we all walking skeletons, after all? Just waiting for the external layer of the deception to fall off?" She smiled with that familiar whimsical smile of hers.

"One way of looking at it, I suppose. I spent two days in this museum and I now have a hard time blaming Cortez for his cruelty. There was a statuette of a man wearing human skin on top of his own. Then these games… I didn't realize that even their games were a ritualized murder. *Palata* or *peleta*, I'm not sure."

"*Pelota.*"

"All right, *pelota*. But you know what I'm talking about, don't you? If, by mistake, the ball ended up flying counter the sun's movement, the whole team would lose their heads. Then they would pile those heads in the central city square. Imagine Aztec children passing by decomposing heads every day."

"Death can be beautiful," said Carmela and smiled again.

"Yes, but every time I'll find myself on the *Zócalo* now, I am going to think about these heads. See, I respect the culture, the tradition. I know these were their beliefs, but the scope of it we simply fail to…"

We were interrupted by a knock at the door. Francisco stood on the porch staring at me. Obviously, he didn't expect to see me.

"Sorry, sir," he said.

"I'm busy now, Paco," Carmela said, and I could feel her irritation. "We're working, Joseph and I. He is going to sit for my portrait. You can come and clean up later. By the way, did you get me some solvent?"

Francisco took a bottle out of his pocket and placed it on the table.

"That's good. Thank you. So, around four or five then, not before."

"*Entiendo*," responded Francisco, softly closing the door behind him.

"I didn't realize you wanted to paint my portrait," I said to Carmela.

"Of course, I do. I'm always looking out for new models. You can only do that many vaginas. Usually people don't say 'no' to me. Everybody wants to have their image immortalized, but the problem is I don't want to paint just anybody. I will only charge you half price. After my death, your portrait will be worth a fortune. You'll make money on me if you ever decide to sell it."

I was taken aback by her intention to sell me something I didn't ask for. But even more bizarre was the casual way she mentioned her own death, as if she was talking about a complete stranger and more than that, she knew exactly when this stranger was going to make an exit.

"You have an interesting face. Quite asymmetrical. I like that. Can you sit for the next twenty minutes without moving at all?"

She positioned me in a chair, then stepped back to her easel, gazing at me intently.

"Tilt your head a little forward, please. That's too much. No, just the way it was before."

"I don't remember how it was before."

She walked over to me, took my head in both her hands and angled it slightly forward, then stepped back to her easel.

"Now you've lifted it again."

"Did I? Should it be like this?"

"No. That's still too much. Don't bring your head so far back. Gives you an air of arrogance. Which is not in your nature."

I was bemused by her perceptiveness. It was only the second time she'd seen me.

"Sit naturally. Relax. And now take this off. Take off your shirt." I didn't move. Did I misunderstand her? "Undress. Down to your waist." It was an order, not a request.

"I thought you were going to paint my portrait... mostly, my face..."

She didn't respond and continued to paint.

When I awkwardly pulled my shirt up, her eyes glided over me, taking me all in. It was a quick evaluating look, both intense and indifferent at the same time. I was no more than an object in space, a form that reflected and absorbed light in a certain manner. Sweat rolled down my armpits. I became painfully aware of dark flabby patches of skin under those armpits, of my grey bushy breasts softened and enlarged by age. I was embarrassed and hunched instinctively, hiding my chest, but then there were my hands: old, knotty and dark against my pale protruding belly. Time has ploughed and plundered my body and I couldn't hide its debris from the young woman so mercilessly and coldly scrutinizing it.

My forehead was soaking wet. Carmela noticed it and handed me a piece of white cloth. Then, with a quick automatic movement, as if unaware of what she was doing, she pulled up her own blouse.

Taken by surprise, I made an involuntary sound. Her breasts were perfectly shaped, though unexpectedly heavy for her slender body. They were lighter olive than the rest of her skin. But her nipples were dark, with large dark areolas around them. I forced myself to look away. Carmela, on the contrary, showed no sign of discomfort – as if stripping in front of a stranger was a very ordinary thing for her.

"Don't move," she said. "I need you to look outside yourself, not inside. Focus on something that interests you. That's why I've undressed."

She started painting again, moving from easel to palette, adding some brush strokes and then stepping away from the canvas. I couldn't but follow each of her movements: the way her breasts sagged forward as she bent over, lifted up as she reached for the upper corner of the canvas, and swayed as she turned.

The sight of her nakedness transported me to a hot and humid afternoon of my childhood, half a century ago: my mother, still young, firmly clasping my steaming hand as she pushed her way through a crowd of women surrounding the tables with heaps of discount clothes in the basement of a second-hand store in Toronto. I must have been nine or ten and I remember black women's torsos brushing against my cheek, the sickening, foetid smell of unwashed flesh... And then – the crackling of static. I was almost blinded, both repulsed and drawn to what I saw: folds of flesh brimming over and under brassieres as women quickly removed their tops in front of my eyes, pulling over their half-naked bodies sweaters and blouses they'd snatched from the tables. I panicked and tried to run away, but my mother held my hand firmly, afraid to lose me in the crowd. And then I saw a young mulatto girl, not older than myself, with the long angular body of a boy. She too took off her top, but to my surprise, there was nothing under it, except for two round, well-formed spheres, lighter in colour than the rest of her body, two alert dark-eyed creatures living a separate life on her small frame. I stared at the girl, transfixed. I was overpowered by a strange sensation: It was the first awakening of desire, but mostly, it was a deep longing for something elusive that I knew even then would always be out of my reach.

"Talk to me, it helps my work," said Carmela.

"What shall we talk about?" I cleared up my throat trying to regain my normal voice.

"Yourself... When people talk of themselves, they are never bored or tired. They come to life and that's exactly what I want in a portrait. Where are you from?"

"I was born in Toronto, but then we moved to Winnipeg." She didn't react. I'm sure she'd never heard of the place.

"Are you a businessman?"

"Why? Do I look like one?"

"You can never tell with foreigners. Some of them look like beggars on the beach, then you find out they are famous poets."

"If I tell you I'm a poet, will you make me look handsome?"

"You are handsome. Very much so."

I found it hard to believe her. Her measuring eyes moved from me to the canvas and back in rapid succession. She wasn't really interested in me – again I became acutely aware of that – other than as a pictorial object.

"Well, I'm not a businessman, but my father was. He owned a factory in China. Made a fortune manufacturing plastic bags."

I don't know why I told her about my father. Did I intuitively sense that some genetic connection with money would make me more attractive in her eyes?

"Boring, no?"

"What's boring?"

"Manufacturing bags."

"Not if it brings you lots of money!"

"You sound like an American."

She came up to me, touched my shoulders and tilted my head. Her naked breasts lightly brushed against my forearm. I lost my train of thought.

"Have you ever been to China?" she asked. "I've always wanted to go…"

"Oh, a long time ago. I was twenty then. My father hoped I would enter the family business and decided I had to see his factory. I met with his employees, Chinese girls, over a hundred of them, aged from sixteen to twenty-five. They lived in a dorm, seven girls per room. My father didn't want them to commute to work."

"Your father was an exploiter, then?"

"No, he paid his workers well. Twenty-five per cent more than anywhere else in China. He was a good man, but I still didn't want to become a businessman."

She put her brushes down and began to smudge paint on the canvas with her finger.

"Money makes life easier. Lots of money, I mean."

"I have never been rich myself. But when my father died, things changed..." I stopped, getting uncomfortable with the subject. "Well now, it's your turn to tell me about yourself."

"What is it you want to know?" Carmela held up the stem of a brush against her outstretched hand, measuring the proportions of my body; then she moved it to the canvas, comparing.

"Your friend, the waiter, said you're already a well-known artist. Yet you're so young."

"Who said that, Francisco? It's true, he admires me. But he knows nothing about art. He is a handyman; makes frames for my pictures. Very good with his hands, but he believes I'll go straight to hell for my pussy bags!"

Laughter overcame her, she put her brush down.

"Oh, look what I did to myself!" She cupped her left breast into her hands and tried to remove the yellowish stain from around the nipple with her finger. The stain smudged.

She came up to me still holding her breast absently in her hand. I felt intimidated.

"Can you lift your head again? Do not tilt it. Just keep it steady. That's it. And stop worrying about your hands. I'm not working on them right now..."

I held my breath, I was so tense. But she stepped back, releasing the yellow-daubed breast just as absently, and I felt somewhat relieved.

"It's true, I got lucky. Had several exhibitions in London as a student, and after that got a green light at home. They love it when the foreign press talks about you."

"Your parents must have given you a good jump-start in life," I said.

"My parents?" She smirked and rubbed something on her canvas with a piece of cloth. "My father I hardly knew. He was travelling when I was a child, and he still is. My mother? She liked to read a lot. Thought it was a waste of time to spend the night sleeping. An insomniac. She was half-asleep most of the time during the day though. I remember I'd ask her a question and she'd look at me, and I knew she hadn't heard. She lives in Paris now."

Carmela fell silent. She glanced at me at rarer intervals now, absorbed more with her creation than with the original. Finally, she declared the session over, faced the picture to the wall – it wasn't finished yet – and cleaned her hands with the solvent. I couldn't tell if she was happy with her work or not.

I felt tired. I hadn't realized how difficult it was to sit without movement. All the time I was aware of her nakedness and my own decaying flesh, and that made me even more tense. I closed my eyes for a moment, but was startled out of my torpor by a light touch on my cheek. I opened my eyes. Carmela quickly and lithely sat on my lap. The weight of her body and the coolness of her stroking fingers on my face were so unexpected that I felt limp, almost paralyzed, but Carmela pressed her naked breast against my cheek and forced her nipple into my mouth.

"Lick that stain off, would you?" she whispered, rising, drawing me with her, manoeuvring me to the sofa.

I finally gave myself up to her body. She exhausted me in what somehow seemed a vengeful, yet delightful delirium, and then I lay there, listening to the waves lapping the rocks at the foot of her house. I listened to the shrieks of the albatrosses; to the subdued shouts of dark-skinned boys selling coconuts. And then my mind drifted away, floating over the ancient and arid land that lay in wait around us with its enigmatic pyramids and the dead cities, long abandoned by priests and gods who had sated themselves on human blood. And somehow Carmela herself was this ancient land strewn with cacti; she was the orange flames of the sunset and the endless sky. She was a high priest ready for the sacrifice, and the innocent girl being sacrificed. The blood of both, the executioner and the victim, ran in her veins.

And then I looked at her, curled in the crook of my arm which had started to go to sleep under the weight of her head, and was struck by her innocent look. Her cheeks were flushed, mouth slightly open, and all the predatory vigour, all the insatiability that had stormed inside her only minutes ago, was gone. The arrogance and the aloofness that she had put between herself and the world disappeared. Here was a young woman, almost a girl, in her most natural and beautiful state. Never before did I feel such rapture and yet such tenderness for any human being. Her clean forehead was like a prism that collected in its focus all my love, all my tenderness, all my old longings. She was everything I had never had: my lover, my daughter, my sister, my wife. The more I looked at her, in that deep repose, the less I could imagine having made love to her, having actually penetrated her – so crude seemed now any such desire compared to the feelings brimming over my soul, feelings for which I had no name.

I had no doubt that Fate had entrusted her to my care. The world was a sleepwalker wandering around with eyes half closed. Now I had to protect her against this world. I imagined myself to be her self-appointed knight in whose presence, finally, perhaps for the first time in her life, she would be able to remove her mask and breathe freely.

My daydreaming was disrupted by a sudden noise. In our bliss, we had completely forgotten about Francisco, who had half-opened the unlocked front door. Carmela grabbed a sheet from the bed, wrapped herself up and went to meet Francisco.

I, a little shaky on my legs, carried my over-pouring heart down the winding stairs into a freshly painted, festive and ever so gentle world.

3

What were the days that followed that magic afternoon like? I couldn't tell you: patches of morning light drifting from the water to the palm trees to Carmela's hair, as she was combing it after a swim; the unhurried movement of her hand; the ocean, the breeze, the sand, hot at noon, slowly cooling after the sunset, the distillation of my perfect happiness, my bliss. That's all I remember. The nights fell upon us suddenly, and the granular light of stars, as if seen for the first time, filled me with fresh awe. They were my witnesses and I thought that my love for Carmela was as uncanny as the light of these stars, created for us and us alone.

Sometimes, returning to my hotel from the cottage of High Sails (that's what I came to call her little studio on the bluff), I asked myself whether I was daydreaming, or simply losing my wits: How could a young, exquisitely beautiful and talented woman fall for an utterly banal old man like myself? But the moment she put her lovely arm around me or looked at me, all my doubts would evaporate and I, covering the velvety inside of her arm with kisses all the way up to a slightly wet, acid armpit, would be instantly thrown into euphoria and feel that somehow I deserved her love, deserved that happiness.

I wanted to be with her all the time, but felt a teenaged shyness in her presence: I was afraid to touch her, but she always took the initiative, relieving me of my fears. She made love to me passionately, with abandon – and that gave me confidence I never experienced before. I was wanted, even desired, in spite of my age and unassuming appearance. All of it was new to me and I gradually began to see myself in a different light. To think of it, I wasn't that old. And weren't the wrinkles, after all, the external expression of accumulated wisdom? No wonder many women found older men attractive. As for the folds of skin hanging from under my chin, when I looked at myself in profile, in dim bathroom light, I could easily see the resemblance to some noble aging Roman Senator, if not Julius Caesar himself.

There were also delightful moments of what she called "domestic coziness." And they, more than intense passion, convinced me of her affection for me. I could see that she, too, needed me, perhaps even loved me.

My utter inability to draw amused her. Sitting next to me, she loved to guide my fingers, awkwardly squeezing the pencil, over the paper. I laughed in disbelief when all of a sudden, out of nothing, emerged a cat climbing a tree, a woman in sombrero sitting sideways on a chair, an Indian boy carving something with a knife. She started teaching me Spanish with a patience that I didn't expect from her. When I asked her once why my knowing her language was important to her, she said that it would make her feel closer to me. I was enthralled. I repeated the sounds of a tongue that I grew to love as mantra, as token of our union.

Every morning I continued to sit for my portrait; then we would have a light snack and go down to the beach with two big towels and a basket of fruit. I was sporting white linen pants and a loose, colourfully embroidered shirt that she bought for me from the local artisans. She had a yellow, wide-skirted sundress and a straw hat with a wide brim that suited her dark complexion so well.

Having grown up inland, I didn't understand the ocean, but Carmela was an excellent and fearless swimmer. Nevertheless, every time her dark head disappeared in the surging green precipices, my heart sank. I felt it was I at the mercy of the waves, for she now became part of me.

"Ask the ocean to throw you the key and then enter," she shouted between her dives, playing with the waves and my fear. The breakers were high, and I stood there helpless, watching her.

She taught me to count waves: While the tallest, the seventh wave, was amassing its strength and then smashing into the beach, I had to run into the ocean as fast as I could, and swim out.

"That's the only way the ocean will let you in," she shouted. "On the seventh wave."

Often, we were the only ones who ventured into the stormy surf, the locals sitting on the beach watching us. What a joy it was after the frantic paddling to finally reach calmer waters beyond the raging surf, turn around and watch the ocean thrust with its flagellating power onto the beach. I would try to keep up with Carmela's quick crawl and hug her in the water, but she would slip out and swim away.

One day she told me she had to leave the beach earlier – a reporter was waiting for her in the studio.

"What reporter?" I tried not to sound alarmed. Her dealings with men, particularly strangers, made me a little nervous. But I didn't want to acknowledge even to myself that these tinkling needles in my brain were the first signs of jealousy.

"A journalist from the local radio station," said Carmela, pulling her sundress on top of a wet swimming suit. "I completely forgot. He's going to run a preview of my September show."

She was in a visible rush now. I helped her stick the wet towels into the canvas bag.

"I'll carry it," I said. "I'm going to walk you to the cottage anyway."

"Oh, that's all right. I can carry it myself." Carmela turned and looked at me. "You know what I'd like to do?"

"What?"

"Guess?" She smiled conspiratorially. "After this interview, I'd like to come to your hotel and stay overnight. I'll be wearing this special dress and I'll pretend I don't know you and then… " She whispered into my ear, then burst into laughter.

Lately, I had noticed a playful side in her that wasn't there before – and I loved it. I lifted her in my arms, overwhelmed with joy. The prospect of spending an entire night with her immediately reconciled me to the impending separation.

At the cottage of High Sails I kissed her good-bye and began to climb up the hill back to my hotel. The sun was getting hot, and I thought I should take a nap to replenish my energy before her arrival later that evening. I almost made it to the hotel, when I realized I was missing my wristwatch. It must have slipped into the sand somehow and I hadn't noticed. Annoyed at myself – now I had to go all the way back to the beach, I reluctantly turned around.

The terrain sloped to the ocean and I saw Carmela from afar. She was on the same spot we both had left ten minutes ago, lying in the arms of a man, her legs wrapped around his torso. Not quite trusting my own eyes, I stopped, then slowly moved forward. I couldn't see the man's face, but I recognized him from the back: It was Francisco. I felt that the world, as I knew it, was vanishing – or rather, the world was still there, but I was no longer able to grasp its meaning. Everything around me became drained of vibrancy. The sky seemed monotonously blue; the sand, painful yellow. I stood there, still seeing and yet not being able to see, a dull drone in my ears. Then I moved forward as if still hoping the mirage would disperse. When Francisco got up, I noticed how muscular his legs were. I stared at his hairy calves and thighs that seemed to threaten me as if they were the focus of my pain. Francisco hopped twice, balancing on one foot while pulling a pant leg over the other. Then he sat down next to Carmela, and she put her arm around him, reaching for her bag with the other hand. She took out some grapes we had brought to the beach, inserted one berry into her own mouth, then took Francisco's head into her hands and pushed it into his mouth with her tongue: her favourite game, the way she had done with me so many times. At the beginning the man was passive, but then they both broke into laughter. He pretended to move away from her but she found his mouth again and they kissed.

I turned around and went back to the hotel.

Without removing my shoes, I collapsed on my bed and covered my head with a sheet. I didn't have any thoughts or feelings. It was late afternoon and the hotel was filled with sounds: People in the hallway were talking loudly in

Spanish; somebody was taking a shower; then there was the erratic noise of running feet. I lay there listening through the sheet, waiting for night to fall. I still hoped for one and one sound only: her light, hesitant tap on my door. What would I do then? Pretend I didn't know anything and forgive her? My heart pumped painfully in my chest, as if somebody was turning a screw-driver inside it with each inhalation. No, I won't humiliate myself with explanations. I will simply leave the room without as much as a word or a touch. I'll get out of the country as soon as possible – and then from a plane I'll write her a brief letter. She will regret what she has done, but it will be too late.

I raised myself to look at the time, but then remembered that I had left my watch on the beach. I must have spent hours in bed, for now it was completely dark. No sounds were coming from the corridor. I realized in an instant that Carmela was not going to come because she was spending the night with Francisco. Though I could imagine her making love to another man, my mind refused to believe it, as if it was somehow against the laws of nature and therefore couldn't be happening to me. That night I was unable to get any sleep at all. One moment, I wanted to inflict pain on her, so that she would know all the measure of my suffering; the next, I wanted to forgive her. For some strange reason, I even felt sorry for her.

I was sweating profusely. Then I started coughing. Unable to contain my fits anymore, I finally got up and went out for some fresh air. In the hallway, a short blonde woman was leaning against the wall, one barefoot leg rubbing the other. The moment she saw me, she snuck her feet into stiletto shoes standing beside her. She watched me struggling with my cough for a while, then unglued herself from the wall and began to twist her foot inside the shoe, rotating her hips in sync with her movements.

"Fucking sand!" she said, balancing on one foot and emptying her left shoe out. "Do you know where the laundry is?" She spoke in a raspy voice with the deep drawl of a Southerner.

"Pardon? The laundry? Sorry, I don't."

"I mean, where do you do your washing?" She emptied her second shoe. "I don't know anybody in this place. Would you like to spend the evening together?"

I looked at her more carefully: bleached hair, a nondescript faded face, a rather plump figure. She looked grubby, second-hand, yet her body had a not unpleasant roundedness about it.

"It must be very late now," I said hesitatingly. "What time is it?"

"I know a very good restaurant not far from here," she said without responding to my question. "They are open till midnight. The owner says his great-grandfather invented Caesar salad a century ago at that place, and they still serve it the old way there."

I lifted my eyebrows in disbelief but agreed to accompany her. Her face lit up.

"Before spending a pleasant evening in the company of such a nice gentleman, I need to have a pedicure done, hope you don't mind." She moved closer to me and I smelled her cheap perfume.

Ten minutes later, we were entering a suspicious-looking den, with several billiard tables and phone booths at the front. A barbershop was somewhere in the back. My companion said something in laboured Spanish to a woman with an apron and pink curls on her head. The woman brought out a copper basin filled with water and placed it on a low stool. With one foot in the basin, the other stretched out in the lap of the pedicurist, my new acquaintance winked at me: "We should get to know each other better. I've had an interesting life, if you are curious."

I said I was, and she embarked on a story that sounded so grotesque that I immediately recognized a fellow tall-tales teller, a kindred spirit of sorts, wondering all along if making up this nonsense was her way of supplementing her other, much more dubious, yet lucrative source of income, or if she did it for pure pleasure – her own and that of a prospective client.

If I were to believe her, she was an orphan, raised by a grandfather who took her as a lover at the tender age of thirteen, and then, in an act of repentance, married her off to his wealthy friend over sixty. His intentions being good, he was unable, however, to restrain his obsession with his granddaughter and continued to demand her favours. It resulted in a ménage à trois that ended tragically: The granddaughter finally poisoned the grandfather, freeing herself from the terrible double bondage. At the same time, she doomed herself to the life of a perpetual vagabond.

"If they find me, I'm finished," said the woman, abruptly slashing the air in front of her throat. Her fear of men was so engraved in her ever since, she added, that she would never think of going to bed before barricading her door first.

Life can be stranger than fiction, they say, but whether there was any truth in her concoction or not, for me her story had one indisputable merit: It distracted me from my own pain. Yet I was quickly getting weary. I paid for the woman's pedicure and was prepared to return to the hotel, when she reminded me I had promised to take her to a restaurant. She was going to take a shower. Could I wait a minute in the lobby?

I reluctantly agreed, but forty minutes later I was still there waiting for her. Finally, feeling exhausted and fooled, I knocked at her door. There was an unmistakable sound of furniture being moved around, then the door opened just enough for me to see a pile of chairs atop each other and a naked arm handed over to me as if for a kiss. I didn't quite know what to do with this hand, but while I was hesitating, the door slammed in my face. I heard the furniture being moved back in place. I knocked again, and was relieved not to receive any answer. The poor wretch didn't know what she did for me: She let me live through the night, not a small gift to be thankful for.

※ ※ ※

I don't remember how I survived till the next day, but by late afternoon I couldn't take it anymore and found myself at the door of Carmela's studio.

"Come on in, Joe," she said, smiling at me as if nothing at all had happened.

"I didn't sleep last night… was waiting for you," I said, half-averting my face. "I know what has happened, I know where you've been." I tried to sound as calm as possible.

"You mean the interview?" said Carmela, turning around and walking into her studio. "I was too tired to come to your hotel afterwards. It dragged on and on."

"You don't need to lie to me, Carmela," I said following her. "I saw you with Francisco on the beach."

"So what?" She turned to me, her eyes squinting. "Can't I talk to another man? What would you like to drink? I have some freshly squeezed mango." She opened the fridge.

"No, thanks. But let's not get off the subject. Why didn't you tell me you had a lover all along? Instead of telling me that he made frames for you and so on. Why lie?"

"What I said was true." Carmela calmly poured herself some juice. "He does make frames for me. He even helped me to build this studio." I noticed the mist gathering on the inside surface of her glass. I felt sudden indifference to everything, but my senses seemed to have lives of their own, noticing everything, infusing every trifle with an annoying significance.

"And that's why you slept with him? To pay for his work?"

"Don't you dare! Don't you ever dare insult me!" Carmela suddenly exploded and slammed her glass onto the countertop. Juice poured over the counter, glass smatterings bursting in all directions. I watched one piece rocking behind the leg of a chair, its amplitude of motion smaller and smaller. Such eruption of rage, even hatred, took me by surprise. But what shocked me even more was that her eyes remained cold as usual. "Yes, he is my lover, and you knew all the time about us and chose to accept it!"

I was appalled at how quickly she had abandoned all her pretence and even the smallest effort to spare me the truth! Had she invented some semi-plausible story, I would've grabbed onto it and lamely, torturously believed her.

"I just want to know one thing. Why did you start an affair with me when all that time you had another lover?"

I felt a sudden urge to relieve myself. I ran to the toilet but stopped short in front of the image staring at me out of the mirror: bulging eyes surrounded by deep furrows, the helpless grimace of a weak, drooping mouth and the long, vertical lines crossing my cheeks all the way down to my neck. There was no way, simply no way, that I, Joseph Parson, 60 years old, could legitimately defend the claims of this monkey in front of that young woman full of life and vigour!

I came out of the bathroom. Carmela was applying some lotion to her face, the way she often did before going to the beach. When I saw that familiar gesture, the helpless ugly ape that had stared at me a minute ago from a bathroom mirror, and with whose behaviour I had nothing in common, suddenly dropped on its knees, grabbing her legs and weeping uncontrollably.

"Forgive me," I sobbed. "Forgive me! I didn't want to hurt you!"

"Why are you so upset?" said Carmela, looking down at me. "It's just sex."

"I thought that you and I... that you loved me a little too; you can't love me all the way, the way I love you, I know that, but I hoped that... " My vocal cords gave up, the sound of my voice thinning into a whisper.

"Well, I like you all right! You're somehow different, and your stories are funny. Francisco is a bore compared to you. For God's sake! He is just a waiter, a handyman who runs on my errands, How can you be jealous of him? Calm down, *querido. No hay que ahogarse en un vaso de agua.* You don't have to drown in a glass of water!"

A hopeless despair overcame me: I was enraged and words came back to me, gushing out of my mouth uncontrollably, without my will.

"So you sleep with everybody whom you find funny, or whom you can boss around and treat like your slave! What about that guy, whatever his name, that drunkard who gave you a diamond? You slept with him too, didn't you?"

"What business is that of yours? I am a free woman."

She took another glass from the dish rack, poured herself some juice, gulped it down and wiped her mouth with the back of her hand.

"After all, we are not married; you can't tell me what to do!"

"You mean if you were my wife, it would make a difference?"

"Oh, sure. Then you could have as much of me as you wished and Francisco would be our handyman, our gardener. He would look after our house for cheap." She paused. "He'd make more frames for my cunts. What do you think?"

For the first time in my life I was about to slap a woman. But I restrained myself. I got up and quickly left, determined never to see her again.

4

Next day I started planning my return to Canada. Looking back at recent events, I saw clearly that Carmela wasn't at all whom I had taken her to be. An imposter with philistine pretensions using art to lure men into bed; a nymphomaniac, manufacturing pussy bags – that's all she was! The more I thought about her, the more my own delusions became painfully obvious to me. I became convinced that she didn't have as much as a spark of artistic talent in her. How then could she have drawn me into all this, making me sit for her for a whole month? Was I completely blind? I had anticipated sessions with her with such impatience! The mere sight of bougainvillea camouflaging the door that led into her world had sent my heart into reverential leaps. Her sleepy whisper in the morning when the first rays of the sun set her ebon hair on fire, that innocent whisper in my half-alert ear made me believe she was a fragile flower in need of my protection, whereas in fact she was cynical and hard as stones and I was an old fool, doting over a predator who toyed with me, her prey, before destroying it.

The memories of nights made for our love now existed solely for my torment. Anger, shame and the old, still unquenched desire for her inundated me: I was out of breath, I was suffocating. The sheets felt wet against my exhausted body. My tortured ear would shut out the drone of the fan only to yield to the cadenced rage of the ocean below as it smashed itself against the sand strewn with dead crabs and empty shells. What was this ocean raging against? The limits imposed by its shores? How pointless, how futile.

Yesterday I spotted decomposing white flesh on the sand. I thought it was a dead dog, but it turned out to be a huge turtle without its shell, its pale sinewy tissue exposed to the sun. The ocean burped it out, then left it there to rot.

※ ※ ※

In the time that followed, I tried not to think of Carmela. But I soon discovered that it was impossible, and the harder I tried, the less I succeeded. My resolve to return immediately to Canada faded into ennui. Slowly, my anger gave place to a dull pain that nestled inside my heart and that I could neither pull out nor ignore. I couldn't hate her: Hating her meant hating myself. But no matter what I did, I was hurting as if I had lost something vital for my existence – a pair of limbs – yet was forced to drag my body through the desert of smiling strangers, pretending that I, just like them, was whole. I knew I couldn't grow new limbs any more than I would be able to love somebody else in what remained of my life. I felt more and more isolated from the world and gradually sank into the realm of dreams that alone seemed to be bringing me some relief. At dawn I would go into slumber and watch the misshapen fragments of my thoughts (ragged little Dali-esque creatures) floating inside my brain. I'd try to pull one out and hold on to it before it dissipated. One rectangular shape took the form of a coffin – at closer inspection, my own. I couldn't clearly see my face inside it: My white sunken cheeks were camouflaged with some quivering shadows of leaves that the trees obligingly lent me. The coffin was drawn by a horse which knew where to go. Nobody followed the procession. My death seemed to be exactly like each of my birthdays, a lonely and redundant affair. Self-pity overwhelmed me and I cried in my sleep. Then I woke up, flipped aside the gauze hanging from the ceiling. I couldn't stand being enclosed in a coffin, a swaddled larva, a mummy, a corpse! I made an effort to get up but my resolve quickly evaporated and imperceptibly I was drifting into another dream. This one shimmered with the glory and sweetness of happiness, as Carmela, my beloved, returned to me as a very young girl, almost a child, whom I had known all my life.

In my dream she was not my mistress, but my wife of many years. We were the same age. We grew up together, married, became old, and then came full circle and regained our youth. Around us, the water was lapping gently, our bed drifting away into the warm, milky abyss. Carmela was both delighted and scared.

"Don't leave me," she said. "I've forgotten how to swim."

"Are you afraid, my sweet? Nothing is gentler than water. I will protect you. I will go anywhere you go. We'll just wait for the seventh wave."

I woke up and knew I wasn't alone any more: Imagining I could preserve the aura of her presence, her smell and her warmth, I skipped my shower for two days. That dream was a turning point in my life. It made me postpone my return home, for now I had an urgent task to complete. I had to secure her new glorious existence inside me: Not only should the malice of the outside world be unable to touch her, but she should be beyond the reach of my own anger, my own jealousy lest they destroy her shining image. I kept listening to the new music that was enveloping my soul with such tenderness. In a strange fashion, we reversed our roles; now she became my guardian angel protecting me from slipping into darkness. How that transformation happened, I don't know. I think it was akin to *satori*, the awakening of the heart, allowing you to see the true nature of the world. That sensation could not have been inferred from any events that had preceded it. Yet it was irreversible. It was then that I forgave her and forgave myself for wanting her all for myself and hating her if she didn't belong to me alone. That forgiveness gave new freedom to my spirit and strength to my body. The world around me was bathing in a warm light of mercy. Now I didn't love Carmela for my own sake, but for her own, and with that, my torment had ended.

5

Two weeks after these – I hesitate to call them events, for they were huge shifts in my consciousness, I received a letter from Carmela. Would I mind sitting for her, one last time? She wanted to finish my portrait. She said she had wronged me, wanted to apologize, and give me my picture as a gift.

Compared to the fragile but strengthening joy I felt in my heart, the letter somehow felt redundant. Yet it burned my fingers. It belonged to the old world of sorrowful vales, while I was hovering in the pure ether. Should I abandon my new beloved, beautiful and full of mercy as my own forgiveness had made her, for the real Carmela? The idea scared me and I hesitated three or four days before finally overcoming my fears.

The door of her studio, so painfully familiar, was wide open. I quietly walked in. I saw her standing in the depths of the hall. The morning light enveloped her in a halo. She stepped out of this glow and moved towards me. I hadn't seen her for almost a month and was shocked at how she'd changed: Her dark complexion concealed neither her paleness nor the bluish circles under her eyes. She looked washed out, pallid; even the well-defined line of her chin seemed weaker. I noticed a shapeless housecoat, so uncharacteristic of her, with an apron stained with paint on top. Apart from these obvious changes, there was a more subtle and yet profound transformation: The dry fire that had stormed inside her seemed to be extinguished.

"Sorry, I was painting, didn't have time to change."

I looked at her again and asked if she was all right. She said she had been sick most of the time we hadn't seen each other, but now she had recovered.

She offered me some coffee, and I politely refused. I was in a rush and preferred to get down to our work right away, I told her. She didn't respond, but it was obvious she knew I had nothing planned. We didn't talk while she was painting. Only once were we interrupted, by an unusual whimpering sound coming from the back deck.

A pelican, Carmela explained, with a broken wing, had landed on her deck that morning. She had tried to give it some fresh fish, but it wouldn't touch it. We went out to see the bird. It sat on the floor clumsily, like a duck, tucked in the corner against the glass pane. With its pouch resting on the wooden planks of the deck, it looked quite grotesque. It was all white with a little red rim around the eye that gazed at us with great suspicion. I tried to go closer. The pelican made a clumsy attempt to dash away from me.

"Better not touch it," said Carmela. "I tried."

"What's going to happen to it?"

"Most likely, it will die. There is nothing we can do for it."

She went back into the studio; I followed her. She turned around and put her hands on my shoulders.

"I'm so glad you came back," she said. "It was all very foolish, I'm sorry..."

It had been a long time since I'd seen her face so close to mine. No dream or imagination could replace the sensation of holding her in my arms, feeling the warmth of her body.

"I love you," I said. "I never stopped loving you..."

She gazed into my eyes, then passed her hand over my cheek. It smelled of paint.

"What answer will you give me then? Have you decided?" She brushed her lips against mine without kissing me, then rested her head on my chest. "Remember? I asked if you'd marry me."

I felt weak in my legs. Of course I remembered, except that the proposition she had made a month ago I had taken as a mockery and an insult.

"Carmela, you don't have to do this to yourself. I know you don't love me. You can't love me. But it doesn't matter, I will always be there for you if you wish. If there is anything you need, just tell me. You don't have to marry me in order to keep me around." My hands started trembling uncontrollably. I wanted to leave. But she prevented me from moving.

"I missed you terribly," she whispered into my ear. "Terribly, I could barely cope."

"Weren't you with Francisco all this time?"

"I'll explain it to you later, you'll understand, understand it all. I was a fool, forgive me – you do forgive me, don't you?"

"Yes," I said feebly.

"I want to tell you something," she whispered, caressing my cheek again. "You're the best. I've never met anybody like you. They all want me for something – for my eccentric art, or because of the people I know. But none of them love me for me, the way you do. You are a true saint." She started crying. I had never seen her tears before. "I know we could be happy together. I will be a good wife to you, you'll never regret it, you'll see. Please, say, *yes*."

I was shattered by her tears and wasn't able to utter a word.

"If you love me, please say, *yes*!"

The despair in her voice! She did feel guilty after all. And if so, didn't it mean that she loved me after a fashion? Wild hope surged in my heart: "Yes," my lips whispered on their own.

"Are you still hesitating? Are you?" She dropped her arms and quickly stepped back. Her eyes were misty.

"No, oh no... I love you. I can't live without you, if that's what ..." I drew her back to me.

"I can't live without you either." She wiped the wetness from her eyes. "Ah, Joe, *corazón*, I'm so tired... Can't even think of painting today." She was now smiling as if relieved of some terrible burden. "Can't we finish your portrait tomorrow? There are so many things I want to do together with you: travel, buy art, entertain interesting people. We will have a happy life, won't we?" She hid her head on my chest, a little girl again.

"Of course, whatever you want, my love... "

On the way back to my hotel, I stopped in bewilderment. What was I doing? One thing was the sublime love dwelling in my soul; quite another was to marry a woman named Carmela. I avoided looking in the direction of that spot on the beach where almost four weeks ago I saw her feeding grapes to Francisco. I knew and trusted my sweet innocent girl. But did I know and trust Carmela? Again I felt that familiar weakness in my legs, that nagging void in my stomach. Remorse apart, it was inconceivable that she would truly want to marry me – that much I understood. What could I offer her? Twice her age, too old to start a family, a foreigner unable to speak her language, knowing not a soul in her country. Could it be my money? She never showed any interest in it, but even if she did, all she needed was to ask. I turned around and retraced my way to the cottage of High Sails. No, it couldn't be true. She didn't love me. I stood there at the bottom of the stairs for a while, hesitating, listening to the wind. Then I remembered her tears, the fright in her eyes. How pale she looked, my poor girl, how tired. Didn't I promise to protect her, when we were floating in the ocean of my dream together? And, further, did I want to live, could I truly live, without her? Not when she said, "I'm yours."

I turned and went back to my hotel.

6

All my life I've suffered from migraines that, contrary to what doctors might think, result from the terrible clutter my undiscriminating memory lumbers upon my mind: a volley of faces, gestures, scenes I strive to yet can't erase. The only time my brain gives me respite and my memory stops collecting its usual crop of disparate impressions is a day or two preceding the onslaught of pain. In those days my sensations are benumbed. I observe life as if through the glass of a fish bowl: the luminescent fan of a tail, the grotesque bulging stare of an underwater monster swooning by.

The days before our wedding were marked by excruciating migraine and, therefore, I only vaguely remember the kaleidoscope of Carmela's friends presenting themselves to her apartment at Chimalistac, a quiet enclave for the well-to-do of Mexico City. All the artists, critics, curators, and socialites that came to greet us. I never got to meet her parents: As usual they were living in their separate capitals of Europe. There was a cascade of multi-coloured boxes filled with jewellery, Venetian and Mexican masks, Talavera pottery, canvases, brushes, shoes, French underwear, embroidered fabric ordered by Carmela and now arriving at our doors with a merry-go-round frenzy. I saw myself from the outside: a short bald man wiping sweat off his forehead and writing out cheques, then retreating to the coolness of the patio to fill up the glasses of yet another batch of guests.

Strangely, the two images my memory was able to salvage from the murkiness of these prenuptial days had little to do with my marital bliss. One was a huge pyramid assembled of pots of red-and-green leafed poinsettia and posing as a Christmas tree near the Cathedral of Santo Domingo in which we were going to get married; and another, next to that tree, a nativity crèche with two sheep, an ox and a donkey grazing at the hay in a manger, surrounded by a crude plywood fence. What made these beasts surreal in this anthill city of twenty million is that they were alive. I remember I had a strong desire to stroke the dusty grey curls of the sheep, but then remembered my tuxedo.

My bride's costume à la Frida Kahlo – the multi-layered stiff lace, the intricately embroidered birds of paradise – seemed equally exotic to me; it outshone everything else in the opulent theatre production that was my wedding. Carmela's black hair, arranged in triple braids on top of her head and crowned with red roses, her pale solemn face, our kneeling at the altar, our exchanging of the vows and rings, my throwing rice behind my left shoulder to ward off the devil, who, I was told, would always hold his grip, given the slightest chance – all of that is no more than an assemblage of indistinct memories. On that stage, I was an uninspired and rather fearful first-timer whom nobody had prepared for his role. The last scene of the show ended with a copious meal. My sense of reality briefly returned with the departure of our last guest, a man who vaguely resembled Francisco.

As soon as he closed the door behind him, I went up to Carmela, took her into my arms and planted a long, breathless kiss on her mouth.

She struggled out of my embrace, pushed me away and collapsed on the bed, the gauze of her dress flaring and burying her head. "Leave me alone or I'll scream my lungs out!" Her cry braced my brain with a cement hoop and I descended into pain that lasted for the next three days, obliterating all sensations and memories.

7

Shortly after these events, we went to Canada to settle my inheritance. The morning after our disconcerting nuptial night, my beautiful bride had apologized for her behaviour. The whole "show" had just been too much. Since I had felt much the same, I was mollified. But I was worried about the trip: What would she think about my almost bare apartment on the outskirts of a snowy provincial city? Of my run-of-the-mill friends, none of whom were artists?

My fears came true: The energy, the sharp purposefulness that Carmela had back home, evaporated; most of the time she just felt bored. Only rarely would she pick up a pencil and sketch the bleak winter landscape that stared at her from behind the window pane: another cement apartment building, two or three cars buried in snow. The climate didn't agree with her; she felt cold and feverish, though I couldn't understand how one could feel both at the same time. Food nauseated her; she found it bland and tasteless.

I noticed the abrupt changes in her mood. She tried to regain the old passion she once, I thought, had for me, but these attempts were so artificial that they left us both greatly embarrassed. After one such bout, she went into a delirium, biting her own fists, beating her hands against the headboard – that wooden, hard, alien sound – and then collapsing with sobs onto the bed. It all horrified me: her violence to herself, her uncontrollable shivering and, worst of all, the way her body would first stiffen, then become soft and listless. I wanted to comfort her, to hold her in my arms, but was afraid to so much as touch her, lest that make her suffering even worse. We were back to the same scene as on the night after our wedding. And I cursed myself for my self-indulgence, for wanting to make love to her incessantly, for believing her when she'd abruptly stop sobbing and jump up shouting: "Do it, go ahead, I can't have enough of you!" Then she'd collapse again, all soft and yielding, weeping like a little girl and asking me to forgive her. She'd whisper into my ear that she knew, she understood it all, oh how awful, how very unfair to me, the nicest person on earth, but one day it would be all over, all resolved, for she'd hide in a remote monastery, with daily *Pater Noster*, just like in her Catholic childhood. And could I please bring her some water and kiss her fears away? I'd soothe her burning face with a wet towel and then she'd finally fall asleep, felled by fatigue.

It was clear to me that we had to leave Canada, the sooner the better, even if some of the business connected with the inheritance remained unsettled. On a plane back to Mexico, Carmela became sick. We were travelling in business class (was there anything I would begrudge her?) and Carmela didn't mind the skilful care of the flight attendants, but to my "ridiculous doting" she reacted with her usual irritation. I was afraid she'd go into uncontrollable fits again when she said, her face turned to the window: "Stop fussing. I'm pregnant and if the nausea didn't stop on the ground, you think it would suddenly stop 15,000 metres up?"

The news that I, in my old age, would become a father, threw me into ecstasy! I awkwardly, sheepishly, pulled myself to her side and kissed her hands. She pushed me away. I sat there trying to regain my breath. I didn't mind her dismissals now. I felt this child was God's response to the vows of love and forgiveness that I'd made in the Zipolite hotel before she summoned me to go back to her. Now the three of us – Carmela, me, and the baby – in the purity of unbreakable closeness. I imagined myself appearing arm in arm with Carmelita at vernissages and cocktail parties: an older man, with a young beautiful wife bearing his child. The truth is I didn't really know what it was like to have a baby around. All I knew was that the baby girl would make my world brilliantly and freshly new. Somehow I was sure it would be a girl, if only because I would have no use for a boy who, by the mere token of our blood connection, would understand my inner workings, a mirror reflecting my fears, my uncertainties, my pitfalls! The girl, on the other hand, would make me feel real, the way I had never felt before; she would expand my shabby self to new dimensions, for she would be of my flesh, yet as different from me as a remote star.

The only thing I regretted is that my poor darling had not told me about her pregnancy earlier. Had I known, I would have seen the tormenting three weeks in Canada in a completely different light. But it was still not too late. I would make up for my previous failures. I'd do anything it took to make her life comfortable, so that she could bring our child into the world without any strain or hardship. I wanted her to remain who she was, a talented and original artist. (I didn't doubt her talent for a moment now! More than that, I was surprised how I could have doubted it in the past.) Yes, we would have a cleaning lady, a cook (Carmela wasn't that keen on cooking), a nanny, and a gardener. She wanted to collect art? I'd buy her art. She wanted to try out sculpture and was talking about going to Italy to buy Carrara marble – yes, we would do that too. A hot wave of gratitude was choking me. I got to my feet, and hugging Carmela gently – not to overwhelm her again – went to the end of the passenger cabin, looking for a place where, unwatched, I could give vent to my sudden tears.

※ ※ ※

We bought a run-down villa 100 kilometres from Mexico City. Carmela plunged herself avidly into grand plans of renovations: She redesigned the layout of each room and made drawings for intricate parquet and wallpaper patterns, drapes, and even furniture. In that, as in everything she touched, she never failed to surprise me. I expected her tastes to be cold, sparse, minimalistic. Instead she was seeking to reproduce a Venetian *palazzo* on a smaller scale. She wanted the warm glitter of gilded surfaces; lush silks on the walls in our bedroom; old armchairs; oriental carpets on the marble stairs. She had her mind's eye on authentic Renaissance furniture she hoped to bring back from our travels to Italy that summer.

She was now four months pregnant and we decided not to postpone our trip in spite of the fact that the villa was not finished yet. Before leaving for Italy, we wanted to spend a couple of weeks at the cottage of High Sails, a place I both loved and hated. But Carmela insisted that we go and so we did.

8

How can I conjure up the days that followed? What can do justice to these most horrible – and in hindsight – most idyllic times I've ever had? The delicious tedium of marital bliss (at times I still couldn't believe Carmela was my wife); the sweet lassitude of hot, lazy afternoons. Pregnancy mellowed and pacified her, and her dependency on me I found deeply touching. It seemed that she had finally reconciled with something that was gnarling at her from inside. Our days rolled on from dawn to sunset like identical smooth pebbles; our laziness, our *dolce fare niente* was complete, permeating the very core of our existence as if some benevolent universal life force was living and breathing for us.

We once spotted a cobweb gently swaying in the air currents between the two potted magnolias in the corner of our bedroom. But to get up with the purpose of ruining the cobweb seemed inconceivable, and so we both stayed put.

After the first three days, we quickly settled into a routine of few words and sparse gestures. I would get up very early and go for a walk along the beach, feeling the cool morning breeze on my face. When I returned, Carmela would be still in bed. I'd bring her breakfast and watch her as she poked lazily into the fruit salad that I'd chop up for her. Her face, bloated from sleep and pregnancy, half buried in her hair, darkly contrasted with a white lace nightgown. I found particularly touching all the signs of her condition, everything she herself was unhappy about: her deformed body, the dark spots on her cheeks, her swollen lips and that enigmatic line that stretched along her belly from her navel all the way down to her pubis.

After breakfast, Carmela would paint for two or three hours, moving around with somnambulist slowness. She wanted to be alone and every time I had to think of a new place to go, of something to do away from the house. She never asked me where I'd gone, or what I'd been doing. I had already explored all the coastal villages and towns, wandered through the dusty streets of Puerto Angel and watched people at Pochutla market. I loved bringing her trinkets from the local artisans: a crudely painted pot, an embroidered napkin, a pair of earrings. She laughed at my unsophisticated taste – and, indeed, I never saw her wearing anything I gave her.

One day it had rained heavily during the night, but let up in the morning, and I wanted to take a bus early to get groceries at the market. By the time I came back, loaded with fish, cheeses and fruit, it was around ten.

Carmela was not at home and I sat for a while on the deck, looking out at the ocean, and wondering where she was. She must have gone for a quick dip: Bathing towel and swimming suit were missing from the drying rack in the bathroom, her nightgown and her house robe scattered over the bed. I felt uneasy about it; we had agreed that she would not go into the ocean alone. But I tried not to be alarmed and made breakfast for the two of us. I sat in a rocking chair pretending to read. Then I went out to the deck again and watched the ocean. Two hours passed and I began to worry in earnest. I went down and walked all the way towards la Playa de l'Amour, the most remote beach separated from our strip by rocks. This was the only gay beach in the country, and affluent yuppies flocked there from Mexico City. I doubted that Carmela would go there but I couldn't spot her anywhere else.

The day was still cloudy, yet you could sense the presence of the hot sun behind the grey puffy veils. I looked at the ocean: Its surface had a menacing steel tinge, the breakers higher than usual. I had heard stories of imperceptible whirlpools or underwater currents that pulled even experienced swimmers out into the open sea. By the time they'd realized the danger and shouted for help, it was usually too late; the powerful beat of the surf would muffle any plea. Carmela loved swimming and she loved risk. But would she venture alone into the stormy ocean in her condition? I tried to think of other alternatives. Perhaps she'd gone to the local bar, or was visiting some friends whom I didn't know. Disturbingly, none of it made any sense.

I went back home, vaguely hoping to find her there. But the house was empty. There was the sound of a tap dripping. I went to tighten it and tripped over a painting leaning against the wall. It was the still-unfinished portrait that Carmela, for some reason, had never wanted to show to me. I don't know what I expected, but what I saw stunned me.

Instead of a face, the figure on the canvas had a yellow oval, empty inside. In contrast to the oval, my hand (the right hand, to be exact) was painted with meticulous verisimilitude; my veins, dark, bluish ropes, branched under the dried skin in all directions. The left arm was replaced with some protruding form that ended in tree roots, growing through the floor all the way down to the earth, full of dead bodies crunched up like foetuses. I was fingering them with my root-like hand. This is how she sees me, I thought, a faceless monster, a deformity, sorting out corpses.

For the next three days police searched for traces of Carmela. On the third day they found one of her sandals half buried in the sand five miles from our house. Her body, partially decomposed and fed on by sharks, turned up in a rocky bay three weeks later. I refused to see the corpse. It was identified by the wedding ring and by what was left of a swimming suit they showed to me.

Carmela's friends and fans organized both her funeral mass and her interment. In the church of Santo Domingo, I stood in a semi-dark corner, away from the crowd, nodding silently to the condolences of people passing by. I didn't know the liturgy and watched the priest moving around the closed casket, waving some incense. At one point a tall dark-skinned man came up to me and said he was Carmela's father. Words stuck in my throat and I nodded to him too, without meeting his eyes. Then, closer to the exit, I noticed a kneeling figure. I recognized Francisco. He looked older and somehow smaller than I remembered him. The intensity of his prayer surprised me – I didn't anticipate such religious fervour from this man. He felt my glance, turned around, then quickly withdrew his eyes. I thought I saw tears in them, but perhaps I only imagined it. Something akin to pity stirred in me. After all, he too had loved her. I wanted to talk to him, but then changed my mind. He, however, got off his knees and approached me.

"I need to see you," he whispered into my ear. "I have something for you. Something from your wife. Where I find you?"

I gave him my address. He said he'd visit in a day or so.

After Carmela's death, I couldn't see myself staying either in her studio on the bluffs or in her apartment in Mexico City and so I had moved to our unfinished villa. There was no furniture there yet, and I dropped my few possessions right on the floor, away from the mounds of shavings and sawdust gathered in the corner. Some window panes were missing: There must have been break-ins while we were at the coast. A mattress and a blanket served me as a makeshift bed, and this is where I spent day after day in a motionless oblivion, feeling nothing, knowing nothing, coming to my senses only through the involuntary stirrings of my body which gave me the immediate anguish of remembrance, and I whimpered with pain in my delirium. I lost count of days and became only vaguely aware that Francisco hadn't shown up as promised. But what was morning? What was night?

I couldn't sleep at night, usually the time of my greater lucidity. But the only thing my senses could be alert to was my increasing suffering. And so I came to hate the nights, their alien life, secreting unknown sounds that tormented me with some vague menace. Yet what was there to be afraid of? What kind of loss or pain was there left after Carmela's death? Once I heard two birds echoing each other: one, with a low forlorn whooping, another with the sharp shriek of a disturbed harlot. I'd never heard anything resembling these sounds, and my soul hung in the interval of anticipation between the shriek and the howl piercing the sticky walls of the night. By the morning, I started hallucinating and saw Carmela materializing out of these sounds, condensed to the size of an unborn foetus. The foetus needed food, but I had nothing to offer it. Next morning I woke to the ring of the doorbell, which I didn't recognize as such: Nobody had ever visited me or rung the bell. I had forgotten all about Francisco, who must have been ringing for quite a while before I opened the door.

He watched me standing in the doorway, a barefoot, feeble old man wrapped in a blanket, my hair messed up from sleep. I couldn't tolerate light by then, and the rays of the sun that Francisco had inadvertently let in blinded me. I observed his tightly fitting black suit, shiny shoes, a silk handkerchief sticking out of his breast pocket. I apologized for my house and my appearance, then began to look for something for us to sit on. Francisco waited silently. I finally fetched two wooden stools, but Francisco remained standing.

"I came to tell you how your wife died. I was there." He fixed his gaze on me.

"My wife drowned in the sea, don't you know?" I said quickly, swallowing a lump of pain.

"Not herself she didn't drown. I fed her to the fishes. She was a witch."

"You're raving mad, Francisco. Grief must've made you lose your mind. Please leave. This is a bad time for me to deal with insanity."

"I murdered her, ok?" he said, without changing the tone of his voice. "She put a curse on me, that woman."

He grew pale. His eyes had the glare of a maniac. I became fearful of him and stepped back.

"I'll call an ambulance – they'll help you…"

"You'll do *nada*, Mister, or I'll finish you too." He quickly stretched his hand towards me. A knife flashed before my eyes.

"Your wife wanted to die. I helped her. Virgin Mary showed me the path, blessed be Her Name." He quickly crossed himself. "The Virgin came in my dream and said: 'Get a boat.' So I did. She herself stood on the bow and pointed to the place, way off the shore." He crossed himself again. "I said: 'We gonna for a swim, Carmela.' Time come we go in the ocean, far, far away. 'You go first, I hold the boat.' She swim way out, I watch. Then she shout: 'Help, I so tired.' But I turn the boat back, as Virgin Mary ordered."

"Did you know… did you know… she was pregnant with my baby?" I whispered, suddenly having a nightmarish vision of being in front of a murderer, not a raving lunatic.

"That bastard? Mine, not yours. His blood on my hands. She told me she pregnant, way back told me. I said: 'Ok, then I marry you.' She said: 'What good are you, fucking beggar? I'm gonna marry the rich *gringo*.'"

Still holding his knife in one hand, with the other he pulled two gold watches on long chains out of his breast pocket. He threw them on the stool. One watch slipped off with a clacking sound.

"Take your bloody gold. She bought it for me with your money. I don't need this shit."

I recognized one old watch that had belonged to my father. The other one was new.

"Your wife was a whore. Paid with your money two

hundred dollars a fuck. I was poor. Forced me come to your house every morning when you in the market. But I'm no slave to a whore, I'm a free man!"

"You're a liar, filthy liar!" I protested in a weak, unused voice.

He cocked his head, then dug a letter out of his breast pocket.

"Read this, Mister!"

I recognized Carmela's handwriting on a bethumbed, crumpled envelope.

"Can't see without glasses..." My dry throat suddenly made a wimpy, puny sound.

Francisco gave me an odd look, then lowered his eyes and shook his head.

"Go find your glasses, *gringo*, I wait."

I hopelessly looked around at the jumble of unsorted things, but was unable to move.

Finally Francisco calmly said, "I'll read to you."

"*Mi pollo...*" He stopped and looked at me. "You understand Spanish?"

I was dumbfounded.

"I translate," Francisco said in a monotone voice. "'*Chicken, why you refused make love to me yesterday? You say it hurt our baby if mother loves his father's verga.*' You know verga?" Francisco pointed to his crotch. "'*If mother love the father's verga, the baby love it too. Come tomorrow by ten, when the old fart is at the market. I love watching the sun shining on your butt! His body cold and wet like worms of death, yours dry and hot, like son of desert. No shade in you, only light. I touch you – I'm on fire. I touch him – I die. I desire you like no other woman desire you. Forget about marrying this slut of yours. You belong to me alone: your liver, your guts, every hair on your chest...*'"

"Enough!" I shouted. "Enough! Get out of here!"

"As you please," said Francisco, stepping back and handing me the letter.

I suddenly woke up. "No, wait! I will call the police, you murderer!"

"I be careful with your words, Mister, if I was you," said Francisco. "I warn you now. One more squeak and you're dead. I'll find you don't matter where." He grabbed me, then let me go. Already in the doorway, he turned around: "As I said, keep your mouth shut, *gringo*!"

I sat on the floor till the night sprawled over my head all its terrifying magnificence and engulfed the crumpled piece of paper lying next to me.

Carmela, O Carmela! Why didn't you tell me? I would've set you free. I would've let you love the man you loved. I would've raised your child. Once in my dream I promised to follow and protect you wherever you went. Will you ever forgive my betrayal? Will you ever forgive my sordid love that has taken away your life? Will you forgive my old dirty fingers for touching your beatific body? Now in death, your soul is pure again, the way it was when I first saw you: your hair like the wings of the soaring eagle, and your eyes sweet and calm like the sleeping water before it rose and took you away from me forever.

CHRISTMAS TANGO

1

"That hole I'm living in, man!" he bellowed in my face, while on his third beer. "I'm glad I'm out of there."

Hunched on a stool, feet dangling, the man was short, stout and sloppily dressed in worn-out corduroys, shirt unbuttoned down to his fat belly. And he smelled.

"Fucking holes, with no fucking *milongas*. Women who haven't got a clue how to walk, never mind dance. I've had it!"

I had no interest in arguing with him. Tango or no tango, wrong city or right, I really didn't care.

"Another beer," the man said, tossing some coins on the counter.

He slurred, his vowels riding over a bumpy road strewn with hurdles in the most unexpected places. I knew he was loaded. Without looking at him, I knew. I felt his back was swaying, while all the time he tried to keep it ramrod straight.

I didn't say anything. He slid off his stool and moved closer, making an attempt to put his arm around me to prop himself up. But I was much taller than him, so he missed the target, staggered, and went high for my baseball cap instead. His hand dropped to half-mast while he tried to pull the peak over my eyes, as if I was still a kid.

"Watch it, pal," I said just in case, my voice drowning in

the racket of three television sets suspended over the heads of the drinkers. The *Montreal Canadiens* had just scored.

"Don't you look at me as if you just snuffed somebody," he said with a sudden influx of energy. "When you feel like blasting the whole world, you go and you tango, get it? You're a lucky son-of-a-bitch. In this city you can do tango Monday, Tuesday, Wednesday, every night you go tango and to hell with it all. Where I live, there is no fucking tango, and I come here and what am I doing? Trying to find that sneaky bitch instead of going to *milonga*! Come on, let's go to Louise. What, you don't know Louise on St. Laurent? Oh, man!" He started laughing.

"You better keep away from Louise, then! Gorgeous woman! Not for brats like you, though! She'll gobble you up! Ha-ha-ha! Know where Louise is? Corner of Bernard. Next to that place, what's it called?" His fingers came together in a soundless click: "Where they used to cut gravestones. Ah, never mind! On Tuesday you go to *Tangueria*, on Thursday there is *milonga* at Geraldo's. Don't go to Juan, though. Juan is full of shit, he gives you all this nonsense about the steps till you drop dead. Forget it! Tango is not in the steps. It's in your fucking soul." He swayed away from me.

"Bartender, another beer for me and my young friend," he called to the red-lipped blonde behind the bar, trying to wave a hand and stay vertical at the same time.

"I have to go now," I said.

"Have to go… He has to go! And what about me? Where do I go? My best friend screwed me. Took fifty grand and buggered off with my wife… I came home – no wife, no money, no furniture, no nothing… But anyway, that's not the point. Forget about it, let's drink."

This man was pissing me off.

"You listen to me. I gonna tell you something that nobody will tell you. You'll be grateful to old Shorty."

Yeah, Shorty, I thought, I'll be thankful alright.

"If you come and the fucker puts you to the barre, and makes you practice with the barre, instead of a woman, that's how you know he is a fucking bullshitter. You practice your *sacadas* and *boleos* with a woman, not with the barre. The barre is dead, it doesn't breathe. You go for the thing that breathes. You get it?"

"Yes, I get it," I said and handed my money to the bartender.

I got off the stool and headed for the exit. I'd had enough of him. I knew nothing about tango, and had no intention of looking for a tango teacher. I had my own life to live, and he was dragging me into his personal problems and his tango crap. Even through his drunkenness, which often smooths the edges out in people, I could sense some sharp, angular madness in him. His obsession running like an idling engine, all on its own. He jumped off the stool in an unexpectedly quick, midget-like movement, trying to prevent me from leaving.

"Come on, have another drink, it's on me." He was now facing me, waving his arms in the air, and then holding them up in front of himself, as if embracing an invisible partner. "I'm telling you it's all in the embrace, it's the energy, it's not the steps. Everybody thinks they learn the steps and that's the dance! Nonsense! It's how you breathe and how you hold a woman."

He moved closer to me. I instinctively stepped back.

"If you hold her right, she will give you everything she has. If she is a good dancer, she knows how to surrender herself. She will be pouring herself into you!"

He shifted ground to whisper. "All you have to do is to take her and lead her wherever you please. You're in control, and if you're any good, she'll let you have it. Never ask for her name or anything. Her life is her business, that's the magic of it... Where else can you get it? This is better than sex, I'm telling you."

The puck went into the net again, and his rumblings sank beneath the cheers of the customers. But I'd heard him, and what I heard tantalized me. Could it really be so easy to get close to a woman? I couldn't even remember when I last had a woman.

I didn't say anything to Shorty, but felt a sudden pity for myself. It descended right to my stomach, making it feel hollow and tight. I suddenly became agreeable and limp, as if all the air had been knocked out of me. Shorty prodded me back onto a stool and ordered another round.

Though I'm almost thirty, I'm still shy with women. I'm not particularly good-looking, you see. My lanky frame does not put its height to any good use. I stoop and walk in long uneven strides, with a slight jerk at the end of each step, an unconscious attempt to make the difference in my shoulders' height less conspicuous. My adolescent bones couldn't cope with rapid growth, you see, and I developed scoliosis, overlooked by my absent-minded aunt.

In my whole life I never managed to figure out what to do with my arms: They often dangle alongside my body without any purpose. But there's nothing wrong with my face. You can't say anything against my face. I'm not particularly handsome, true, but I am not unattractive either. My eyes, for example. You'd always want to look at them again. Out of curiosity. It's their colour, mostly: washed out blue, almost white but with a dark rim around the pupil, unusual for a man. Redheads and albinos have such eyes, but I have a mass of dark hair on my head, and a shy little smile that doesn't expose my teeth. Lately, I've been trying to grow a small moustache.

Even though my features are not irregular, they must harbour some warp, an intangible swerve, a deeply hidden deformation that more than anything else may explain why it's so difficult for me to meet ladies. Women intuitively feel that I align myself with some asymmetry lurching out of every corner if you want to really look. They find it disturbing. Women like a straight line. And where can I get that line with my constant self-doubts, empty pockets and a hole in my socks?

One girl – nice legs, otherwise nothing special – burst into tears at that very moment when normal women are supposed to melt into blissful fatigue. Anyhow, this girl sobbed into my ear: "You hate me, because you hate yourself!" Where did you get all this pop psychology crap, I wanted to ask her, but didn't. Because women don't hear you anyway. And why would I hate her? I didn't care one way or another... But later I thought, she might've hit onto something here! You dislike others as long as you dislike yourself. Ha! That's a thought! That sort of makes sense to me, come to think of it! By the way, I never claimed I liked myself. As for other people, what's there to like? Well, women, maybe. Maybe. Only if you know how to handle them.

What I mean is that women expect a man to know "what he wants, and where he's going," as they say in sitcoms.

How can I know what I want? Every minute I'm pulled

in opposite directions. To go for one thing means to deny myself another. And if I deny myself that other wish, I'm only half fulfilled, while the other half of my confused, contradictory self remains forever needy and orphaned!

For some men all it takes is to narrow their eyes just so, and say nothing; stand and sway lightly on their heels, hands in their pockets. That's it! Say nothing at all, don't even smile, just squint your eyes like so, and she's done, she's cooked. Deep down, every woman wants to give herself up, to surrender completely, body and soul: "Just take me, lift all the responsibility off my shoulders, and I'll be yours." Scary business!

What spoils the game for me is that I always give away my eagerness. Too much yearning in my eyes, too much *I'd give anything to have you*... True, I sometimes manage to put a stern mask of indifference on my face, and then there is no way out of it, except rubbing my mask against theirs – a dance many of them are so good at.

And yet if only you knew how I see you – you stern secretaries, you tight-lipped accountants, short-skirted administrators! I see you as enigmatic sirens, bred by the high tide of the sea, beautiful, serene and enticing! You're holding wreaths of glory in your marble arms, and sing the songs that make the earth whirl around. Why don't you sirens ever scribble me your phone number on a scrap of paper under the dim light of a street lamp, fumbling in your handbags? Sorry, no pen, will a piece of lipstick do?

Of course, it will! I accept telephone numbers written in blood.

2

On windy December nights the world is aloof and unyielding. Rare passersby in the street, brooding lonely ghosts. You can't approach them and strike up a conversation. They'll cross over to the other side of the road before you get close.

I have only one tool for probing this hostile world – the joyful and persistent alertness of my private parts. While I myself, in my absent-mindedness, can overlook things, my privates react instantaneously to minute changes in the brightness of the world's feminine filament, standing to full attention at the sight of any skirt swaying by, feeling the mute, dark necessity for action even in the presence of a long-legged, vapid billboard girl sporting a modest bikini. At the same time, the most far-fetched congruity of images can subsume my tool's primitive power into sublime bliss.

Last year, in a rare moment of peace, I stood beside a small pond of lilies in a city park. It was early spring and the sight of the lilies, the exquisite purity of their half-closed curves, suddenly catapulted my hair-trigger instrument into a state of euphoria. After that, how could I underestimate this crude tool that could so easily, in a blink of my own eye, elevate me to such metaphysical heights? It has been alerting me to the state of world affairs since I was six. After all, this possession of mine is the only thing that makes me real in the phony world and makes the phony world real for me.

After meeting Shorty in the bar, one thought kept rankling me: What do men do with their tool of cognition under certain circumstances? Or, to put it bluntly, how can they avoid a hard-on while dancing tango? Do they get so used to women that they stop feeling any excitement and become completely desensitized?

One Sunday night, when I had nothing much to do, and nobody to call, I decided to satisfy my curiosity and take a tango lesson. Who knows whom I might meet there?

But it was the middle of the month, and no studios accepted drop-ins. I had to pay cash for the rest of the course, seven or eight classes.

I took my grandfather's old chronometer that was collecting cobwebs in the corner of my room into the antiquarian marine shop. The two hundred bucks that I got solved the problem.

I discovered quickly that Shorty had lied to me about tango. Indeed, tango *was* in the steps: in the endless repetition of the basic steps and turns. But the clean, precise, sharp yet unhurried footwork combined with the leisurely nonchalant attitude ("I may turn when it pleases me or not turn at all") was completely beyond my reach. Yet, difficult as they seemed, turns were easier to execute than tango walking. "Walk like you breathe, *tranquillo, tranquillo,*" commanded Alfredo, a dark Argentinean in black soft velvety pants and a massive golden chain showing through the open collar of his loose silk shirt. "It's easy," he said.

Thrusting back his gelled pitch-black hair, he walked with the confidence of a commando, and the regal sleekness of a cat. He firmly, but gently, probed the floor with the tip of his arching foot, caressing it ever so lightly, and then thrust his hips forward, while his torso was still slightly tilted back. Never, never could I learn to walk like that!

There were twice as many women in the class as men, and I had to dance with each of them to be fair to all. In tango jargon, women are called "followers" and men "leaders". Most of the "followers" were plain-looking, rather tired middle-aged ladies who had summed up youthful buoyancy for the occasion; only two women were in their twenties, and of those two one was pregnant. Like me, these women were struggling with their steps. Awkward and gravity-bound, they sheepishly trod the floor, as if stepping into a capsizing boat. They jolted in the most unexpected places; or came to a sudden halt, abandoning the music completely.

But I had an even harder time with the whole thing than these women. While "followers" at least could focus on their steps, I had to choreograph those steps for them, all the time paying close attention to the music. I had to watch out for other couples, and navigate the floor, always counter-clockwise. Leading turned out to be tricky and I sweated profusely. Besides, how do you silently communicate to a woman what you intend to do next?

"With your whole body, not just your arm," explained Alfredo.

"Hold her light, but firm, Chasen!" That's how he pronounced my name. "Where your hand, where your body? The arm on her back, the body went out for lunch. They together, your body and arm, no?"

"They should be," I conceded.

"Put your hand over there," he said, pressing my listless hand against my partner's back. "Strong, but easy, don't push her. She feel your power through your chest. From the waist up you one creature. Make senses, no? Make senses." He answered for me, as was his habit.

"Move closer to her, no fear."

I hesitantly did as he told me. Fear I sure had. Plenty of it. Expecting at any moment my extra-sensitivity to come springing forth, as it were. But nothing happened. The woman against whom I pressed might as well have been a washing board. I felt nothing.

"She's a woman, you're a man, no? Ladies? Leave your head home, ladies! Walk like an expensive cat, like this! That's better, Claire. I don't want your head. I want your body! This is tango! In Buenos Aires we dance close embrace, you better get used to it now. Men, ankles together, ladies, knees together. Don't look at your feet, close your eyes, ladies, feel the man. You don't feel him, he don't lead. No lead, no dance. It's not your husband, don't boss your man here! And we go now. One, two, three, four, five, six, seven, eight! Now, the music!"

My only saving grace was my sense of rhythm. I had come to love tango music and gradually it entered my blood stream. It took me five months of steady practice to learn to walk. And then it came to me! It happened to me, it entered my core: Together with the music, I cried for the world, I wept, I melted with sorrow. Tango both humbled and raised me out of the ashes, all in a single note, sighed out by a *bandoneoni*. Sometimes fear would overcome me again, and I'd become uncertain of my steps. Then I would breathe the air of movement and hope, right through my core, through the centre – no, not through the lungs, through the diaphragm, as Alfredo used to say. And the greatness of tango filled my heart, loosened my legs.

I walked to the sad and solemn sounds of the *Cumparsita*. I was that soul in the masquerade, a soul waiting at a wharf in an alien port while the foreign ships, ablaze with garlands of light, came and sailed away, and left me waiting.

> *La comparsa de miserias*
> *sin fin desfila*
> *en torno de aquel ser enfermo*
> *que pronto ha de morir de pena.*

I now felt the addiction of tango. It was like life itself: repetitive, yet always new, full of unforeseen trickery, archness and drama. It teased me with rich promises that were immediately taken away, and bestowed upon me sudden, unexpected blessings. Like life, it had a powerful undercurrent, an all-penetrating pulse that could drown you if you were not attuned to it. You had to dissolve yourself in tango, in music, and let the music carry you to the place of your greatest fear and sadness, and take you out of it and bring you back, while you had to take its dark throbbing into your very veins, and look into the abyss it was leading you to. You were naked in tango, you couldn't hide, no more than one can hide from life. You had to trust tango as a new-born baby trusts his existence. You had to be exuberant, cruel but gentle, while the music was still playing. You had to draw the knife at the sight of treachery but then pause and tuck it away and turn around and forgive, forgive that woman.

And sometimes, in moments of confusion, you had to stop moving and absorb the stillness; for there was a pause in the trajectory of the flight.

I discovered that there were women who knew the steps and danced well; but then there were others whose knowledge of the technique was deeply buried inside them. They could stop and do nothing at all or take the risk and accompany you on a perilous journey because they trusted you. They had an uncanny knowledge of how you were in the world and how you breathed; they intuited your next step and moved together with you effortlessly, with a certain languished passivity, as if they had no will of their own; they did not devour your freedom; they just followed you along the undulations of the music. These women were the very best dancers and most in demand.

A long time ago I passed the point of no return. To pay for more and more classes, I sold antique jewellery my mother left me. I moved into an even smaller flat further east, and supported myself doing odd jobs during the day while continuing to dance at night.

Yet at the beginning tango didn't make my life easier. The contrast between the times spent in the studio and the drawn-out hours I wasted in the room I could never call home made my solitude even more unbearable.

I remember one occasion especially, when I stepped into the night, after practicing tango, and saw the stars over my head dry and shiny, freshly washed. I couldn't bear the immensity of the sky and looked down. The city, sullen and empty, lay deflated under my echoing footsteps. On a night like that, it stops sprawling upwards; instead, it topples over on its back like a hibernating beast, horizontal, forcing its infinity on my ant-like crawl. I inspected the cracks in the pavement, vaguely hoping to find a key to their intricate pattern, which I sensed would be less inscrutable than the enigmatic blueprint of the starry void above me. But the meaning of both eluded me.

I remembered the pain of a year before. That's when I lost my last job and I'd been looking for a new one ever since, but nothing had panned out. People in the old job humiliated me. And I wouldn't have it. I might starve but I won't tolerate the slightest sign of disrespect. Ever since then I'd got into the habit of roaming the streets. I think I was vaguely looking for a miracle in the low-lying winter-frozen spaces of the city: a chance encounter, perhaps, a freak opportunity that would never stroll into the four walls of my drab attic.

What I met through my nocturnal wanderings was the wind. Indiscriminately, using the props afforded to it by every season, it piled up spectral slabs of chaos on the sidewalk. In autumn it sated on leaves – dispersing, then spinning them into ephemeral castles. In summer it clogged the passageways between houses with mobile hordes of dust and crumpled balls of paper; it leafed through the fat weekend *Le Devoir* editions page after page, exposing stale news to the indifferent legs of passersby.

In winter, when there was no snow, and the unswept leaves, dark and oblong, like ancient Egyptian boats, got frozen solid into the ground, the wind's credibility hung solely on aimless phantoms like myself. It fingered my spine under my shabby loose coat, vertebra after vertebra, all the way down to the tail bone, till it found an exit through the hole in my pocket.

Just like the wind, I kept up an appearance of movement under the monotonous absence of change. In order to stretch my dwindling budget, I moved from one crummy room to another, all the time staying put, so to speak. All these rooms were carbon copies of each other: all on the top floor, right under the roof. They all had wallpaper of an indefinable colour coming off at the junction with the ceiling and most had showers that didn't work. Since I was often late with my rent, I kept my mouth shut about the shower and didn't wash for days.

I wish the wind would stop. Its aimless wanderings disturb me. Sometimes I fantasize about my city. I imagine that in the past it was all soft and pliable: wax-like gyrating staircases climbing along the faces of the houses; the houses themselves soft, framed with trees, lithe like lianas. Then, I imagined, the wind came along and stiffened all form, so that nothing was left from the initial design. Skeletal branches knock against the window panes along the dark façades.

I even imagined that the cracks in the crooked sidewalks were also the wind's work; that the wind had slanted the pavement towards the middle of the road and swept the few pedestrians away. Now people walk in the middle of the road, forcing the infrequent cars to swerve into the oncoming lane to pass them.

I too gingerly step into the middle of the road. I give nothing of myself to the city. And the city closes on me, begrudging me every speck of itself, till one day I finally venture to a real Saturday *milonga*. And that changes my life.

3

At first, to avoid embarrassment, I decided to ask only the beginners to dance, leaving some possibility of an escape in case I completely screwed it up. But I was mistaken in my strategy. Though good dancers were seeking out partners of equal skills, there were many other forces at play that I couldn't quite grasp at the time, and which I still don't understand. There would be a girl – a young, smooth, insipid creature, hardly able to make two coherent steps – in the arms of an experienced, even excellent dancer, usually an older man. Perhaps, I, too, in the inversion of roles, could ask a good dancer without feeling I was going to crack.

At my first party I felt elated. I liked the muted ambiance: the flicker of candles on each table; the smell of perfume on the women's heated skin mixed with cigarette smoke reaching the floor from the stairwell where people puffed between *tandas*, two or three dances forming one theme. The fact that I could always go to the bar, have a glass of beer or whisky and watch others dance in case I suddenly got cold feet, suited me just fine. I liked the way men quickly sprayed breath freshener into their mouths before inviting a woman onto the dance floor and then put the spray into their breast pocket with the same quick, clandestine gesture. I liked the provocativeness of the women's outfits: their black shimmering skirts with slits at the side that bared their fishnet-stockinged thighs; their see-through tops held in place on the flimsiest promise of an imperceptible strap. I liked the way women closed their eyes while dancing, as if in complete abandon. Sensations overwhelmed me. The most powerful of all was the heat, coming from my partners' bodies after I danced two or three tangos in a row. Some women felt like balls of fire, all burning and melting inside, my only protection a layer of clothes – the silk, the velvet, the chiffon. Underneath the fabric I could feel the clasp of their bras.

I instinctively avoided placing my hand on women's naked backs (I noticed that other men did the same), and moved it to the area safely protected by fabric. But once, inadvertently, my hand slipped up my partner's bare shoulder-blades: They were cold and sticky with sweat and I was struck by the unpleasantness of the sensation.

If my right hand, always resting on my partner's back, had some level of defence (no matter how light and transparent the fabric usually felt), then the left was completely exposed, and I semi-consciously hoped for the exchange of some silent messages, some mysterious current travelling from her fingers to mine... But nothing was communicated to me and I was left disappointed.

Dancing the tango, I discovered how different women's hands felt: some very soft, others dry and rough as men's. What kind of lives might women with such hands have had?

Then there was the sensation of their breasts. In *calesita* women leaned over me at a sharp angle, their bodies linked to mine at the chest. It was a never-ebbing excitement to feel the weight of a woman's body so publicly placed on top of mine. Some women's breasts felt small and firm, some were big and soft, and I learnt to transport the tactile sensors from my fingers to my torso. Not an unpleasant experience, misplaced as it might seem.

※ ※ ※

Two women in particular attracted my attention.

One, in claret-coloured tight pants and a tunic, with a pale face and emaciated, almost breastless body, had a languid, careless way of moving. She danced obliviously, as if divorced from her own self. Her long ash-blond braid, too, seemed to have a life of its own, only remotely echoing the turns and twists of its owner. I was mesmerized by these double unsynchronized rondos, the way this ankle-reaching snake lightly swept against the floor when the woman suddenly went into a deep lunge. When I finally plucked up my courage to approach her, fish-like unsmiling eyes transfixed me. I thought what an excellent dancer she was, in her strange, inflexible, rake-like way. Yes, in my mind, I thought of her as a rake, and was both repulsed and attracted by her. She was staring right through me. What would it feel like to hold her in my arms? The more I desired her, the less I was capable of inviting her.

And then there was another girl, almost as tall as me, with wide hips and chocolate skin that brought the azure waves of the Caribbean to lap at my feet. I started walking towards her, but she was quickly intercepted by another man. And then I watched the oily smoothness of her dance, and I imagined her in my arms. Sometimes she was a goddess, and sometimes a mysterious creature out of the depths of the ocean, a mollusc in search of its form. And I was the shell that could absorb her and give her this form, had she only trusted me with her exquisitely slow undulations.

The music stopped. At that moment the yellow band holding the Carib girl's voluminous hair back slipped off her head, and she bent over to pick it up with a careless gesture. She was now an ordinary girl perhaps, accessible. Desire burned inside me.

"*Aimeriez-vous danser?* Would you like to dance?" a high, somewhat childish voice asked, breaking into my reverie.

"*Bien oui.* Sure," I replied to the owner of this voice, who, to my surprise, turned out to be a short, middle-aged woman.

Must be in her late forties, early fifties, I thought. Much shorter than me (a disadvantage in dancing), but it was the first time that a woman had invited me for a dance, and I felt flattered.

"My name is Pauline," she said, switching to English when she heard my laboured accent.

"I'm Jason."

I was trying to catch the beat of the music before making the first step.

"Have you been dancing for a long time?" she asked.

"Oh no, I'm a beginner."

"That's all right. It takes a while, but you'll learn, you'll see."

I was slightly annoyed, first, at her patronizing kindness, but more by the fact that she needed to talk to me at all while we danced: It prevented me from concentrating on my steps. Her bleached blond ringlets were at the level of my chin. I didn't see much of her face or her body, but she felt cosy and feminine in my arms, with those neat unhurried steps of hers. As if she were crocheting something with her small feet. I noticed her wasp-like waist neatly emphasized by a tight black belt that set off her generous hips. I also liked the feel of her fuchsia dress. It was soft, old-fashioned, with loose translucent sleeves falling all the way to her shoulders when she raised her well-shaped arms. A row of small pearly buttons rose to an upright collar that left only a small wedge of flesh at the top of her neck exposed. There was something touching about her being so old-fashioned. As I was leading her into forward *ochos*, I caught a glimpse of her knee: It was smooth and round, a gently outlined slope that seemed to be completely boneless. Pauline's whole body didn't have one sharp line. Her shoulders and her chest were cosily plump, and fitted perfectly in my arms, in spite of the fact that she was so much shorter than me.

While dancing with her, I became aware of a peculiar fragrance. It wasn't the smell of perfume – I don't think she was wearing any – but rather, that of her skin. It reminded me of something remote, long forgotten, and I couldn't figure out what it was. Then, in a flash, in cadence with the music, an old country house in England came back to me.

In the year of my mother's death, my aunt took me there to spend a summer with her. I was ten years old and we were slicing up juicy green apples from our garden and spreading them over towels on the floor of our little shack at the back of the property. I thought then that they looked like small round moons, those apples. Later, when the air cooled down, and the real moon and the stars came out, we had a sudden visitor: A hedgehog came trotting along with the heavy tread of a trooper. He rolled onto the apples, hooking with his needles as many he could. Then he disappeared. Pauline's skin smelled like those slightly withered apples, twenty years ago, in the August of my mother's death.

While dancing, Pauline didn't fuss around on the floor, nor did she press me into constant movement. I could stop and relax to the point of not thinking about my steps anymore. Most of that evening we danced together, and I felt no need to change partners.

But when I got home after midnight, I felt completely spent. Taking off my shirt, I saw a damp spot on my upper sleeve left by Pauline's armpit. The smell of apples kept haunting me.

4

I was soon spending my days in anticipation of the weekends. My head was filled with scraps of music and vague yearnings for Pauline whom I now danced with regularly. One night was particularly disturbing: I dreamt about making love to her incessantly. When I saw her the next Saturday at the dance studio, I felt embarrassed and invited other women to dance instead. When I finally danced with her, I avoided looking into her eyes.

Between dances Pauline and I hardly talked to each other. I knew nothing about her life. My arms knew her body, but otherwise we remained complete strangers. I liked this anonymous intimacy of the tango. I found the physical proximity to a woman who was old enough to be my mother exhilarating. It intrigued me, and raised me up in my own eyes. I felt like an iceberg, the whole of which nobody, not even me, could see.

Pauline was one of those rare, superlative dancers who wasn't flashy on the floor, but could intuit your slightest move.

At a special *milonga* the night before Christmas Eve, we danced far beyond midnight till the candles were extinguished and the chairs put up on the tables. We came out into the street and were confronted by a ferocious gust of wind.

"Where do you live?" Pauline asked.

"Ten blocks away from here, on Park Avenue," I said, lying. I didn't want her to know that I had no car and had walked across half the city to get to the *milonga*.

"I'm driving in that direction. I can give you a ride."

"Well, I could walk… but sure, if it's not out of your way." Climbing into her white car, I noticed a pair of crutches on the front seat next to her. She must have read a silent question in my eyes.

"I fell down and broke my… *cheville*… how do you say that? …my ankle. That was two months ago and now it's much better."

I recalled then, through the unconscious memory of my arm, that in *ocho* Pauline would lose her balance for a split second and lean more heavily than needed on my arm. She did have that imperceptible limp.

"It must hurt when you dance?" I asked.

"It hurts some, but I'm used to it now. Another three weeks, the doctor said, and it'll be completely healed."

What a devotion to the tango, I thought, and what endurance! A hard little nut in spite of her delicate looks.

"Could you stop right at that corner, near this building, please? I live over there." I pointed to a nondescript façade that I thought could pose for my apartment.

"It was wonderful dancing with you tonight," she said hugging me good-bye. "*Vraiment.*"

She pressed her body to mine, and I held her for a minute, postponing the inevitability of having to get out of the car. I wanted to continue what we had started on the dance floor, though I wasn't sure what that might be. So, I kept holding her.

"I know it's late, but I wish I could dance one last time with you… Today is Christmas Eve. We should celebrate…" I was whispering in her ear, taking in the sweat mixed with apple fragrance again. "What if we go to… I mean, would you mind if… I have some good CDs, but my sound system is not working... I mean, it's in the shop... In the meantime, could we not, perhaps, dance at your place?"

She gently freed herself from my arms and paused. Then she turned off the engine. We were now sitting in the car in darkness. There was no sound, except the wind gnarling at the car's flanks.

"*Mais*... I suppose we could," Pauline said finally without looking at me. "But it's late now and I'm tired." She paused again. "I need to go to work in the morning."

"Pauline," I said, almost losing my voice, "you're the most beautiful woman I've ever met. Dancing with you is like... it's really very powerful! I can't imagine waiting till next Saturday."

"Ah, *mon Dieu*!" She chuckled, then patted me on the cheek. "You don't need to flatter me, you know. I'm an old woman..."

"What has age to do with it?" I said with some vehemence. "You have experience. You have that special beauty of maturity... And you're a wonderful dancer!"

"Oh that – perhaps!"

"Don't ever say you're old, even as a joke." I caressed her hand. Pauline laughed faintly but didn't remove her hand.

"I'm not that old, just old enough to be your mother."

I let go her hand, moving away from her. She gave me a long sideways glance.

"Oh, okay," she said with averted eyes. "I guess we could stop at my place. For a very brief while."

"Yes, for a brief while," I replied. I reached for her chin, turned her face towards me and kissed her. Her lips felt soft. She didn't resist. While she was driving, I put my hand on her knee.

We were now in Outremont, and she finally parked the car in the driveway of an old Edwardian house. While she fumbled for the keys in her purse, I stared at the stained glass in the porch door. Not shitty. She has a good life, this woman. I wiped my feet on the doormat, a straw elephant dangling a BIENVENUE! sign in his trunk.

Inside, I smelled a suffocating mixture of dried flowers, baked pies and the familiar fermenting apples. It was warm, even stifling, as if the house was seldom aired. The hallway was full of antique low tables, chiffoniers, baskets. A bouquet of tulips splayed out of an elephant-shaped vase served as a lamp. Each tulip was made of coloured glass, with a bulb inside. I noticed that there were no Christmas decorations of any sort.

"Would you like some tea?" she asked. "I don't drink wine so late at night. Wake up with a headache in the morning."

"Tea is fine," I said, somewhat disappointed.

I followed her to the kitchen. There I found myself in an elephant kingdom run amuck. Gaudy beasts with trunks lifted like trumpets winked from the tea towels, curtains and tablecloths. There was a tiny elephant sitting on top of each canister; there were elephant mugs and pots and cups on the shelves. The tea cosy was an elephant and so were the backs of the chairs around the table. Two of the four chairs were occupied by huge stuffed beasts with erect trunks, all four pillar-like legs up in the air. One beast was pink, the other blue. The blue one was staring at me, the pink one at Pauline.

"It'll take a couple of minutes before the kettle boils. What kind of tea would you like?" she asked, leaning against a cushion where two crocheted beasts intertwined their trunks like the copulating snakes on the caduceus.

Under the bright kitchen light Pauline looked much older than in the semi-darkness of the dance studio. She was obviously tired. Her smudged make-up revealed all the trappings of age: the swelling under the eyes, the deep wrinkles around her nose, the sagging skin of her cheekbones. Perhaps aware of the effect that her face had on me, she turned off the overhead light, and lit two candles. Two sharp shadows reached the middle of her cheeks with their narrow tongues, then licked her nose, her lips, cutting her face into swiftly moving triangles.

"Your elephant collection is quite remarkable," I said, avoiding looking at her. "I've never seen anything like it."

"Not mine," she said. "My ex-husband's. We travelled a lot. We lived in the Congo for several years and there he took up carving. Elephants were easy to make and we brought back quite a few. Friends assumed we collected them. For each birthday party or anniversary somebody would bring us an elephant. And then I guess we fell into this trap and started looking out for them in different countries. Some are made of real ebony, some copper, there are even a couple of gold ones... More than 600 in this house. Would you like one?"

She got up and reached into a small shelf where a family of black elephants was walking trunk to tail along a crocheted meadow towards the frosted window. She removed the smallest baby elephant, last in the file, and handed it over to me.

"Thank you," I mumbled, slipping into my pocket the silly little thing.

"For luck," said Pauline pouring tea out into two elephant cups and handing one to me.

"Have you ever had your palm read?" Pauline asked, sipping her cup. "This is one thing I'm really good at. If I look at your hand, I can tell everything about your character, your past and your future. Give me your hand."

She held my hand in both of hers; her clasp was cosy and warm.

"Oh, what a big palm! Nice shape, too! You've had a hard life," she said, gently unfolding my index finger. "It's because you're a dreamer and an artist. You're very impressionable, very soft inside."

"How do you know?" I asked, smiling and drawing her closer to me.

"The palm tells it all. See, between the valleys of Venus and Mars there is a little mound, and then there is a line, separating those two valleys. Yours is very deep. Only artists have it."

"Can you foretell the future as well?"

"Yes, there is lots of travelling ahead…"

"Travelling and a big fortune, right?" I said, laughing. "They always say that. Do you really believe in this?"

"Big fortune, hmm… that *je ne sais pas*. But travelling, that's for sure. Look!" She showed me some more lines on my palm.

"Where should I go? Is that also written on my palm? How about going to Buenos Aires together?" I now took her hand into mine and pretended I was studying it. "Let's see if your hand says you agree to travel with me. This line, right?"

"It's not that simple," she said, laughing. "You have to look for a pattern, not just one line…"

"All I want to see is if you're going on a trip to Buenos Aires with me," I said half-jokingly. "That's all I care about."

"Oh, don't be silly!" She puffed up her cheeks and, with a little smack of her lips, let the air out coquettishly. She was suddenly acting like a little girl.

"No really, I'm dead serious! If I have to travel, why don't you come with me? Everybody goes to Buenos Aires: Alfredo, Jorge. The whole gang. Sebastian has a place people can stay. I think he's turned his own house into a hostel for tango people. And he doesn't charge that much."

She looked at me with a mixture of surprise and incredulity.

"Are you serious? You're talking about it, Jason, as if it was, I don't know, a ride to the Laurentians or to Toronto, at most. Just hop on a plane, and you're there. Plus" – here she hesitated a moment – "we hardly know each other."

"So, that'll give us a chance to get to know each other better…"

"You're a dreamer, I was right about that!" She was laughing now in an easy, light-hearted way. I had obviously managed to amuse her. But she didn't take me seriously, I could see that.

"Look, it's not impossible," I said, persisting. "We just have to plan ahead. You said you work? I mean, can you take a leave?"

"Sure, I work. My next vacation isn't till September."

"So, we'll go in September. It's nice there in September, not too hot; the tourist season will be over. It would be wonderful, I promise!" Her girlish laugh excited me. "Well, then?"

I saw that part of her wanted to be persuaded. I moved closer to her and took her in my arms. I couldn't restrain myself and started kissing her neck, her hands. My breath was short.

"We'll walk down those streets in Buenos Aires, the same barrios where our tango started."

I said "our" as if we already had some mutual history, as if "our" life was just a continuation of what started generations ago in the Southside docks and brothels of Buenos Aires and all I had to do now was to resuscitate this life.

"Don't think about money. I'll get what we need from my cousin in Toronto. He has a shoe store and he is rich." I was lying, I had no cousin with or without money, but I wanted her badly. "Please, Pauline, say yes!"

I put my hand on the smooth knee showing through the slit of her skirt. I had wanted to touch this knee for a long time. Words poured out of me, uncontrollably, rapidly.

"I want to hold you in my arms forever. I want to carry you – to protect you... I don't care what people would say... I've always been looking for a woman like you."

"Oh, stop it. It is just tango, that's all there is!"

"Why don't you believe me?" I desperately wanted to make love to her.

"I believe you, all right, I believe you!" She suddenly started to sob.

"What's the matter? Why are you crying?"

"I'm sorry, this is silly. I'm really sorry."

"Did I hurt you?"

"No, Jason. It has nothing to do with you. It's been a year today since my husband left me. Anniversaries are hard."

"How could he have left such a wonderful woman? Especially at Christmas?"

What I said was stupid, of course, and I meant it as a joke, but my hands were working up her black-stockinged leg, words were popping out of me, and I didn't care about them anymore.

Pauline quickly removed my hand from her knee and pulled the two parts of her skirt together. When she burst into tears I was completely confused. I never know how to deal with female tears. To me they're a punch below the belt, a plea for help that hardly leaves me any room to manoeuvre, urging me to act without telling me what I'm supposed to do. They make me feel guilty. But what am I to blame for? That her husband left her? That the world is such a fucked-up place? I didn't create it, it's not my responsibility.

"Were you married a long time?" I asked, unable to think of anything else.

"Almost 20 years. They were happy years, we never quarrelled, not once." There was a pressing, raw sincerity in her voice.

"It must have been hard on you. But all that's in the past. Forget about it. It's time to turn over a new leaf." I scooped her into my arms and started to undo the upper buttons of her blouse. She resisted.

"Don't," she said dryly. "Don't."

"Why not? Please..." My voice became coarse, a stranger's voice.

"Don't, I'm telling you."

But it was too late. While my left hand was travelling down her back in the attempt to undo her bra, my right hand dipped under the bra's wire. Oh, the delicious sensation of soft female flesh! One more second... and I pulled my hand away in disgust. Instead of the breast, I had run into a flat surface, hard as a board.

"What's that?" I asked, not trusting my own hand anymore.

"It's what's left after the surgery," she said calmly.

A mixture of horror and cold curiosity suddenly took hold of me.

"Show me."

"No."

"Let me touch it, then."

"No. Please don't. My husband left me because..."

"Because of that?

"Yes. Two weeks after the surgery."

I unclenched her fingers grasping her blouse. Yes, I had to see it for myself. Removing her top, I gently ran my finger over her former breasts, first the left one, then the right. Strangely, it wasn't as horrible as I expected. There merely were no breasts anymore, just a flat surface, much like the chest of a man. There was even a residual layer of fat, between bone and skin. How cleverly she had camouflaged it while dancing with me, I thought.

I felt a sudden overwhelming sense of fatigue, as if something had changed in the air. Perhaps the wind had abated. It was eerily quiet. Pauline slipped the top back on, leaving the padded bra where it had fallen on the floor.

"It's late," I said. "Time for me to go."

"Yes, of course. Shall I give you a ride?"

"No, thanks. I need to walk a little. It'll be good for me to walk."

"I understand... I know you live far away... though you said you live nearby. Sure you don't need a ride?"

How did she know? But I felt too tired to think. After all, I'd danced well past midnight. It'd been a very long day, and frankly I didn't care.

"Merry Christmas to you," I said.

"Merry Christmas," she responded. Then she closed the door behind me.

I took in my first gulp of fresh air. Then wiped my feet against the straw elephant holding out his "BIENVENUE" trunk. That was weird. I wasn't coming. I was going. But then everything felt weird at that hour of the wolf on Christmas Eve. Tango seemed repulsive to me now. And I couldn't fathom what on earth had moved me to squander my last money on it. Tango was a deceit, a chimera. Women were a chimera. So was life.

I walked out into the street gasping for the crisp, frosty air that felt like a special gift for my oxygen-starved lungs. The delicious fragrant chill caressed my skin. Oh, the joy of escape, of moving again wherever one pleased in brisk carefree steps!

It didn't bother me in the slightest that I had to cross half the city to get to my place. Something had indeed changed around me. A strange quietness clad the city, as if a voice had been cut short in mid-phrase. Yes, the wind had stopped. The wind that had been whistling down the streets for months, that wind had dropped its daggers and left the city. Gone, as suddenly as it had arrived, replaced by white spectral mourners that had alighted on the ground in complete silence: whirling around broodingly; powdering houses with snow; frosting trees, shrubs, porches and the sharp peaks of the fences; cushioning sidewalks; and sweeping over the minute untidy indecencies that had been revealed by the wind.

Within half an hour, the city was fully dressed in its new attire. It lay there in solemn purity, white and sinless. It seemed to become lighter with each thrust of snow, as if ready to ascend. I, too, felt I could rise to the skies; all I had to do was to get rid of the ballast that kept me earthbound.

Slipping frozen hands into my pockets, I felt something smooth and solid. Pauline's baby elephant. It still retained the warmth of the house I'd just left, much warmer than my hand. I held it for a minute. Then threw it into a freshly blown mound of snow. Softly it sank down into the white shroud, legs and trunk up, making no more then a dent. I stood and watched it quickly disappear under the abundant whiteness falling from the night sky.

ANGELS ASCENDING, ANGELS DESCENDING

About human life, there are only two or three lines to be written.
I. Bunin

1

Asya Alexsejevna Letnevskaya, sixty-two, was too nervous to comprehend in full detail what the doctor had just told her. All she understood was that *not* going for the five-hour heart surgery would leave her a year to live, at most. Whereas, agreeing to surgery would offer her "a forty percent chance of survival."

Finishing his explanations, the doctor pushed away the diagram pierced with red pencil arrows – as if Amour had taken aim at her heart – and finally raised his eyes to his visitor: "It's up to you to *choose*."

Asya Alexsejevna glanced at his sinewy hands, his knotty fingers soundlessly tapping the table, and saw no possibility of *choosing*. Neither there at the doctor's office, nor later at home, where she lived alone with her cat Proshka.

There was no other creature in the world who would feel the same fit of nausea as she did at the idea of her annihilation. Cat Proshka didn't count: Like all cats, he seemed quite indifferent to the fate of his owner.

Asya Alexsejevna was childless, had never married. A

puzzle for those who knew her. Even now, her former beauty left indisputable traces on her face, especially when in profile. Her late mother, having a presentiment about her daughter's destiny, used to say: "Better to be born fortunate, than beautiful." As if her daughter had any say in the matter. But Mother proved to be right: When Asya Alexsejevna was younger, men couldn't imagine a woman of such looks to be available. They suspected a horde of wooers lurking in the background. That she could be wanting anything was beyond their comprehension.

Asya Alexsejevna spent her youth doing what most girls did: waiting for the "True and Only Love" she'd recognize from its first light tapping at her then wonderfully healthy heart. But men proved imperfect. Lacking. They knew not how to express the mysterious ecstasies of the spirit. They circled around her like bees with a taste for nectar, then took off for much less spectacular meadows. And gradually, the patina of disappointment dimmed Asya's dreams. Her lonely struggles wore her out.

At forty, a melancholy mask looked back at Asya Alexsejevna from her bathroom mirror. Eyes framed by dark shadows. Deep vertical burrows running along the wings of her nose all the way down till they met a thin, dry line of a mouth. If it were indeed her face, she didn't want to know it any more.

At fifty, she let go of life's grip. Hopes imperceptibly slipped from her the way ballast pushed overboard slips off an overloaded ship. And just like the ship, the void, the emptiness inside her, suddenly made sailing much easier. She also discovered that her withered looks, the very face she avoided looking at, protected her as the *burka* protected Muslim women.

At sixty, she froze. Secretly, she was proud of achieving the state of "inner readiness," as she called what other people would consider *resignation to death*. Asya Alexsejevna counted that state of mind among her fortitudes: It had helped her to endure years of solitary struggle.

Now this visit to the doctor. It shuffled all her inner tides. Broke her defenses. Death was both unthinkable and unfair. It would deprive her of any chance to correct errors she had made in life, to grab the opportunities she had so foolishly missed. Now she desperately wanted to live.

Yet who could give her that chance? Who was responsible for, or even slightly interested in, her continued existence?

She had to make a rational decision about the surgery, yet she was lost. A sudden urge to survive at all costs somehow felt wrong, a weakness undermining her resolve, her tight-lipped endurance of many years.

No matter how hard Asya Alexsejevna tried to reason, reason alone couldn't provide her with the answer. At first in jest, then quite seriously, she began to seek out signs that would point her in the right direction. She began to pay attention to the most insignificant objects, silently asking them for a benevolent intervention in her destiny.

If the knife slipped out of her hands (which happened more and more often lately), it meant surgery; if it were a fork or a spoon, the right thing would be to stay away from it. But often the signs were hard to interpret. A black cat crossing your path usually means trouble. But what exactly did it mean in her case? Going for surgery or avoiding it?

It was during these days of tormenting uncertainty that Asya Alexsejevna decided to put her papers in order. Just in case.

She opened discoloured folders – a jumble of old postcards and letters; sepia clippings from the newspapers; photos of her parents against the fountains in Petrodvorets; old embroidery patterns; the notebook she kept as a young girl, with citations: "A man is made for happiness, like a bird for flight. Gorky." These were followed by her own comments in an upright, large, childish cursive: "Yes, he is ten times right and I will prove it with my own life!"

Or: "There exists a certain kind of inner confidence in oneself, when a man can do everything. He can almost instantaneously write poems that posterity will keep repeating for centuries to come. He can encompass in his consciousness all thoughts and dreams of the world, only to hand them out to the first stranger he encounters and not regret it a minute. Paustovsky." ("I wish I could write as beautifully! But I have not a grain of talent for anything!!!")

Or: "Really, about human life, there are only two or three lines to be written. Yes, only two or three lines. Bunin." ("This I don't understand. He must have had a terrible life, this writer! Should ask P.")

Who was P.? thought Asya Aleksejevna. The name behind that one letter had dissolved in the fog of the past. Still trying to remember, she opened another envelope. Her fingers stumbled on a dried flower, a daisy, which she had neglected to press. Carefully, she unfolded the clump of greyish petals. Among them the faded eye of the flower was still intact. Without thinking she started to peel off its petals, one by one: to go under knife, not to go, to go... Then she remembered.

2

That summer Asya had celebrated her seventeenth birthday and just graduated from high school. She was strikingly pretty: slender, willowy, light on her feet. A mass of dark curls contrasted with the deep violet of her eyes, framed by thick, velvety lashes. Perhaps it was the tone of her skin, alabaster pale, contrasting with her hair, that gave her the aura of such radiance.

She knew she was beautiful, and aware of that beauty's power reflected in the expression on men's faces, both young and old, when they caught a glimpse. Or in the tremble of old women's fingers as, waiting in grocery lines, they wanted to touch her, to stroke her long hair.

"The darling little sweet one," they'd say.

The way her math teacher glanced at her and her alone while explaining new material to the class both disturbed and flattered her. And sometimes, when riding on a bus, and holding with both hands to the overhead railing so that her whole body stretched upward, lifting the full breast and exposing her slim waistline, she had a strange and embarrassing fantasy: that some man would silently come up and "measure" her waistline, encircling it in his powerful hands, marvelling at the compactness of the circumference.

But, in spite of her looks, Asya was shy. She blushed easily, masking her embarrassment in little giggles, then getting even more embarrassed. As if in playing the unfolding sonata of her own self, she still pressed the wrong key every now and then.

She had a quick mind, however, and things came easily to her. She loved literature and wanted to teach it to kids. She also drew. What came out of her pencil were phantasmagorical cities: columns gyrating like eels; towers inlaid with gold and precious stones; fanciful porticoes and bridges intertwined with grapes and bright tropical flowers; courtyards with statues, fountains and hanging gardens. And lately she had got into the habit of mentally redrawing every building she passed: taking away here, adding there, till the existing city, house by house, grew to resemble her own imaginary one. After doing this for a year or so, she concluded that architecture was her true vocation.

When a distant relative invited her on a hiking tour of ancient Russian churches organized by Kurchatov's Institute of Nuclear Physics, she hid in the toilet and sucked on her finger, which she'd done since the age of three when upset or excited. Camping in the woods, singing along to the guitar around the fire, wandering from village to village in search of old churches – how lucky she was!

The guide, Konstantin Evgenjevitch Kramov, a senior research physicist, had gained quite a reputation in semi-dissident artistic circles as a poet and self-styled expert on Russian medieval art. Kurchatov's Institute was known for its brilliant young scientists. In the great intellectual competition of the sixties between the "lyricists" and the "physicists," the latter easily beat the former. Physicists were erudite; they knew languages and literature; they were great wits.

And, unlike philologists, nuclear physicists were equipped to uncover the mysteries of the capital "U" Universe: If they hadn't done so yet, they would in the very near future. Every young girl wanted to marry a nuclear physicist or at least to know one.

The intense excitement of anticipation made Asya restless. But a day before the trip, her relative called: An emergency at work prevented him from coming. It was decided that Asya would catch a later train on her own.

By the time she got off the train at Buryatino, it was dusk. After the nauseating stench of the crammed Friday night train, the sharp, fresh coolness of the countryside made her swoon.

She stepped under the dark canopy of firs. The last rays of the sun fingered the tree branches, dappling the grass under her feet with intense, swift-moving golden patches of light. The night sharpened all the smells and Asya stopped for a moment suddenly feeling all soft inside, and free. She inhaled a subtle and tender fragrance: The lily of the valley must have been quietly blooming somewhere in the moist secrecy of under leaves, away from her eyes.

In the total stillness, a cuckoo sounded its melancholy call, as if looking for an equally mournful soul-mate. Asya counted: five, a pause, another three, and then silence. The somnambulant murmur of water signalled the presence of a brook. The campsite must be somewhere nearby, then. Asya followed the sound, looking for a clearing with tents in it. Behind the thicket of trees the earth sloped down. She picked her way through a shallow ravine, over a ponytail trail overgrown with thistles and burdock. Her feet were all wet with opulent dew. The ravine opened into a meadow and in the darkness Asya caught a glimpse of a fire. Quietly she approached.

There were two men around the fire. One was smoking a cigarette, squatting and squinting into the flames. The other, younger looking, stirred the coals of the dying fire.

"'Fitful flame...' you couldn't have said it better," the older man said reflectively. "'Fitful flames...' How does it go? 'The darkness lit by spots of kindled fire, the silence, like a phantom far or near an occasional figure moving...' Now, let's see... the next line must be something like this: 'O tender and wondrous thoughts, of life and death, of home and the past and loved, and of those that are far away.' He is so 'un-Russian,' Whitman is. Yet, somehow, he affects you... he gets under your skin. You've seen Chukovsky's latest book? What do you think of his translation?"

"I think Chukovsky did a superb job," said the man rearranging something in the fire. "I got the book last week at Razval's for twenty roubles. You know its real price? Fifty-five kopecks. Well, I splurged. Free verse is tough for a Russian ear. I know Turgenev tried his hand at translation too, then quit."

"Strange that Turgenev was even tempted. Two worlds apart."

"You know who'd have been perfect? Mayakovsky. I think he imitated Whitman a lot."

"Oh, come on. Mayakovsky imitated Whitman? Both are supermen, of a Nietzschean fold. In that sense, they had somewhat similar sensibilities. But imitation? Sorry, I disagree."

"I don't think Mayakovsky tried his hand at translating anything, did he?"

"Was too busy writing all that drivel in the last years of his life."

"Leave the great man alone. He paid dearly for wasting his talent."

"I think he was sincere. A true believer. Or tried to be one as best he could."

Both men fell silent. Then the one stirring the fire said: "You say Whitman is un-Russian. Who could be more Russian than Tolstoy? Yet he loved Whitman…"

"What makes you think that? Tolstoy thought Whitman was a nut case, a writer of gobbledegook."

"That's at the beginning, but then he really got to appreciate him."

The man who had been reciting Whitman reached to the side to pick some twigs and then he saw Asya. She had been standing motionless all this time on the other side of the fire, listening intently.

"Here is the phantom Whitman must have been talking about. In the flesh, so to speak. If all phantoms were this pretty, there'd be no reason to fear the afterlife. Welcome to our abode. I'm Kirill and this is Alexander."

"Hello," said Asya quietly, approaching the two men and taking off her rucksack.

"Finally! And where is the boss himself?" asked Alexander, examining Asya with curiosity.

"Grigoriy Arkadievich is not coming. There is some problem at work."

"Well… I would have been surprised if he'd made it. Not that I mind his replacement. Not at all. Are you hungry? Or shall we continue our poetic debates? Ask Alexander, he'll treat you to some superb fish soup." Kirill smiled up at her. "If you're nice to him," he added.

"Thank you... but I..."

"Don't say no until you try it," said Alexander. "It's very fresh. You'll gobble it up together with the bowl. We were fishing almost till dark. Lots of gudgeons here. Straight into the broth. You must like fresh-wriggling gudgeons, don't you?"

Asya smiled at the joke, then squatted at the fire.

The fish soup was barely lukewarm. It smelled of ash. But Asya felt great hunger the moment the thick liquid touched her palate.

"Where do you wash dishes?" she asked, finishing the meal.

"In the creek below. But there are lions and tigers roaming in the dark. So, we'll do dishes tomorrow. And I'm afraid I'm out of tea. See that tent over there? There must be a free spot for you." Alexander rose to his feet and aimed a flashlight into the forest. It glided over the dark crowd of trees surrounding the clearing before snatching some tents out of darkness.

"The one on the very edge," said Alexander, pointing his light.

Asya picked up her backpack and followed the path blazed by Alexander's flashlight.

Closer to the water, the earth was cooling unevenly, releasing the intense heat of the day. Over the invisible brook, mist hovered low in flat milky strips. Asya lifted her head and gasped: Around her the sky was breathing, throbbing with life. The stars were huge, streaming with pure light, the way she had never seen them in the city. Her heart pounded at the almost frightening beauty suddenly revealed to her.

Gently, trying not to disturb anybody, she opened the flap of the tent. She expected to find several people inside, but her own flashlight revealed only the figure of one man lying on his side, breathing rhythmically in his sleep. He was wrapped in blankets, his head covered. Asya paused, then quickly and soundlessly took off her wet shoes, then her sweater, and slipped under the other sleeping pad trying to leave as much space as possible between herself and the man.

She was tired and sleepy, yet sleep wouldn't come... the sharp, poignant smells of night, the clusters of stars separated from her only by a layer of old tarpaulin, a man lying next to her – everything was so strange and mysterious... And these physicists! How clever they were, how knowledgeable! They discussed things she had never heard of! She too wanted to do and know many things; as many as there were stars in the sky. She would build beautiful cities, never seen before! And that would make everybody kind and beautiful... But how to go about it? Where to begin? Like the stars, her longings seemed to be beyond her grasp, or her comprehension.

The frogs croaked. A gust of wind swept over the tent. And then, a light patter above her head, as if some elf-like drummer was climbing onto the roof to try out his tiny instruments. A minute later, he slid to the ground and disappeared into the woods. The rain had stopped as suddenly as it began. A single cloud, straying from its path to the land of rains, must have unburdened itself over her head, and now, light and hollow, was catching up with his rainy brothers in the dark ether... Asya finally fell asleep.

She woke up to a sensation of a bright warmness enveloping her whole body. Under her closed eyelids radiant arcs throbbed, changing shape and colour. Smooth semi-circles of intense orange, blue and purple, transformed into horns and protuberances as she tried to unglue her eyelids. Vaguely, still in a semi-dream, she took the shifting shapes she "saw" for the mercurial insides of the kaleidoscope she received as a birthday present when a little girl. She remembered the sheer happiness, the almost unbearable delight that the luminescent, swiftly sundering and reforming constellations stirred in her. She sensed similar enchantments coming her way now.

But something was pressing down on her. She opened her eyes: Her hand was enfolding the stems of a huge bouquet of daisies. Moist with dew, they must have been recently picked.

Asya looked around: The place next to her was empty. The man she had been sharing the tent with was gone. As were his belongings. Before disappearing, he laid a blooming meadow into her hands… Asya examined the bouquet: It was loosely arranged, daisies on the fringe, cornflowers in the middle. How did he guess cornflowers were her favourites? She buried her face inside the azure foam of narrow, delicately carved petals and was transfixed by their scented warmth, the essence of earth and sun and the fields of early summer. And for a moment it seemed to her that she herself was that meadow, that field of rye quivering under the hot rays of noon and the shadows of night, in all eternity and the pain and ecstasy of being.

She put the flowers down. It was hot in the tent. The day must have begun long ago, and she was missing its wonders! But what will she say to the stranger who gave her this gift? How will she recognize him in the first place?

She breathed in the slightly bitter scent again. A ladybug fell out of the bouquet into her hand.

To give her *all that* was to say "Thank you." But what was the man she never saw thanking her for? Asya sat up thinking: This stranger woke up and there she was, sleeping. Just as last night, she raised her head and there they were, the throbbing stars... She suddenly knew the meaning of his gesture: He was simply thanking her for her existence.

Asya imagined herself throwing flowers high up into heaven. Thank you, stars! Here are more for you! Oh, how silly. She fell on her back laughing. In her childhood she believed that stars *were* flowers, only they lived in the sky, while their earthly twins lived here in the meadows.

I wonder what *this stranger* looks like, she thought. Must be tall, broad-shouldered, with flaxen hair and blue eyes. He will be so easy to love!

But what if he is... no, that cannot be! As Chekhov, her favourite writer said, in a man everything has to be beautiful: his soul, his thoughts and his clothing. He said, *his soul* and *his thoughts*, he didn't say his height or the shape of his nose!

What to do with the flowers, though? Leave them in the tent? *He* might think she doesn't care about his gift. On the other hand, showing up with a huge bouquet is like bragging, thus betraying *their* secret... She pulled several flowers out of the bunch at random, stuck them in the breast pocket of her shirt, and crawled out of the tent.

Oh, how sweet and fresh and lovely the air and the sky were! What lightness she felt in her whole body!

People around the fire were already finishing their breakfast. She recognized Kirill and Alexander. They nodded to her; she smiled back. Then she looked around: Two women, the wives of the physicists, were puttering around the tents; the rest were all men in their late twenties or early thirties. They looked so unremarkably plain! Sweat pants, keds, shirts, khaki backpacks, khaki jackets... Nothing in their faces or their manner betrayed great intellects at the cutting edge of the most important science of the country.

But one man looked different, though he was older than the rest of them, thirty-four or even thirty-five, that old. He was examining the map spread in front of him on the grass. His right arm was in a cast, with a sling over his shoulder. There was sharp-focused intelligence in his face: You wouldn't want to say anything silly around this man, that's for sure. With his pince-nez and pointed beard, he resembled Chekhov on the wall of their literature class room. Only this face looked thinner, more austere, closed into itself. This was Konstantin Evgenjevitch, the leader of the group. What a distinguished name and how it suited its owner! "This must be *he*!" Asya decided with a little jerk of her heart. Her tent partner. But – she dug at a mole hole with the point of her shoe – would he pay attention to a little girl like her, serious and thoughtful as he seems? And to pick flowers with one arm just for her? Unlikely.

"Kon, this is Asya," said Alexander. "She arrived late last night."

So they call him "Kon." She wasn't sure she liked it.

The man detached his eyes from the map and shot a quick sharp glance at Asya. A whiff of a smile touched his lips.

"Your first time? I don't remember seeing you on other trips."

"Yes, it's my first time," Asya breathed out.

Again he smiled, then his eyes returned to his map. What a beautiful velvety baritone he had. In a split second, he took her all in, and now knew her.

"The menu today is as elaborate as usual: porridge and tea," Alexander said. "The product of Lesha's tireless imagination."

"Five minutes of delay, and she'd have had to sate on air," said Lesha, appointed cook of the day. "Folks here are a hungry bunch."

"She wouldn't be the first!" said a man with a broad peasant face. "In Australia one clever dodo claimed he could live on air alone. The guy had quite a following."

"Max, stop hanging macaroni on our ears with your tall tales."

"No, I'm serious," said Max. "You should read the newspapers, rather than show your ignorance in front of a young lady. Asya, you've got yourself into the midst of a totally uneducated and narrow-minded bunch who don't even…"

"Max, fold your peacock feathers and leave the lady alone," said Alexander. "Better throw your considerable intelligence into a collaborative effort to make up our lunch menu. Lesha needs your brain, your honesty and your consciousness."

"Asya, do you see what they are doing to a poor hapless youth who is trying to enlighten them?" protested Max.

Asya laughed, furtively examining Max. He looked funny, walking with lanky uneven strides, from time to time forgetting to bend his knees – which made him look as if he were on stilts.

Asya headed toward a pile of washed dishes and stumbled over thick roots hidden in the grass. She would've fallen nose down had it not been for somebody's firm grip on her arm.

She looked up: An intense pair of eyes nailed her to the ground. A naked and unapologetic desire glinted in them.

"The nearest hospital is 60 km away," said the man tightly holding her arm. "We would have to leave you here oozing blood." There was not a shadow of a smile on his face. When she rose to her full height, she saw that her "saviour" had a diminutive, almost childlike frame. His eyes were hidden under a low, protruding brow.

Her lightness left her. "An ape," she thought, "an ugly ape."

She flushed with embarrassment, quickly got up and ran towards the stack of clean metal bowls nestled in a hollow between the roots. She ate her porridge, then ran down the slope towards the creek to wash her plate.

The brook turned out to be bigger than she'd imagined the night before. Bird cherry trees in full bloom leaned over the flat banks. The tiny white crosses of their flowers dotted the silvery ripple of the water. The soil under her feet was slippery clay. Holding on to a bird cherry, Asya examined the shallow backwater at her feet: Two tadpoles chased each other in the liquid mud of the bottom. A little distance from them, she saw a sleeping mermaid. Stalks of grasses close to the surface swayed gently by underwater currents were her hair.

Asya sat on her haunches, looking for a cleaner patch of water to wash her dish. Through the befuddling, almost bitter, smell of bird cherry, she sensed something sweeter, and gentler: Mignonettes must be hiding near.

She was about to leave when she caught a glimpse of a

young man half hidden by bushes. His hands buried in the fluffy cloud of his hair, elbows propped on his knees, he was examining something on the ground. Asya stood behind him waiting. She picked up a little dandelion parachute. If I blow it towards him and he turns around, it means *he is the man*. If not... A diffuse milky cloud alighted behind the man's back. The young man turned around. His green eyes, positioned wide apart, wandered over her. Again she felt that lightness.

"Hello," she smiled.

"Ahh, helping flowers to procreate? Very thoughtful."

"No, it was... no, nothing. I was looking for a cleaner spot."

"It's all mud down there. But here is not so bad. Look at this, though!" He pointed to the plate on the ground between his legs. She came up and squatted next to him.

"Most amazing creatures these are. One finds the path, and the rest follow... I've been watching them for half an hour; a little more time and the whole colony would move here."

Asya looked closer. Several ants were pulling at a clot of porridge stuck to the plate. It was too big for them, but soon others came along to help.

"How do they tell each other what to do?"

"That's still a mystery. Apparently they leave some chemical substance on the path; other ants follow the smell."

"Look, look, this one is pushing, the other pulling," whispered Asya.

"Yes, an amazing cooperation between these ladies."

"Ladies... That's funny!"

"The worker ants are always females, didn't you know?"

"And what do males do then?"

"The usual. They copulate with the queen and then die. A discarded material."

Asya pursed her lips, not sure how to respond. The man quickly glanced at her:

"Do you know ants have a strict social order? And they learned agriculture millions of years before people did."

"Really?" she said immersing the plate into muddy, dim water.

"They have special underground fields where they grow mushrooms needed for their larva. What they do is break leaves, chew them, then use them as compost. Clever, eh?"

Asya looked at her interlocutor with wide admiring eyes.

"Wff," the man blew into Asya's eyes. "That's better. At least when you blink, I know these are real eyes with lashes, not violet butterflies."

Asya quickly covered her face with both hands. When she removed them, the man was standing in front of her. She noticed how tall he was.

"By the way, I'm Boris Zhukov." An open, friendly smile, curly flaxen hair.

In an instant she became certain it was *him*.

"Have you... was it you who ...?" Asya breathed out as if plunging headlong into icy water.

"Who did what?" Boris smiled conspiratorially.

"Oh... I was simply wondering, have you been on trips like this before?" said Asya, suddenly scared by her plunge.

"With Kon?"

"Yes... going to churches, like that?"

"We used to lead these trips together. He is my old friend, Kon. But he is much better at this than me. So now I'm simply enjoying myself."

Asya stretched out her hand to the sky.

"Is the butterfly going to leave me? Dallied on a flower and off she goes..."

"Starting to rain, it seems..." Asya passed the hand over her cheek. "It rained last night too. Did you hear?"

"Kon and I spent half a night arguing, as usual. By the time we fell asleep, only cannons could have raised us."

Everything sagged inside her. If Boris and Konstantin Evgenjevich or Kon, as they called him, had shared the same tent, neither of them could have slept in her tent and therefore...

"What churches are we going to?" Asya asked, trying to mask her despondency.

"You never know with Kon. He chooses sites nobody else would."

There was an ironic glint in Boris's eyes.

"An unusual man. With his own ideas and convictions. And a good poet too."

When Asya and Boris returned to the camping site, all the tents, including the one she had slept in, had already been packed away. Her rucksack was sitting in the centre of the clearing, the clothing she had left in the tent stacked on top of it. Next to the pile was her bouquet of flowers. Somebody was looking after her. But who was it? She picked up her bouquet, her backpack and joined the campers.

3

They walked through woods that grew thinner and thinner, finally leaving a few birches as sentries before yielding to the field of rye. Asya found herself next to one of the two women.

"Is that where you picked your daisies?" asked the woman as they stepped on a trail running through the field. The timid scraggy ears were swarmed by weeds and wild flowers, and in some patches had given in to them completely. "You must have gotten up early to get to this place!"

"Yes. I mean no," mumbled Asya taken by surprise. "I mean when I woke up, there were sort of... there were already flowers there. Somebody left them in the tent."

The woman stopped. She gave Asya a look. "Flowers in a tent? That's interesting!"

Asya felt earth parting under her feet. She was ready to flee.

Why is *he* hiding from her then? What is *he* waiting for? Or is *he* testing her somehow, wanting *her* to guess who *he* is? If so, why wouldn't *he* give her any sign? Well, then. *He* embarrassed her in front of this woman and she is going to challenge *him*. She will make *him* take off the mask... She stopped for a moment pretending to examine something in the grass and letting everybody pass by her. High over her head the lark trilled in the vivid blue of the sky; far on the horizon, soft puffy clouds were coming together.

Asya opened her fist, letting the flowers slide to the ground. They fanned out on short stubble, the cornflowers still fresh and pert, the daisies already showing signs of decay.

"What are you up to?" she heard a vaguely familiar voice behind her. The "ape man" was breathing heavily. He must have lingered at the camp and now was catching up with her. His eyes were burning with the same nasty flame that had put her off in the morning.

"Was that yours?" she asked firmly meeting his eyes and pointing to the flowers.

"What?"

"These... Did you give them to me?" With all her heart she hoped he hadn't.

"Should I have?"

Asya felt an immediate relief. No, it wasn't him, she was certain of it.

"It was a joke. Of course you shouldn't have."

She turned around and ran towards the hikers. But the "ape man" was running alongside with her.

"Why are you always trying to escape? Did I do something wrong?"

"No, I just don't want to miss anything," she gasped, her only desire being to get rid of the man.

She finally reached the group, who had left the field and were now stepping into a village. Old apple trees in full bloom hung over dilapidated timber huts that appeared empty. Everything seemed motionless, except the fences frozen in their flight: some leaning backward, some forward. Like drunks they swayed, waiting for a strong gust of wind to collapse.

"I passed by this place two years ago," said Konstantin Evgenjevitch, "and there were still some signs of life. Now it's as if the wind had swept everybody away."

The windows of several huts were barred.

"It was autumn then... and apples fell off the trees, hitting the roofs like hail. A dull kind of a sound. Pum, pum. Nobody picked them up. It was an eerie feeling." He looked at Asya. She felt that his quiet, almost intimate tone was now addressed only to her. She glanced at him gratefully and then looked askance as if returning to others the trophy that couldn't belong to her alone.

"See that church on the hill over there?" said Konstantin Evgenjevitch. "That's what we're going to start with."

What he called a church was a dilapidated structure long abandoned. The stucco had fallen off the walls, revealing white stone dirtied with soot. The church must have endured fire. There were no doors, and the three entrances were now large ragged holes. They stepped inside. The summer day melted away and the cold-grave smell of earth embraced them.

"Well, here we are," said Konstantin Evgenjevitch, walking forward and stopping in the middle. People gathered around him amidst burnt planks and construction rubble. Empty bottles and fish cans littered the stone floor. Somebody must have picnicked here.

"We're now in the central nave," he said with quiet solemnity. "The Greeks called this central part *afolikon*, which means the Centre of the World. Standing here, we're embracing the Universe. This is still a created world. But it is already the world touched by a celestial flame, and therefore pardoned."

"What do you mean, pardoned?" Boris gave voice from the edge of the crowd. He was so tall that he towered over the rest.

"Don't interrupt," Kirill said. "Let Kon say what he has to say."

"Here, right here," Konstantin Evgenjevitch turned around making a sweeping gesture with his free left arm, as if inviting invisible witnesses. "Here is the New Earth ready to accept the New Sky." He fell silent, observing the effect his words had on his listeners.

"The church is the Universe, isn't that true? But at the same time, it is built in the image of Man. How so? Now, here is the mystery. Come, come closer please." He waved his hand, eyes searching out Asya in the crowd. When she approached, he continued:

"Why is the church, any church, even this scorched and raped one, a symbol of the Universe and Man at the same time? Look how it grows upward!" He lifted his left arm to the dome yawning with holes. "It grows towards Heaven. It aspires to Heaven, just as our souls do cry for Heaven with invisible tears. And this is our dilemma. We are still inside the created world. We're part of matter. Matter that will sooner or later rot and perish!"

Again he paused, his face now a mask of quiet suffering.

"But will we die altogether? Die entirely? No. When we're here, in this sacred space, we're on the threshold of a New Kingdom... Standing here, we are accepting into ourselves the celestial flame!"

"You call this a New Kingdom?" said the man resembling an ape. He kicked a can with his foot. It rolled with a discordant clatter through the quietness.

Konstantin Evgenjevitch turned around. "No, this is not the New Kingdom! This is human negligence and the desire to destroy. Now, look up."

He pointed upwards. "The church has a dome. Think of it as our head. The church is our body. God dwells up there, in the dome. Always depicted high up. Looking at us from on high. Pantocrator, the All Ruler, the Sovereign Lord. One dome means there is only one God."

Through the gaps in the dome the irregular squares of the sky, criss-crossed by the dome's skeleton, looked painfully blue.

A flock of crows sitting on top took off with raucous cries.

"What if there is more than one dome? What does that mean?" said Asya bravely, trying to distract everybody's attention from the ugly noise the birds were making.

"Three domes would mean the Holy Trinity. Five domes, Christ and His four apostles. Isn't that so, Boris?"

"I suppose. You know better."

"By the way, pay attention to the shape of each dome. What does it remind you of?" The question was addressed directly at Asya. She looked around, hoping for support. But the crowd was silent.

"An onion," she said uncertainly, half-hoping she wouldn't be heard.

"An onion?" Konstantin Evgenjevitch shot a stern glance at the girl. "Nothing better than that? Well, the ancient domes emulate the helmet of a Russian warrior, defender of his country. But of course, each dome standing on Russian soil is also a flame. Our soul burns like a solitary flame with the desire to know God and to serve Him. Our whole life is a sacrifice to God! Isn't it so?" He closed his eyes. This time nothing broke the silence. Asya saw his eyelids tremble slightly. He must be praying.

Then, as if coming to his senses again: "But God is unknowable. Forever we yearn for God and in our immense, boundless yearning, we're like a solitary flame saying to God" – Konstantin Evgenjevitch raised his voice in passionate supplication: "Show me Your face, I implore You, show it to me before it's too late and my life is extinguished and my powers to pray are nil!" His head lifted in a gesture of supplication, then he froze: "And the only place we can know God face to face, God's terrible and frightening yet merciful face, is here, in the church!"

Again, he fell into silence. Nobody dared to interrupt him.

"But a man praying in the church usually looks down. He seldom lifts his head up to see God. Confronting God happens slowly. The believer enters in the West, though the main entrance." He suddenly turned around and walked back to the hole through which they had entered.

"What does the West mean and why do we enter from the West? The West is the Land of the Dead, that's where the dead were buried in all ancient churches. It is also the site of Hell. Here, on this wall" – he pointed with his left hand in the direction of the wall – "the Last Judgment is usually depicted. Terrible scenes of Hell and its tortures. So anyone entering the church comes from the site of the Dead, from the secular life of the flesh, equated with Hell. But then the man who entered the church inevitably goes forward. He goes towards the altar, isn't that so?" Konstantin Evgenjevitch took a few steps forward to show how it happens. "The altar is always in the East. And what is in the East, Asya?"

"I am not sure…"

"What is in the East, Igor?" He addressed the "ape man."

"Igor is counting crows as usual," said somebody in the crowd. Through a gap in the wall, they saw Igor sitting on a pile of coal smoking.

Kon finally replied to his own question: "The East. What is the East? Symbolically, the West is darkness, the East is light. The West is ignorance. The East is knowledge."

"Oh, cut it out!" somebody said.

"Excuse me," said the woman who had asked Asya about her flowers. "I thought we were on an architecture tour. Suddenly, it's ideology all over again."

"Ideology? But this is a fact. The ancients believed that Paradise was located in the East, and therefore…"

"Wait a minute. It's the same old song, isn't it?" The "ape man" dropped his cigarette and hurriedly joined the group. "You're trying to tell us that the West is rotten, and the East is where the light will come from, right? Meaning Russia is enlightened and the West is ignorant?"

"I believe the West came to the end of its historical mission. It ran out of new ideas. If there is any renewal in the world, it is to come from Russia. Yes, I do believe that."

"Kon, it's unfair to use this as an occasion for propaganda," said Boris.

"Folks, let's just get off this. You and Kon are old time opponents, everybody knows that… let's focus on architecture."

"So far, we haven't heard a word of it," said another woman, with cropped hair.

"Thank you, Boris, for letting me express my beliefs before you interrupted. My goal is to demonstrate how everything in this world is connected with everything else. The church, therefore, is a geographical expression of the soul's spiritual journey. Isn't it so, Asya?"

"Yes!" exclaimed Asya. She'd got to like and anticipate his "isn't it so" and was prepared to catch it now as if it were a ball served specially to her.

"The eyes of the believer," Konstantin Evgenjevitch continued calmly, "are affixed on the splendour and glory of iconostasis hiding the altar. The believer walks towards it with hope in his soul and tears in his eyes. From Darkness to Light. From the Land of the Dead to the Land of the Quick. From Despair to Hope. From the Hell of earthly existence to Spiritual Paradise. The journey is full of spiritual peril but if we persevere, we're at the Gate of Heaven, just as Jacob was when he saw the ladder... The Church is Jacob's Ladder... Approaching the altar, we approach Heaven. Here the transition has been finally completed."

Konstantin Evgenjevitch stepped back and leaned against the wall. "Any questions?" he said, his voice now flat, his face showing great exhaustion. Suddenly he looked so old, so lonely. Asya's heart went out to him.

"Why did we come here, to this filthy dilapidated place?" asked the ape man. "Aren't there better places?"

"There are. And we will see them today. This sacred place is ruined. It is raped as a virgin might be. Yet God's beauty still shines. Through all the desecration and humiliation, isn't that so? And I thought, if you can glimpse the divine light here, right here, how much more you will appreciate something untouched by human degradation.

And talking about architecture" – Kon's eyes searched for the ape man – "talking of architecture, Igor, I believe that this church is a prototype of the famous Church of the Intercession of Nerly. It's an early rehearsal, so to speak."

"What makes you think that?" asked Igor.

"The same structural organization. The same great economy of means. See the middle window? It is slightly lifted, there is an asymmetry... that's how this effect of lightness is achieved. They did it at the Nerly church too. Like a pillar of air running upward. Come, let's look outside."

They trooped back out of the cold into the vivid brightness of the day.

"See these little sculptures? Normally, there would be an acanthus running all around the curved wall." He turned to Asya again.

"Where?"

"Look straight ahead and up. See? There's usually a leaf motif running all along the wall. But here instead of the conventional vegetation ornament, you've got these young women's faces carved out of stone. A very unusual feature! Only at Nerly and here!"

"What does it mean?" asked Asya.

"What does a lovely girl's face mean? I think it means the same thing in all times and places: beauty. Isn't a woman's face God's loveliest creation?" Kon looked straight into Asya's eyes, smiling. Asya looked at Konstantin Evgenjevitch and forgot to breathe.

He was allowing her to enter, in fact inviting her into *his* spiritual worlds, worlds full of mystery and beauty. Immediately she decided she wasn't going to be a literature teacher, nor an architect. She would restore churches instead. That way she would have something to share with him. A soul-mate proximity to this deeply-spiritual man.

Rambling from village to village, they saw five more churches that day. But none of them, beautiful and in full repair as they may have been, impressed Asya as much as the first ruined one. It was there, among debris and human excrement, that she could feel – for the first time in her life – the real presence of God. And she was rapidly falling in love with the man who pointed Him out to her. With his austere, reticent face, ignited by faith, he belonged to a higher caste of human kind. Could she follow him? Could he love her back? She was a pygmy; she knew nothing, he knew and felt all.

Yet his eyes searched for her in the crowd. He wouldn't begin his explanations till she was at his side. At the beginning it surprised her. But as the day progressed, she got used to it. And yes, she was his grateful and compassionate listener. She strove with all the powers of her mind to reach the lofty tidemark of spiritual tension that his exalted insights demanded. God was near, as long as this man was next to her.

The morning with her silly hunt for a man who gave her flowers, this morning seemed no more than a mirage.

But the all consuming effort tired Asya. She could no longer understand the words she heard. Instead, she lolled in the soothing modulations of his baritone. But when the journey came to an end and the voice ceased, she felt the umbilical cord connecting her to this true and only life was suddenly severed. She looked at Konstantin Evgenjevitch and panicked.

He, in the meantime, was counting the hands of those

who wanted to see the Nerly church next Sunday, on a one-day trip.

She heard him saying, "Asya, I hope you're coming?" But she didn't clue in right away, and only with some delay, weakly breathed out: "Oh yes, yes... Of course."

❄ ❄ ❄

To live though a week of waiting was to cross a scorched desert. Asya's parents were insufferable, their conversations empty; her friends' interests shallow. Only the night brought her some relief: Staring into the darkness she dreamt of future happiness. Suppose Konstantin Evgenjevitch fell in love with her? Anything is possible. Natasha Rostova fell in love with Andrey Bolkonsky, and he was 13 years older than her. No, 12. She should look it up, their age difference. The point is it didn't matter for them. Why should it matter for her? Surely, they would have married, had Andrey not been killed at Borodino. If she marries Konstantin Evgenjevitch and they have a daughter, they will call her Natasha, and if it's a boy, they'll call him Andrey, and if it's both... But he is so accomplished, has such a rich inner life. He must have all kinds of interesting friends and colleagues, while she, she has her parents, and her friend Dasha who has just had an abortion and who comes to cry on her shoulder every evening while she, Asya, doodles her phantasmagorical cities.

4

The next Sunday Asya frantically ran out from the subway entrance to the railway station. She had taken the wrong exit, the one furthest from the railway station, their meeting place, and now was almost ten minutes late. Another minute, and they'd set off without her... From afar, she discerned his face among the dozens flickering by: He was leaning against the marble column at the subway station pavilion, waiting.

"You're the first one, Asya! Folks are too lazy to get up on time Sunday morning. We'll wait."

Relieved, Asya caught her breath, straightened out the blouse with pearly little buttons. It was her best blouse, put on specially for him. Having Konstantin Evgenjevitch all for herself even for a short while was thrilling. The pounding of her heart resonated in her throat.

"Hmm," said Konstantin Evgenjevitch, looking at the clouds scudding though the skies. "You think it's going to rain? Maybe that's what scared our people off."

Asya's heart froze. Her frenetic rush, her fear of missing it all...and then the avalanche? Her new-discovered God will not allow that.

"Oh, there's Alexander over there!" she cried waving her hand to the man she spotted in the crowd. But she was mistaken. A man she took for the Whitman aficionado passed by without turning his head in their direction.

"Looks like it's just the two of us," Konstantin Evgenjevitch announced, consulting his watch five minutes later. "Shall we cancel or not?" He looked at her, smiling.

"I don't know," Asya whispered lowering her eyes. Yes, the inevitable was coming. It was terrible. She wouldn't survive it.

"Well, since we've already made the effort to come this far, why don't we carry on?"

Konstantin Evgenjevitch began to walk away from the railway station.

She followed him on cotton-wool feet. Suddenly it didn't matter any more. She had no will of her own. The higher power was leading her. But in him too there was some change; something different from a week earlier, but what was it, she couldn't quite tell.

"Aren't we taking a train to Vladimir?" Asya asked as if finally waking up. She knew the Vladimirsky region quite well, having spent several summers there at her relative's cottage.

"My car is around the corner. Since it's just you and me, we might as well get there in comfort." He turned around and lightly touched her shoulder: "You think you could put up with my company?" Only then did she notice that his arm was free of its cast.

"People's interests are shallow, isn't it so?" He opened the car door for her, courteously waiting until she got in. "Or maybe I bored everybody last time. What do you think?"

"How can you say that, Konstantin Evgenjevitch? You talk like... like nobody else could!" She smiled brightly at him, her eyes alight with joy.

"Well, then... the only explanation is that people can't sustain any deep interest in anything these days. Impatience, superficiality, the search for immediate gratification."

They were now leaving suburbia, the white drab five-story boxes flicking by on both sides of the road.

"We are losing our eyes, our souls, monkeying the West, isn't that so?"

"Yes, of course!" she agreed quickly, triumphant that he was addressing her as his equal.

"But Russian culture is by definition a deep, attentive culture, inclined to philosophical contemplation. The Russian soul digs down. It doesn't flit from flower to flower for the easy nectar of entertainment as the Western soul does. It contemplates one object, one phenomenon, drawing the deepest conclusions from its observations, sometimes of global significance. Wouldn't you agree?"

"Yes, of course..." whispered Asya, watching the light play hide and seek on the motley trunks of birches. How brilliant and fresh was the day! It was only just unfolding, and though each moment of it was filled with small wonders, the charm of the day lay in the miracles to come. And Asya was ready. Everything filled her with delight: the electrical poles, rare cows in the pastures, women on the curb selling potatoes out of metal buckets. And then this wonderful masculine smell in the car, a mixture of tobacco with something else; the confidence with which he drove; and the shape of his beautiful hands calmly poised on the wheel. The right hand looked pale and anemic after months of incarceration in a cast. A ring was glittering on his finger. Konstantin Evgenjevitch fond of jewellery? How unlikely! She looked more closely: It was a wedding ring.

The wooden poles along the road cracked and broke in half; the asphalt always running in front of the wheels lost its solidity and melted.

Married! Asya forced her tears back. But the lump in her throat made breathing difficult. Konstantin Evgenjevitch took his eyes from the road.

"Are you all right?"

"Yes," Asya said, nodding while looking straight ahead. "I feel dizzy in cars sometimes."

"Why don't we stop and rest?"

"No, I'll be all right."

"Here is something for you then!" The hand with the wedding ring disappeared into a pocket, then dived out holding a piece of paper.

"I'm reading my poetry in CHL on September 8th. You're welcome to come."

Automatically, keeping her eyes on the road, Asya took the printed invitation.

"Do you know what CHL is?"

"No."

"The Central House of Literati, near Bolshoy Nikitsky. You'll come then?"

Asya didn't reply.

"But what's wrong? What's the matter with you, all of a sudden?" There was impatience in his voice.

"Nothing," said Asya, continuing to look ahead.

She now remembered how in the village where she had spent her childhood summers the boys plucked feathers off a live chick and let it go. She watched the chick squeaking in horror and pain. Instead of running away from its tormentors in a straight line, it twirled around in circles. She felt she was that chicken with feathers plucked.

"So, tell me then," Konstantin Evgenjevitch said cheerfully. "What have you done with your wonderful life so far?"

"Nothing, really... nothing much," she said, miserable with longing for the world she had just lost.

"You're a university student?"

"No, just graduated from high school."

"And what are you planning to do next?"

"I don't know... I thought I wanted to restore churches..."

"You must like churches then?"

"Yes, well... architecture in general. When you talked about churches last Sunday... I liked your talk."

"And what did you like most about it?" Again he treated her like a child.

Asya couldn't think clearly. Finally, making an effort and in order to say something, she said: "Jacob's Ladder. I liked when you... you said something about...some connection with the church."

"Good! You remembered the important part! Do you actually know what Jacob's Ladder is?"

"No," said Asya indifferently. She didn't have to conceal her ignorance anymore. Nothing really mattered.

"When Jacob fell asleep he dreamt of a ladder going all the way up to the sky. This is in Genesis and the Gospel of John, by the way. And on this ladder he saw angels descending and ascending. And then he saw God standing right next to him. And God promised him the Promised Land and the Heavenly Kingdom. Jacob woke up in awe, but he also felt protected. After that dream, he always had an angel at his side."

"I don't understand..." said Asya, unable to follow.

"What do you not understand?"

"This ladder thing..."

"Ah, you're not the only one. The ladder has been debated over centuries. One interpretation is that it links Earth with Heaven. In that sense, you can symbolically think of a church as Jacob's Ladder connecting two planes of existence, the higher and the lower one. Does that make sense?"

"Nothing makes any sense," said Asya.

For a moment neither of them spoke. Then Konstantin Evgenjevitch broke the silence:

"Yes, there are days when nothing does. It happens to everybody. In our lives, we too climb a ladder, a spiritual one. One step at a time. Getting closer and closer to God. And it's hard; we have to apply ourselves all the time."

"To apply how?" asked Asya with inner desperation.

"Striving for spiritual knowledge, for a certain purity of the heart."

"And if we fall, then what?" For the first time she looked at him.

"Then we hope Jacob's angel will catch us and raise us up... That's why the angels descend... in order to come to our rescue when we're in need."

"And the ones that ascend, are these the same angels?" There was mockery in her voice.

Konstantin Evgenjevitch cast a long glance at her: "That I don't know," he said seriously.

The highway turned into a dirt road flanked on both sides by sombre firs. Konstantin Evgenjevitch stopped his car on the verge.

"These are mushroom places," he said. "Lots of *boroviki* in the fall. Let's walk a bit along this trail."

The trail meandered through dense forest, then came to an abrupt end, blocked by a fallen tree overgrown with brambles.

"Konstantin Evgenjevitch, there is no path here!" exclaimed Asya as he came to a stop at the barrier.

Her guide hurried back to her.

"Why don't we rest here then? You seemed to be unwell in the car."

He pointed to a mossy hillock under the firs. His voice sounded strange. Asya looked up at him. He abruptly wrapped his arms around her and drew her face close to his. She lost her breath as he kissed her on her lips, then her neck, then hair. Startled, she tried to tear herself free.

"Careful with my arm! It hasn't healed yet."

"Konstantin Evgenjevitch, what are you doing?" she exclaimed. "Please, let me go!"

"Call me Konstantin, simply Kostya, will you? Let me kiss you here, let me." He roughly pulled her in again, forcing the collar of her blouse to burst. Small pearly buttons came jumping down like hail.

"I couldn't sleep all week... your eyes were haunting me... your hair, your lips..." He slipped his left hand inside her loosened blouse.

"I beg you! Let me go!" cried Asya. But he wrestled her down to the moss. With his left hand, he managed to pull the blouse up from her trousers, and because he was using only one hand his actions felt grotesquely brutal. He buried his face in her naked belly, greedily kissing her flesh.

"I had to see you alone, I had to touch you..." Her body went limp.

"So you knew nobody would come, then?" she whispered.

"I certainly hoped so." His words were muffled by the slack muscles of her abdomen. "I postponed the trip till next week. Please, let me... I'm not going to do anything bad to you. It will be pleasant, you'll see..."

Sudden anger stirred in her. She collected herself and forcibly sat up, dislodging the man.

"All right, then. Do it. Do it fast. Or you'll miss dinner with your wife."

He moved away from her, letting her go. Her belly, burning from the contact with his beard and now suddenly exposed to the air, felt cold. Their eyes met. She had never seen such an expression on anybody's face and for a long time afterwards was haunted by it. His face was the face of a dead man, ashy, pallid. And he looked at her with the fawning eyes of a beaten dog.

"You don't like me then?" he asked quietly, now rising to his feet.

"No."

"Not at all?"

"No, not at all."

"I'm sorry. I thought maybe you did. It seemed so to me."

Asya lightly rolled onto her knees and tucked her breast back into her blouse. She noticed that the three upper buttons were gone and suddenly felt terribly sorry for herself. These were buttons you couldn't find in the store. Now she might as well throw away the blouse.

"These buttons, they're special," she murmured, rummaging around. He understood her anguish and squatted next to her. Combing through the moss, their fingers met.

"I'm sorry," he said, quickly pulling his hand away.

He found one button and handed it over to her. For a second, it glowed with a feeble light in its pearly convex depth.

"I have a spare sweater," he said in the car. "You can put it over the blouse if you're cold. You don't need to return it to me."

"I have a warm scarf in the backpack," she replied.

He dropped her off at the nearest metro station, and suddenly, when she was getting out of the car, he held her arm: "Forgive me, Asya. You will, won't you?"

She nodded, unable to speak.

5

Most days of that summer, the last summer of her innocence, Asya spent on the sofa staring at the dark jacquard circles of the old upholstery. She wondered how, though she'd been staring at them since her early childhood every evening before falling asleep, she had failed to notice their disgusting resemblance to skulls. She felt herself totally boneless, her body heavy and useless in a dull, grown-up, stolid way. She refused to eat and didn't want to talk on the phone. Only once did she yield to the pleading of her mother and presented herself, emaciated and shaky, in front of the Exam Commission of the Architectural Institute. She failed the very first exam, an essay, and with a relieved heart, returned home, to her sofa. The next year, she didn't attempt to compete again, and became neither literature teacher, nor architect, nor restorer of churches.

But by the end of that disastrous summer of Konstantin, when the heat in the city had subsided, she finally began to leave her flat. Her walks had no purpose; however, she loved the dry, wasted rustle of the autumn leaves under her feet, the bitter smell of autumnal air. A little boy stopped her once near the mineral water machines. He asked for a three-kopek coin to get a glass of fruity water. He had but one kopek, enough only for a non-fruity glass. She fumbled in her pocket and together with a coin pulled out a crumbled piece of a cardboard: an invitation for a poetry reading.

Again she hid in her room. The tears she wasn't able to squeeze out of herself for the whole summer were now unstoppable. After a week of renewed agony, she put on a blue dress that complemented the violets of her eyes and went to the Central House of Literati. She came deliberately late to avoid meeting anybody who might know or recognize her. The hall was overcrowded and she was let in to stand in the aisle behind the curtains.

And then she saw him, alone on the darkened stage, in a bright circle of light. She could hardly recognize him, his black turtleneck, black leather jacket and beige trousers giving him an unfamiliar air of art world elegance. But then she heard him and once again was mesmerized by his voice. She couldn't tell if his poetry was good or bad, nor did she care. She loved this man, more than she loved herself, and the modulations of his voice – now slow, now passionate, now tender and contemplative – were all she had: That voice was hers, the way the man wasn't and never would be. And so the vortex of her love was now centred not on his face, too public and almost too handsome, but on his voice alone. She closed her eyes and listened, tears running down to her blue dress.

For a moment, it seemed to her that he had noticed her, had singled her out of the crowd. That an invisible cord ran between them over the heads and eyes of all these strangers. That, like two months before, he was uttering his words for her and her alone. But perhaps it was just an illusion. She glided out of the applauding hall without waiting for the end.

6

Holding a dry daisy in her hand, the daisy she had almost de-petalled, Asya Alexsejevna envisioned again that summer of forty-five years ago… With her inner eye, she saw young men reciting poetry around the fire amidst the silent, nocturnal woods; saw the sun-drenched meadows, the dandelion fluff, the pearly buttons glittering in the moss. And she recalled her passion for another man of which nothing was now left. Nothing, except a sad and still poignant memory.

And then it seemed to her she could feel again the scent of wild flowers put into her hand by another anonymous man, who saw her in her sleep in the brightness of the morning sun, and admired her and fell in love with her, but had chosen never to reveal himself. It occurred to her that there had been no better tenderness and no greater beauty in her life ever since.

But now, almost half a century later, she couldn't but think tenderly of both kinds of love, for after all, they were two faces of one great and mysterious force that both graced and burnt her. It occurred to her that if there had been such a weekend in her life, one weekend, it meant her life was not wasted.

❊ ❊ ❊

Next day Asya Alexsejevna made an appointment for the surgery. She had been never happier than in the month preceding it. She made plans to do many things after her convalescence. That she would be fine, she now had no doubt.

First she wanted go to the Black Sea together with her friend Dasha and her two grandchildren; then she would make it to the famous church on the Nerly River... And she would start with a piece of fabric that had sat in her wardrobe for the last ten years.

Summer was coming and she needed a sundress.

NOTES

Page 97: *MTS – Machine Tractor Stations (Mashinno-tractornaia stantsiia) were created in the 1920s as a means of collectivization, prohibiting individual farm households and whole villages from possessing motor power. MTS became the symbol of Soviet power in rural areas.*

Page 97: rasshibalku *and* pristenok – *games played against a wall using coins, stones or puck-like objects.*

Page 201: *A masquerade of miseries/ marches endlessly around me./ Soon,/ I too will die of pain.* (Translated by the author.)

❧

Much gratitude to Michael Mirolla, my publisher and editor at Guernica Editions, who laboured patiently over each sentence, as well as to my friend and editor George Payerle, a compassionate midwife of the first draft; to Kim Smith, and always to Włodek without whom the book would not have seen the light of the day.

The resistance of the human spirit in face of time, disloyalty, and oblivion is the theme of Marina Sonkina's new collection of short stories. Her seemingly naïve and helpless protagonists inhabit disparate social stations, geographical locales and cultures; all are persons displaced in their own lives. But in their struggles for survival, they discover the redeeming and dangerous power of unconditional love – the only weapon available to them. Strange and incomprehensible, love makes its sudden appearance to an eight-year-old hunchbacked boy in the title story of *Lucia's Eyes*. As he brings the gifts of his artistic imagination to Lucia, a refugee from the Spanish Civil War, the bleak and cruel reality of Stalin's Russia dissolves into magic... In "Runic Alphabet," a Polish-Canadian painter plants a tree that brings to life memories of a woman long dead who remains the only true love of his life. In "Carmelita," an aging man from Winnipeg, vacationing in Mexico, falls in love with a young Mexican painter. In "Christmas Tango," a jobless drifter in snowy Montreal discovers tango, inadvertently transforming his own life and the lives of those who come in contact with him. In "Tractorina," a hard-working crane-operator, retired in post-Gorbachev Russia, is driven into a rose-tinted abyss by her stepson. In "Angels Ascending and Descending," a young girl is initiated into the mysterious symbolism of Russian Orthodox church architecture by a priestly man who hardly lives up to the spiritual heights he preaches. Full of unexpected turns and twists, sadness, joy and humour, these stories reflect life, itself always a surprise, and always a miracle.

"These stories display a masterly range of emotional tones, from ice-hard brilliance to mordant wit to sheer lyricism. Marina Sonkina's characters rise from the page to become people we know and understand, although they live at widely distant points of the compass, spiritual and geographical. It's clear that she loves them all, with a passion that forgives their weaknesses. In "Runic Alphabet," a painter plants a tree that, as it grows, awakens memories of a lost love. In "Christmas Tango," a chance encounter with a drunk in a Montreal bar sparks a new meaning in a man's life. "Carmelita" takes us to a small Mexican town where a Canadian expatriate becomes a victim of his newly acquired wealth. All of these stories reflect Sonkina's erudition, skill and versatility. She is a writer to treasure; she tells memorable tales in succulent, satisfying and elegant prose." – Martha Roth.

"Marina Sonkina's stories give us unexpected characters in surreal situations presented with unflinching verisimilitude in prose that is at once forceful, lyrical and filled with scepticism. This is not the stuff of European fiction, nor of the multicultural mainstream in North American post-20th century writing. This is more like Mavis Gallant in reverse, a shrewdly observant fictive sensibility self-transplanted to the New World from the old. The fact that English is Sonkina's most recent language (after Russian, Italian, and French) gives her writing the linguistic piquancy of a fusion cuisine. These stories don't taste like borscht or pea soup. They taste like fillets of elk in a hot paprika sauce." – *George Payerle*.

Marina Sonkina was born in Moscow, Russia. She taught literature and linguistics at Moscow State University till she escaped – with two then small sons and two suitcases – the Soviet Union. It took her more than a decade to settle into English before she dared to brave its waters with pen in hand. She lived in Toronto and Montreal where she worked as a CBC producer and broadcaster, documentary film researcher and translator. She taught Humanities at Dawson and Vanier College in Montreal and now shares her time between teaching at Simon Fraser University and the University of British Columbia as well as writing. She has published two collections of short stories and two children's books. Marina lives in Vancouver.